BRIDE OF THE CRUEL ALPHA

SEA KING ALPHA
BOOK ONE

OLIVIA BHELLE KILDARE

To my boys, who support me in every way in everything I do, and to my husband, who shows me every day that fated mates exist in real life, too.

CONTENTS

A BRIDE FOR A POWERFUL ALPHA

Lyra

"Do you honestly think that wolf king will actually notice your looks?" My oldest sister sneers at me as I apply my makeup.

I watch in the mirror as my eyes redden at her harsh words.

"Daddy's giving you away as a sacrifice," she continues. "That filthy wolf will probably eat you alive after having his way with you. Disgusting."

The knot I'd felt growing in my stomach all morning suddenly feels like solid lead. I meet Anastasia's gaze in my heart-shaped vanity mirror, my eyes wide. "Do you really think he'll kill me?"

I'd heard as much, especially as the servants gossiped in the castle since I'd been promised as a bride to the Sea-King Alpha. Some say he is hideous and smells of raw sewage mixed with brine. Others say he is the most beautiful man in the world, with a physique so powerful no mortal man could ever best him. But *all* of them say he's a beast, a cold-hearted murderer that my father must appease, or our people will no longer be allowed to harvest the ocean's bounty.

She smirks, pulling her lips to the side under her prominent nose.

"Of course he will. Did you really think you could marry a wolf shifter and still be alive after the wedding night?"

"Anastasia, stop it." Ailsa, my other older sister, younger than Anastasia but two years older than me, marches into the room, her golden hair flowing over her shoulders like silk. "You shouldn't scare her like that on a day like today."

Anastasia shrugs and shakes her head at her only full-blooded sister. "I'm just trying to prepare her."

"I'll be the one to prepare her, thank you," Ailsa tells her.

"Okay, well, bye 'sis,'" Anastasia says to me, her final word dripping with sarcasm as she slinks out of the room.

"Don't listen to her," Ailsa says, grabbing my pearl-studded brush and gathering my hair. "She's jealous."

"I don't see what she has to be jealous of." I inhale slowly, trying to calm the jittery butterflies that have taken residence right above that lump in my belly. "She's a high princess, betrothed to the handsome Ethan Snowthorne of the Winter Realm. I'm just a low princess, being thrown at an angry wolf king so he doesn't kill us all."

She pauses, holding my hair in a ponytail before twisting it into an updo. "Stop calling yourself that, Lyra. Your mother is just as loved by our father as hers and mine was, maybe even more. And my mother would roll over in her grave if she knew how Anastasia had turned out. You have to ignore her."

"Ignore who?" My mother, Queen Consort Iridessa, steps into my room with her usual graceful countenance. Her sleek auburn hair is several shades darker than mine, which is more of a copper-tinted blonde so bright I often hide it under a hat so I don't blind anyone.

From the moment I was old enough to know I was a princess, I wished I were more like my mother: brilliant and confident, with an unmistakable air of elegance. If one hadn't known my father had a former wife, the Queen Regent Amelia, it would be impossible not to see my mother as the true monarch. But because she is his second wife, the kingdom does not recognize her as a real queen.

"Anastasia," Ailsa replies. "She's been bothering her about her fiancé again."

"I'm sure your sister is just being protective," Mother says.

Ailsa finishes up my updo, leaving curled tendrils hanging on the sides, then she pins in my small tiara. She leans in and pats my shoulder. "You look beautiful. I'll give you two a moment to say goodbye. I'll see you downstairs."

Goodbye…

It's not a word I wish to say to my mother or to Ailsa, and moisture soon pools in my eyes as my sister quietly steps out the door.

"You look so beautiful, sweetheart." My mother adjusts the puffy shoulder on my dress sleeve, though it's already fine. I've chosen my favorite gown for the trip, a soft lilac A-line with lace embroidery. She holds her gaze down, but I still see the glint in her emerald-green eye as tears begin to well up. "The Sea-King Alpha is a lucky man."

"Have you ever seen him?" I ask, hopeful.

But she shakes her head. "I have not. Only your father has, when they were arranging your union." She bites her lip and continues. "You mustn't worry about the chattering around the castle."

So, she has heard it too.

"Those people have never seen the man, either–or any shifter, for that matter." She holds up her head, forcing her lips into a smile. "I'm sure he's handsome, given that he's the king of all the sea-facing lands."

I nod, trying to fake a smile, but it's not his looks I'm worried about.

I stand, and she pulls me in close, the scent of her gardenia cologne sweet and comforting. "I will miss you," she whispers in my ear. "I'll find a way to visit you soon."

We pull apart, and I'm already sobbing. "You won't be at the wedding." It's a statement, not a question. Such things have already been decided without our input.

She places her index finger softly on my chin. "I will always be with you, my little Lyra. Just look in your heart, and you will find my love." She pulls something from her pocket, a velvet box. "I want you to have this. It's from my mother, your grandmother, whom you've never met." She pulls out a diamond necklace, its main stone encased in an elaborate floral setting.

"It's beautiful," I say as she wraps it around me, fixing the clasp behind my neck.

"And so are you, Lyra." Reaching for a tissue on my dresser, she dries my tears and adds a little more mascara. "There. You're all ready to go, my dear little girl."

I giggle despite my sadness. "Mother, I'm twenty years old, not little."

"You'll always be a little girl to me," she insists.

She leads me by the hand down the many hallways and out to the courtyard, which is bustling with activity. Servants load the festively decorated wagons with a trunk of my belongings, along with several goods donated by our fishermen, farmers, and merchants who wish to find themselves in good standing with the Sea-King Alpha.

I suppose a nervous young human bride isn't enough of a prize for a wolf shifter king like him.

We approach my father, who is directing all the activity as if he's conducting an orchestra. "That goes in the carriage with my daughter," he tells a man with a small, locked box. "The finest jewels should not be stored along with salted fish!"

"Father—"

"No, no, no, man," he tells another servant, ignoring me. "The Sea-King standards should be displayed in front of ours, so they identify the caravan as it approaches. Now, behind it, be sure the acrobats perform perfectly. We can't embarrass the people of Maelie."

"Father, I'm ready to board the carriage," I manage to say.

"Oh, splendid. Splendid." But he doesn't even look my way. Instead, he sprints over to a man carrying a wine barrel, insisting on having the man set it down so he can take a taste and be sure it's perfect.

"Your father is busy," Mother says, her voice pleasant yet sharpened with an edge of annoyance. "Let's just get you settled."

"Your Highness, allow me to assist," my lady's maiden, Cally, says as I approach the gilded carriage. The horses pulling it are some of the finest in our kingdom, bred to feature long, fluffy blond manes and wearing the bright blue standard of the Kingdom of Maelie, the largest human civilization on the Pearl Coast.

Though we stand at the mercy of the wolf shifters, who rule over all.

Cally adjusts my dress when I sit on the velvet-lined seat, and Ailsa jumps in for one last hug. "I'll write to you every day," she promises. "Don't worry."

The drivers call out that they are ready, and Ailsa jumps off as they close my carriage door. Through the small window, I see my family, except for Annastasia, who is nowhere to be found.

My mother blows me a kiss, Ailsa waves frantically, and my father looks toward the wagons handling the cargo trunks as my carriage pulls away. The few friends I've made in the royal school are somewhere lost in the crowd, and it's hopeless to try to find them.

I leave behind everyone and everything I've ever known and loved.

I'll be the bride of the Sea-King Alpha, Cassian Oliver, living my life in a strange land with strange people.

If I survive the first night.

THE SEA-KING ALPHA OF OCEANA

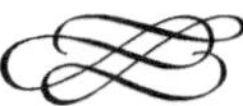

Lyra

DAYS HAVE PASSED, AND I'M SO EXHAUSTED FROM THE JOLTING AND rocking of the carriage that I'm ready to crawl into whatever bed the Sea-King Alpha provides me, no matter how frightening he turns out to be. Cally has fixed my makeup so many times that it must look caked on ten layers thick, and she's redone my hair twice as often.

But finally, the sharp, crystal spires of Oceana Castle, home of the Sea-King Alpha and his royal court, finally appear in the distance. I hitch a breath at its wonder, at least three to four times the size of my home back in Maelie. I always knew I'd been born into privilege, the way my father's castle was covered in gold and jewels, and I always had anything I needed. It's why I try not to complain about my betrothal to the Sea-King. Our people rely on the ocean so much for food, trade, defense, and survival.

But this place...

The castle and its land sit against a sharp cliff with ocean waves pounding the rocks below. The outer walls, made of thick, impene-trable stone and adorned with iridescent seashells glistening in the sun, stand far outside the castle itself, leaving a massive expanse of protected grounds within. The castle itself rises vertically far into the sky, its upper-floor windows appearing like specks of dust.

Yet despite its size, it gives off an aura of belonging, as though nature itself had formed the structure eons ago. I stare in fascination as we approach the castle walls.

I'm startled out of my thoughts when our caravan stops suddenly, just feet outside the boundary.

"What's going on, Your Highness?" Cally asks, pulling back a curtain.

I shake my head. "I don't know. Maybe there's a problem with one of the wagons."

But I'm wrong.

Within seconds, a swarm of wolves surrounds our caravan, their eyes flashing red, and their sharp fangs jutting out of snarling mouths.

Cally gasps in shock and jumps backward, practically landing on me. "Y-Your Highness!"

I inhale sharply, pulling her back onto the carriage floor. "Stay down."

She nods rapidly, leaning against the seat I just vacated and holding herself tightly, her knees up against her chin. I close the curtain quickly but leave a small crack of it open, just enough to see what's happening outside.

Right away, I regret the choice. One of the wolves, a slightly larger, black one, begins to transform, his body contorting rapidly while he stands upright, black fur melting away to be replaced by skin— human, naked skin.

I break my gaze instantly, my heart pounding frantically as I try to catch my breath. I'd heard the stories before, of course. Men shift into wolves and back again effortlessly, a power we as humans can't quite fathom. But I've never seen it happen with my own eyes before.

As the newly shifted man starts to speak, I sneak another glance through the crack in the curtain, amazed to see that somehow, he's now partially dressed.

"I am Beta Turgan Rumok of Oceana," he hollers, his voice firm and frightening. "What the hell is the meaning of all this?"

The head of the Maelie Guard dismounts but does not step far from his horse. As he speaks, his voice is edged with a slight tremor. "His Royal Majesty King Chez Molliton of Maelie extends his wishes for a fruitful marriage with his daughter. He has provided these gifts as a—"

"We don't need any of your fucking gifts," the Beta interrupts harshly. "And who the hell are these clowns? This isn't the circus!"

"His Royal Majesty wished to provide entertainment for—"

Again, the Beta cuts off the guard mid-sentence. "The Sea-King Alpha has no need for your entertainment or your gifts. Do you think we do not amply provide for ourselves?"

"His Royal Majesty did not wish to offend," the guard says, his voice squeaking a little.

"Quit wasting our time," the Beta grumbles. "You're to bring a bride and leave. Did you not bring a bride?"

"Her Royal Highness Princess Lyra Molliton is in the carriage, and—"

The wolves don't wait for the guard to answer before they all start shifting. Within seconds, my carriage is surrounded by men—naked men—who throw open the door and reach for me.

I scream from the shock of it all as they haul me out the door. I catch sight of Cally running after me, but the men grab her and start to pull her away.

"She's my lady's maiden!" I holler.

"Take her," the Beta says calmly, and soon they're dragging both me and Cally toward the castle.

I catch a peek back at my caravan, where the wolves who are now men are grabbing all the crates, boxes, and trunks and throwing them all over the cliff into the ocean.

"Those are my things!" I scream as they take hold of my trunk, trying to run back, but a powerful arm grabs me and turns me around, pushing me forward.

"You have no need for human things anymore," he says sharply.

I glance at Cally, whose eyes are wide as the guard holding her shoves her forward. I give her a nod, trying to be reassuring. After all, I was given to the Sea-King Alpha, so I'm sure he will provide me with whatever I need. She relaxes and stops fighting the men, as do I. It's useless anyway.

This is my fate.

As we're led through the castle entrance, I look up at the terrace above, locking eyes with the most handsome man I've ever seen in my life. His physique is tall and powerful, with solid, defined muscles visible through his tight shirt. His eyes are bright silver, rimmed with crimson around the irises, and his hair is nearly white with a silver tint.

I hitch a breath as his eyes meet mine, chills rushing up my spine and raising the hairs on the back of my neck. I freeze in place, my feet no longer moving behind me, and the men behind me start pushing me forward.

The handsome man above breaks his gaze, turns around, and walks away, leaving my breath caught in my lungs as I struggle to walk into the castle.

It takes a few moments of being out of his presence before I can walk again. Now that I do, I try to walk quickly. The sooner they take me to my room, the sooner I can relax and be alone for a moment to recover from the shock.

All my beautiful dresses, my precious books, my keepsakes I've had since childhood... they've all been thrown into the ocean currents, never to be seen again.

My old life has likewise been cast off, leaving me no choice but to accept this new role as the bride of this Alpha.

Was that him I saw on the balcony?

If so, I now know which rumors of his appearance are true. But despite his stunning good looks, only a cold-hearted man would treat his bride this way.

Am I really stuck with this evil man forever?

The grand hallway entrance is not what I'd expected. Back home, everything is covered in jewels and gold. Here, simple, natural materials fill the room, and despite my rattled nerves, somehow, the place feels elegant and welcoming. I'm curious what my room will look like.

But instead of heading up the staircase to the living quarters, we descend into a hallway that leads down below the castle. After walking for several minutes, I catch a whiff of… a horrible stench, a terrible combination of sweat, urine, and mildew. With a turn of the corner, I soon see why.

I'm in the dungeon.

I barely have time to recognize my predicament before Cally screams. Though it's getting darker, there's no mistaking it. She's being dragged off in another direction down a long, empty hall.

"Hey, she's with me," I assert, stopping and turning to one of the guards.

He just grabs me by the arm and pushes me forward with a grunt.

As Cally's screams disappear into the distance, the guards shove me into a cage. One of them moves to close it, but he stops and looks at me first. Stepping in, he moves toward me, and I back up quickly against the cold rock wall behind me.

He smirks, reaching his hand up toward my chest.

Is he going to—oh, no!

Panic rushes through my nerves as I try to block him with my hands. "I-I belong to the king!"

He won't dare put his hands on me if I remind him of that, right?

But instead of touching me, the man grabs for Mother's necklace, yanking it off. "So does this," he snarls, slinking back out of the cage and slamming the door shut behind him.

As the group of guards walks off, laughing, I sink down to the filthy floor, my lavender lace skirt flopping into the grimy dust. I reach up to my bare neck, letting the tears come.

What does this Alpha even want with me?

I guess I'm not his bride, but his prisoner.

FOR THEM

Lyra

I DON'T KNOW HOW LONG I'VE BEEN IN THIS PLACE, BUT I CAN'T CRY forever. If I spend too many tears, I'll become dehydrated, and I'm beginning to get thirsty.

Realizing that I'm completely dependent on these guards to stay alive, I take several deep breaths to calm myself.

I am a princess of Maelie, and I'd better start acting like it.

I rise, wiping my eyes off with the only clean part left of my sleeve and walking the edges of my cell to get a better handle on my surroundings. Strangely, it's a single cage, with no others attached or nearby.

From what I can tell, I'm at the end of a hallway, lit by a single torch on the wall several feet down the corridor. I shudder, acutely aware that the guards can extinguish it just for fun if they'd like, leaving me in total darkness.

There's nothing in the cage but an old, dirty, smelly blanket and a bucket for… my needs. I suppose these are my only possessions now.

But before I cry again, I remind myself that there are subjects in my kingdom with only a few more possessions than these. What food they can acquire from the sea is all they have to eat, and if the Sea-King Alpha decides Maelie can no longer access that, these people will starve and die a silent death.

Thinking of them, I feel foolish, worrying over trunks of mere possessions thrown into the sea. I don't need beautiful dresses. I don't need to read books that those people can never access. I don't need diamonds, even those my own mother fastened around my neck.

I am here for them. No matter what this Alpha wants with me, if he wants only to keep me as a possession in this dungeon forever, or if he wants me to perish here, I will do it.

For them.

As Lower Princess of Maelie, I am here to serve my subjects. And the only subject I have here in Oceana is somewhere in this dungeon.

"Cally!" I call out.

No one answers, though I try several more times.

Resigned to my fate, I return to my spot near the wall. I sit cross-legged, staring into the dimly lit hallway. Silence envelops me, except for a faint, eerie hum reverberating through the stone walls.

I close my eyes, picturing the few glimpses I've had of the castle above me, so elegant in its simplicity, so similar to the feel of the entire palace. I suppose people who can turn into wolves are more in tune with the wild world around them. Maybe that's why they build with the natural materials they find on their lands.

Unlike my father and Anastasia, they don't need gilded walls.

But does that mean the gossip about the Alpha King's cruelty is real? Maybe that connection to nature grounds them to their darkest inner instincts.

I shudder at the thought.

Hours, maybe days, pass, then footsteps approach, and I rise to greet them, hoping it's someone who will let me out of here. Appearing in the dim light is a guard and another man, a servant holding a tray. I'm silent as the guard unlocks the door, feeling vulnerable in the dark, empty cage.

But as soon as the servant sets the tray down, and the guard locks the door behind him, I feel safe again.

"The woman who was with me," I say. "Is she safe?"

Neither man answers. They simply turn away and walk down the hallway, disappearing into the flickering torchlight.

"Thank you," I call after them.

I turn my attention to the tray, my stomach growling as the smell of food wafts toward me. It's a simple meal, bread and vegetables, for which I'm grateful. A large carafe accompanies it, and I take a long sip, savoring the cool, clear water.

I eat slowly, aware that I can't be certain how long I've been kept here, though I know it's long enough that my stomach isn't used to this much food. I save half the bread, hiding it in my dress pocket in case I'm not fed again for a while.

THE DAYS DRAG ON. AT LEAST, I THINK THEY ARE DAYS. I'VE USED MY finger to mark each time I've been fed in the dirt beside me. From the level of my hunger, I've deduced that they're feeding me once a day, though different guards check in more often, usually to replace the torch in the hallway.

And so, this patch of dirt is my calendar, proof that I live, for now.

I'm sitting, admiring it, when I hear more commotion than usual, and several figures start to appear in the torchlight.

One of them has a familiar voice.

"Where are we going?" Cally demands, her voice sweet yet firm.

My smile is instant as I rise, sprinting toward the bars of my cell just as she catches sight of me.

"Your Highness!" she cries, shoving away the men's arms and rushing toward me, her eyes wide.

We hug through the bars, and I allow the tears to flow again.

One of the guards opens the door while two others pry us apart, throwing her into the cage with me and slamming the door again. We just laugh through the tears and hug again.

"Thank you!" I tell the guards.

One of them grunts. "Anything to shut her up."

I frown at the guard as Cally pulls back. She instantly starts straightening my hair. "Goodness, Your Highness. How could they treat you like this?"

I shrug, pulling her hand down. "It's the same as they've treated you, for which I apologize," I tell her.

"None of this is your fault," she insists.

I shake my head. "I can't say it isn't. But anyway, are you well? Are you hurt? Did they feed you?"

"Well enough, Your Highness," she replies. "I was more concerned about you. I kept insisting that I needed to be with you because it's my duty."

"We're equal here," I insist. "Maybe it's time you just called me Lyra. We're friends, after all."

Her eyes go wide, and she lets out a tiny gasp. "I don't know if I can."

"Try it."

"Lyra." She giggles. "I like that. I've always thought your name was beautiful. Your mother named you well. You're just as lovely as your name."

"I certainly don't feel lovely right now." I let out a sigh, jiggling the cage a little.

"Well, this Alpha wanted a wife," she says. "Why he's treating you like this, I have no idea. But I don't think it'll last forever. I have a feeling you'll be at his side soon."

"I'm a little afraid of that," I admit. "I mean, the man turns into a wolf. Does that happen all the time? Can he even control it?"

"I think they can, judging by what I've seen." She sucks in a breath. "Did you see that gorgeous man when they were leading us in? Up on the ledge? Do you think that's the Alpha?"

"I don't know, but he seemed… unique." A feeling I don't understand flows through my arm at the thought of him, erupting my skin with goosebumps.

"I'll say." She bites her lip. "I guess what they said about him being gorgeous was true. I just hope that once he gets to know you, he apologizes for treating you like this."

"Maybe someday, he will," I say.

I doubt it.

But right now, I don't care. Cally is safe.

I lead her back to my spot by the wall and show her my makeshift calendar. I'm still a prisoner, but having Cally here makes me feel like one day, I'll get to be that bride.

I suppose I'll find out eventually.

NO TIME FOR BRIDES

CASSIAN

'ALPHA, HE WANTS TO PARLEY WITH YOU.'

My Beta's voice shoots through my head in the mind-link just as I make the final blow to the brown wolf in front of me, sinking my fangs into his neck. The taste of copper drips from my tongue, and I survey the battlefield.

It is true; the Mountain-King Alpha's army is backing off, though my people continue to chase after those who try to escape their immediate fights.

'Hold.' I command in the community mind-link.

Immediately, my warriors stop their aggressions, stepping back to form a line, waiting.

'Where is he?' I ask Turgan.

He runs up beside me, his black fur shimmering with the moisture of fresh blood. 'Over the east hill ahead,' he answers. 'Shall I come along?'

'Aye.'

He follows as I sprint up the hill, along with my foot servant, who remains in human form far behind me, holding my bag.

As expected, King Cobour awaits our discussion in human form, sitting in a gem-studded throne under a woven tent.

'He has a lust for wealth,' I remark to Turgan.

'Quite,' is his only response.

My Beta and I shift, the foot servant handing us pairs of pants to slip into as we approach.

"Sea-King Alpha Cassian," the enemy king greets me.

"Cobour." I refuse him the formal title, knowing its absence will bite.

My tactic is awarded with a low groan escaping his lips. He knows my army has the advantage, so he doesn't dare correct me. "I would like to find a way to end this conflict."

"As would I," I agree. "Unfortunately, this battle is not of my making."

He grimaces, knowing he was wrong to ever dare step foot in my kingdom. "I had hoped to negotiate."

"Your company will leave my lands in its entirety, never to return," I say simply. "These are my terms."

He betrays his disappointment in his eyes. "Perhaps we could discuss fishing rights in your northwest quadrant."

"You know well we will do no such thing," I insist. "Those who come at my kingdom with violence instead of negotiation get no part in the spoils of my land."

He pauses for a moment and inhales slowly. "I'll take my leave, then."

"Yes, you will."

I stand firm while he calls to his troops, who ascend the hill toward their camps, shifted back to human form, their expressions deflated.

"Take your dead with you," I add over my shoulder as I walk away, expecting no answer.

"I'll leave it to you to see that he does as he's told," I tell Turgan when we return to my army. To the community mind-link, I add, 'Let us go home. These fools waste our time.'

Turgan walks with me for a few steps before leaving. "Shall I arrange a scout of the southern lands?"

"Aye," I reply. "This asshole kept us busy while other more pressing matters are closer to home. Cobour is a joke next to Assanan." I stop and look at him. "What count do you have of the Forest-King Alpha's troops?"

"It's difficult to calculate given their stealth," he tells me. "But I am estimating high and reinforcing our ranks to meet the challenge."

"Excellent." I blow out an exhale forcefully. "Keep me informed. I think it's best I get back to the castle."

"We'll break camp and be back this evening," he says. "I trust Helmswood to tell me if Cobour and his army stick around."

"If they do, they die."

"Aye," he answers.

Without another word, I shift, the power of my white wolf urging me into a swift run. The exhilaration of freedom quickens my steps, the cool salt air breeze rushing through my fur as I race to my castle.

I arrive refreshed, and another foot servant greets me at the castle gates. "Congratulations on your victory, Your Majesty."

I snort as I shift, accepting the clothes from the man. "How did you get such swift news?"

"Your return is news enough," he says with a smirk.

I'm still chuckling as I step into the castle, intending to go straight to my quarters. But my mother interrupts my plans.

"Cassian," she calls from a side hallway. "Are you back from the battle?"

"I am, Mother," I say gently, turning to her.

She smiles, the lines around her mouth more pronounced than I remember them. "I'm delighted to see that," she says. "I hope you taught those awful mountain people a lesson."

"I did," I confirm, a light smirk on my lips. "Mother, did you need me for something?" She is getting more forgetful with her frail health and advanced age.

"I-I was hoping you'd consider bringing the girl to your chambers," she says quickly.

"Girl?" It takes me a beat to recall her foolish idea of accepting the offer of the human bride, an idea I neither wanted nor needed. "Ah, the human princess. Mother, I will not take a wife, much less a human one."

"I don't expect you to make her your Luna," she argues. "I would just like to hold grandchildren in my arms long before I die. You've denied all the eligible ladies in the court, so I have lost hope. However, it's a fact that even a human can bear shifter children to royal wolves, so this union could work."

"Do not speak of dying," I order her. "And I do not wish to waste my time on a human female when my future heir will come from a pure shifter union, as my father's did."

Her face brightens, but I shake my head.

"And such is a fate I am not willing to partake in for many years to come," I remind her.

"Very well." Her features sink into her face. At first, I think she's just frowning, but it's soon clear that half her face is frozen.

'Come immediately!' I command the healer in the direct mind-link, catching my mother as she begins to fall to the ground. 'My mother has had another attack!'

The servants around us jump into action, fetching water and warm towels, but I pick her up myself, carrying her to the nearest sofa.

"Mother," I say softly.

She tries to smile, but her face will not allow it. The healer rushes in carrying her bag of herbs and remedies, directing the servants to assist. I stand back, waiting as my mother's color slowly returns.

'This one occurred suddenly,' I tell the healer privately.

'Yes, Your Majesty,' she agrees. 'She's been under a lot of strain lately, and it's taxing her mind.'

'What can be done?'

'All we can do is help her relax,' she explains. 'Whatever she needs or wants, just do it. Tell her whatever you know she wants to hear. It is for her own good.'

'Of course.'

After several moments, my mother sits up straight.

"Don't rush it," I warn her.

"I'm fine, Cassian."

A servant offers her a cup of water. She takes a sip, closing her eyes to get her bearings. It's clear she has recovered.

"I need to go, Mother," I tell her. "I expect trouble from Assanan soon."

"And the girl?" She looks at me hopefully.

"I truly don't have time for this, Mother," I argue.

But she looks at me again, her eyes dripping with hope. "Could you at least get the girl out of the dungeon?"

"She's there for her own protection."

"Are you telling me my son, the Sea-King Alpha, cannot protect the inhabitants of his own castle if they're not in a cage?" she asks, knowing full well it will rile me.

Just do whatever she needs or wants for her own good. No doubt, the healer's words are wise.

"Ready a room in your wing," I tell her.

She claps her hands happily.

"But don't expect me to be anywhere near the human girl," I add. "I have a war to fight."

"Of course," she says, her tone suspiciously sweet.

I walk away, rushing toward my quarters to prepare my next move before the Forest-King Alpha makes his move.

Does she really expect me to take a human bride?

I don't have time for this shit.

I HAD ONE JOB

Lyra

EVERY MORNING—OR RATHER, EVERY TIME I WAKE UP, SINCE TIME doesn't seem to exist down here, I check to see if Cally is breathing, my heart thumping with relief when I discover she is. This morning, it's labored and wheezing, but at least she's alive. I step up to the cell bars, gazing into the dim hallway.

Being in the Sea-King's dungeon is a tortuous life. I've become so accustomed to the stench, I hardly notice it anymore, but the air itself sits heavy and thick, building up in my lungs as they gasp for oxygen.

It doesn't seem to bother the guards. Either they're used to it, or wolves have some sort of miracle lung capacity that lets them thrive in this hellhole. It seems strange since wolves have such a strong sense of smell. I would think they'd be horrified to have to spend more than one minute down here.

But I hear them all the time now, just down the hall, and it's almost like they're throwing a party, playing cards, talking about women... about us, sometimes. I can tell they're drinking because their rank breath chokes me when they bring us food or come by just to gloat and gawk at us. I can't understand why the king would want his men to ogle so crudely the woman who is supposed to be his bride.

I guess, maybe I'm not his bride. Maybe this is all just a cruel joke.

I know Cally is suffering. She's had breathing problems since she was a child, so this existence is likely killing her. Each time they bring food, I beg for her release, but the guards just laugh and jeer.

Her pain burns deeper in my veins than my own.

I turn as Cally starts to stir. A fit of hacking coughs overcomes her, and I hurry over to pat her back gently. She waves me off, looking up through puffy, exhausted eyes. She only sleeps for a few minutes at a time at most.

"I'm okay," she tells me, though I know it's far from true.

"We need to get you out of here." I try to run my fingers through her matted hair, but it's impossible. Normally a lovely butter blonde, now her silky locks are filled with dust and sludge.

"Please do not worry about me," she insists. "They even hold you here, the bride of the king! There is no hope for a mere servant girl. I have accepted my fate."

I shake my head vigorously. "No. I'm going to get you out of here."

"Someday, we'll find a way out together," she promises.

I see the hope in her eyes, and I can't be the one to extinguish it. "Okay," I agree. "We'll get out of here together."

But even as the words leave my lips, I know this will never be. Stone walls surround us on all sides, leaving only the guarded hallway to hint that there is any life outside this cage, though in my state, weak from what must be months of little food, muscles atrophied from the cramped quarters, it's foolish to think I could even unlock the cell.

There is no escape.

But I keep these dark thoughts from Cally. "Let's play a game," I suggest.

Even in the dim light of the torch, I can see her eyes brighten slightly. "Tic-tac-toe?"

"Yes, if that's what you'd like to play," I tell her. We have few choices, with nothing but our fingers tracing the filthy dirt floor to work with. "You take the Xs, and I'll take the Os."

She nods enthusiastically and draws her X on what is now a permanent game board on the floor, its frame deep from so many weeks—months?—of play. I add my O far away from her turn. Time passes slowly, the meager enjoyment of the game occasionally broken by one of her coughing fits.

"You're letting me win," she complains finally.

"No." I've lied to her face, and regret boils through me. "You're just very good at this."

She doesn't argue, but she scoots toward the back wall and sits in the hard dirt. I join her, wrapping my arms around my knees so we can stare into the silence.

The guards arrive again, and I close my eyes to focus on their banter, pretending I'm home, sitting at the corner table during one of my father's noblemen parties with a glass of bright pink punch. Then, I tried to ignore the endless conversations around me, thinking them silly and pointless. How I wasted those moments wishing I was somewhere else when I should have been soaking up the joy of sharing that time with the kingdom's subjects.

Life's lessons hit hard, ruthless.

"Thorne is losing again," Cally whispers softly.

I nod, having just deduced the same. We've come to know the men by voice, some by sight. "His wife is going to kill him, losing his whole week's pay."

We giggle softly, covering our mouths to stifle our amusement. We'd been refused food for at least a full day—it was hard to tell—the last time we laughed at one of the guards.

The air changes then, but only for a second as the torch flame flickers in the hallway. Cally and I stand quickly, trying to inhale a fragment of freshness that will not penetrate the dense air near the floor.

A man has entered, his voice unfamiliar but strongly commanding. "Is *this* how the Alpha King is rewarded for the gold he pays you miscreants?"

A cacophony of shuffling follows, the familiar guards grunting and falling into line.

"No, sir!" one of them, Lazareth, offers pathetically.

"Luckily, I don't give a shit what you're doing down here, as long as the prisoners stay put," the new guard answers. "Where's that human girl?"

I stiffen at the words, and Cally's frail body shakes beside me.

"She's down the north hall," Lazareth answers quickly.

"Take me to her now," the new man insists. "We're ordered to bring her topside."

Joy rushes into my heart, and I turn to Cally to meet her arms in an excited hug.

"We're getting out of here!" she whispers blissfully.

"Finally," I agree. "Be sure to do as they say so they don't change their minds."

Cally nods, biting her bottom lip.

It's hard to stay calm as the guards slowly make their way down the hall, and I nearly squeal with delight when one of them opens the lock.

"Which one is it?" the new man demands. His face is contorted with disgust, but I don't blame him. He's clearly not used to the stink down here. His robes seem regal, so he must be a king's guard.

"The redhead," a guard says.

"And which fucking one is that?" the king's guard spits out. "They both look disgusting. Who can distinguish hair color?"

"That one," another of the guards, Henry, says, pointing at me.

"Bring her," the king's guard says, and he turns to walk off.

Henry takes my arm and pulls me out, but my heart slumps into my chest when he locks the cage behind us.

"She's with me!" I protest loudly, my nerves screaming at me to go back to Cally. "She needs to come with me!"

The king's guard turns around, impatience filling his eyes. "I have orders to release you, and you only," he grunts. He turns around and walks away despite my continued pleas. "Why the fuck are they always so difficult?" he complains, without another glance at me.

"No!" I scream as Henry drags me down the hallway. "She's with me!"

"Do not worry about me!" Cally yells after me, her voice hoarse and weak. "It is you who is important!"

"No!" I repeat, but Henry is already pushing me forward.

The last I see of Cally, her weak, sickly body slinks to the cold hard floor, her hands grasping the cage bars to steady herself.

I had one job, one person to protect, and I've let her down. I don't deserve the fresh air I'm forced to breathe, and I choke on it as they pull me up the stairs.

SOMEWHERE IN THE MIST

CASSIAN

I DETEST TRAINING IN HUMAN FORM. THE SCRATCHY, THICK TUNIC beneath my armor barely holds its shape and does little to abate the chafing from the heavy metal plating. Swords and shields feel foreign in my arms, though I wield them with ease from years of training.

I would much rather feel the grip of my teeth as they bear down on my enemy's neck.

But Phelan favors the old ways, a time when wolf shifters fought for—and won—control of all the lands. That was the time when wars meant lines of soldiers in glistening armor, their swords and shields falling with a clank against those of the enemy. It was a time when we fought as human as a nod to our past—when we were human.

No one remembers the first child born with the ability to shift, nor does anyone remember how it occurred. Those days are lost in the mist of cold, ancient memories. Now, we train in human form because some of the elders think it makes us stronger.

I beg to differ.

Phelan approaches, his smile wide against the tanned, leather-like texture of his skin. Somehow, my father's best friend has found such peace in his old age that smiles come easier than the grimace of a warrior, though deep furrows are still burned into his forehead. "The warriors have done well today," he says.

"Then we should stop this foolishness and spar as wolves," I suggest.

His smile just gets broader. "I've no objection, so long as they also practice handling weapons. You young people don't realize it, but it's a useful skill."

"For one without fangs, maybe." I ignore his chuckle in response and address the warriors. "That is all for today."

They show me the sign of respect, and I watch them clear out from the training grounds in an organized fashion. I turn back to Phelan when the last warriors have stepped away. "Has there been any more word on Assanan's movements?"

"No." His easy smile fades. "Most likely, he is recovering from his last battle from the east, restoring his ranks."

"But you have no doubt he'll strike here next," I finish for him.

"No doubt," he confirms.

For a second, I see the flame of anger in his eyes that erupts, despite his normally peaceful manner, whenever he speaks of the man who killed my father. He and my father, the Sea-King Alpha Hedroin, had known each other since childhood, just like Turgan and myself. "We'll take him down," I assure him.

Phelan nods lightly, and the flames extinguish in his eyes. Instead, they brighten with another thought, one I'd rather he keep to himself.

"What of the human girl?" he asks.

I feel my chest tighten. What is it with these elders that they continue to insist I marry some human princess? Or marry at all? "What of her?" I reply.

He chuckles again, and my blood comes to a mild simmer. If it were anyone other than my father's Beta, he'd be flat on the ground already. But my respect for him as a man and a leader outweighs my anger. When my father fell, he stepped in as a guide and mentor to me as best he could.

"Dyanne says she's bringing her up from the dungeon today," he says.

"My mother is persistent, and this is her choice alone," I explain. "Healer Elara suggested I appease her wishes to avoid further attacks. My mother is not well."

He exhales softly. "She has been through so much. It's the worst thing, to lose a true mate."

"And this is why I don't understand why so many of you insist I marry this human," I tell him. "Suppose I find my true mate when I have already begotten children with this woman? How could I ever reconcile this?"

"Perhaps this is why your mother insists on it," he says quietly.

I shake my head. "I don't understand."

He pats my shoulder again, a habit of his when he is in a fatherly mood with me. "Perhaps she feels it's best you never experience the pain of losing a true mate, and—"

"And she knows the human would not be her," I finish for him.

"Precisely."

"And you, Phelon?" I ask. "What is it you feel is best for me?"

His lips rise once again, and he gestures for me to sit on a nearby bench. We settle in, watching the clouds sail past against the deep azure sky.

"Your father always looked to the clouds," he begins finally, breaking the silence. "We were young, so much younger than you are today, just boys, really." His eyes turn distant. "He said his grandfather told him that all the ancestors of the ages are right there in the clouds. When they pass, that means they're checking up on you, to see how you're doing. When they're not there, it means they know all is well."

"He told me the same," I explain, a sigh escaping me. "But I didn't believe him." I turn to meet Phelon's gaze. "Do you?"

He shrugs and looks up again. "I don't know if it's true, but it's a fine idea. So, I believe your father comes to us the same way, just checking in."

It wouldn't be a bad thing if that were the case. I look up a thick, billowing cloud just above us.

"I think he would want me to give you this advice," he continues. "If there is a true mate for you out there, you should do all you can to find her."

I gaze back at him, furrowing my brow. "Strange advice, coming from a confirmed bachelor."

He chuckles lightly. "I never said I didn't try to find my own."

"I'm sorry." Guilt chews at me. I always wondered why the Goddess didn't bless such a kind, dutiful man with a mate.

"No reason to be sorry, Cassian," he insists. "My life has gone well enough. But I'll never forget the day your father found Dyanne. I'd never seen such happiness in his eyes." He turns to me. "I don't think he would want you to be denied such joy. I don't think your mother does, either. She is just lost in her own sadness right now."

I nod, knowing it's true. Father always told me I should find the one, that I shouldn't settle for anyone who isn't a true mate.

"Anyway," he slaps his knees and stands. "This hard bench is no place for an old man with a withered back. Perhaps I'll go find some breakfast leftovers from the cook. Are you coming along?"

I shake my head. "No, I think I'll sit here for a while."

He pats my shoulder once again. "We'll talk later, then."

"Yes," I say.

I watch him walk away, a slight limp in his step now that his back is in pain again. Once alone, I look up at the cloud, which has lingered despite others having passed over and moved on.

"I'll wait for the one," I say out loud, hoping that somewhere in the mist, my father hears me. "There's no way I'm marrying a human girl when there's someone out there you and the Moon Goddess want me to meet."

BY ORDER OF THE QUEEN MOTHER

Lyra

CALLY'S EYES KEEP FLASHING IN MY MIND, EXHAUSTED, DEFLATED...
sick. The sound of her cough keeps echoing through my head. I've
heard her erupt in fits of coughing so many times.

But I trudge forward, the hands of the guards burning against me
as they shove me every time I try to stop. In my weakened state,
there's nothing I can do to stop them.

There may be nothing I can do even when and if I regain my full
strength. These are wolves who can tear my head off in an instant.

But I don't believe they will do that as long as the king wants me.
And since he has sent for me, that must be the case. My only hope is
to beg for Cally's release once I meet him face-to-face.

Though the very idea of that terrifies me.

The ache in my stomach grinds as we reach the top of the long,
slanted hallway leading up to the castle, the one they forced me down
when I arrived. *How long ago was that?* There's no way to tell.

Henry opens the top door, and powerful rays of sunlight strike me like a bullet, blinding me so harshly that I yelp, bringing my hands to my eyes to cover them.

"What the hell's the matter with you now?" Henry snorts, shoving me forward so hard I nearly fall forward.

Instinctively, I reach my arms up to stop myself, but I have to close my eyes. At least I won't have to see the floor barreling toward me before my face hits it. But again, the men's arms stop me midair, holding me up long enough to gain my footing so they can keep pushing me through the castle.

I've never had so many men grabbing at me. I've never had *any* man grab me. As a daughter of the king, I've been completely off-limits while Father decided the most strategic use of me, which apparently, is selling me off to a cruel wolf king who enjoys watching me suffer.

Slowly, I'm able to blink my eyes open, and my fuzzy surroundings come into focus. I'm now acutely aware of eyes all over me. I don't understand why the king would want me paraded around in public as soon as I came out of the dungeon. And I don't understand why he wanted me in the dungeon in the first place.

Thankfully, we pass into a hallway and leave most of the curious onlookers behind. Grand archways tower above me, simplistic and functional but somehow… elegant. I'm unable to distinguish a seam, soon realizing they are carved out of a single massive stone. My breath hitches as I now understand why the entire castle seems to fit so well in the landscape.

It is the landscape.

It wasn't made from the materials in the cliffs. It is the cliffs.

Somehow, these people—wolf shifters—had tamed the highest cliff face, turning it into a massive piece of architecture fitting for those so in touch with nature.

Impressed as I am with the surroundings, I can't get Cally out of my mind. Whatever happens in this place, I have to stay alive so I can save her.

My stomach churns as we approach a set of massive double doors carved from what looks to be mahogany wood. Each panel shows a scene—stories perhaps—of wolves and ships and all the creatures of the sea.

Surely, the Sea-King Alpha is behind these doors, and I'm about to see him… again, I realize. That must have been him who met my eyes on the balcony that day when they led me inside.

No other man besides the Alpha King could have such a commanding presence, could be so handsome and strong.

Butterflies flutter in my chest as the guards open the door.

But all it is… is another hallway, some sort of entry into a larger suite. I brace myself as Henry knocks on the interior door.

Maybe these are his chambers.

I hitch a breath as the door opens, but it's just a woman who appears. Specks of gray hair pepper her temples, her eyes the color of cold steel.

"I've got her," she snaps. "Leave."

Without another word, Henry and the others spin around and leave me there, clicking the huge mahogany doors closed behind them.

I feel the woman staring at me, but I keep my eyes on the floor, mindlessly tracing the intricate patterns of the hardwood as it winds down the hallway.

"Look at me, girl," the woman orders.

It's a struggle to raise my gaze against the weight of her presence. When I finally do, hers narrow, flitting down and back up, assessing me. I fight to swallow against a dry throat.

A judgmental grunt escapes her lips. "Hmm. I thought you were a princess. Well, you hardly seem regal to me. But you're human, after all." She sighs, exaggeratedly. "Can't expect anything more from that sorry lot. Anyway, I won't permit you to see the Queen Mother in this state. Get inside, and we'll get you cleaned up."

"Queen Mother?" I ask.

She snorts. "Oh, so you do talk. Of course, the Queen Mother. She's responsible for the household affairs until the Alpha King finds a suitable Luna. Of course, that won't be you." She lets out a snide chuckle. "Well? Get inside. The bathing suite is that way."

Her tone has me hurrying past her, trying to reach the bathing suite before she shoves me like the guards did. Something tells me that would be even more unpleasant than the male guards.

The massive soaking tub is already prepared, steam rising from the water, scented of lavender and rose. It's been so long since I smelled something pleasant, I'm surprised I even recognize the fragrances.

"Strip down," the woman orders behind me, her harsh voice so contrary to the warm welcome of the bath in front of me. "We'll throw that… garment out in the trash."

I run my fingers along the lace of my purple dress as I obediently remove it. It's been my favorite for such a long time, but now, it's nothing but tatters, worn so thin it's hard to remember it ever being the luxurious gown I wore to my father's events.

It's the last thing I have from my past, but I suppose it is better left forgotten in a pile of rubbish.

"Get in," she says harshly.

"I-I have a lady's maiden who can assist me," I explain. "But the men wouldn't bring her up with me from the dungeon."

"I know nothing of a maiden," she insists. "Get in."

I'm accustomed to ladies assisting me in my bath, so I do as she asks, though she scrubs my back harshly, erasing any pleasure that should have come with the first moment of cleanliness since I'd been forced into the darkness below the castle. I remain still as I do for Cally, or any of the maidens from my castle back home, all of whom would have assisted me with a much gentler touch, though I'm sure the thickness of the dungeon grime may have required more effort.

After the tub is drained three times, and several forceful dips to wash my hair, I'm finally soaking in clean, floral-scented water, but the experience is cut short.

"Get out and dry off," the woman orders me. "Your gown is on the bed in the bedchambers. I'll return to fasten it for you."

With that, she disappears, and finally, I can breathe. I close my eyes, spending a few moments in the still-warm bathwater, inhaling nothing but beautiful fragrances for the first time in… I don't know how long.

But guilt eats at me soon, remembering Cally, still trapped below, still filthy, still starving, still sick.

I exit the tub, drying myself off and wandering naked into the bed chambers, where a simple but lovely blue gown is draped across the dark purple bedclothes.

The woman never told me her name, and I don't really want to know. But she mentioned the Queen Mother, not the king. Maybe the Queen Mother is the one who ordered my release from the dungeon.

I suppose the Alpha King still wants nothing to do with me.

And maybe that's for the best.

SOMETHING IS WRONG

Lyra

SEVERAL MINUTES PASS, AND THE WOMAN HASN'T RETURNED TO HELP ME fasten my dress. I sure don't miss her company, but I feel the cool air on my bare back and hope the Queen Mother doesn't walk in to see me like this.

There's a dressing area in the suite, so I figure I can at least do something with my hair in the meantime, sitting on the velvet bench in front of the vanity.

I hardly recognize my reflection when I look up at the mirror. Though clean and wet, tufts of my hair stick up over balls of mats, and my heart sinks. It will take forever to comb these out.

But I have to try. The alternative is having that cold-mannered woman come back and start ripping half of it out of the follicles.

So, I find a brush in a drawer and start working on the ends, gently pulling as I work my way up. It's a slow process, but it's working.

I catch sight of my eyes in the mirror. Blotches of bluish-purple form a half-circle underneath them, the skin hollowed out. The whites of my eyes are speckled with tiny red veins, and even the green irises seem faded.

My mother always said she loved my emerald-green eyes. The thought of her births an ache in my heart. She said she would try to visit. Would the Alpha King allow it?

Will I ever see my family again?

But I shake my head. I can't think about this now, not while Cally is still suffering in the dungeon. I have to make myself presentable for the Queen Mother so I can beg for my maiden's release.

The door opens, and a cold shudder rushes over me, sending goosebumps prickling over my arms.

"There you are," the same woman says sharply. "Get up."

I obey without hesitation and feel her cold fingers fastening the back of my dress.

She sighs, exaggerated frustration biting at her next words. "I suppose we have to deal with this hair. What a disgusting mess! Give me that."

She reaches around me and grabs the brush out of my hand. Instinctively, I tighten my grasp, but her strength against my weak muscles is no match. I close my eyes, bracing for the pain, and it doesn't disappoint.

My scalp screams as she yanks on the knots, her long, bony fingers dropping the hair she tears out into the vanity wastebasket. But I don't scream. I don't complain.

This woman could turn into a wolf and bite my head off, too.

Besides, I need to be compliant so that the Queen Mother has no reason to refuse my request.

When she's done, she spins me around harshly. "Ugh, you look awful. I suppose that's a human trait. I doubt the best makeup in the kingdom can fix that, but I'll try, nonetheless. Hold still."

My stomach turns in on itself while she holds my chin roughly as she dusts on powder and blush. I breathe as shallowly as possible so I can avoid moving, closing my eyes when ordered and opening them reluctantly.

When she is finished, I finally let out a breath, relieved for the end of the torture. I turn to the mirror, hitching a breath when I see the impressive results.

Now I look alive, at least, though I still don't feel like it.

"Good enough," she snaps, though her tone betrays the words. "Follow me."

She points to a pair of shoes on the floor, low heels that match the gown, and I slip them on before following her out the door. She walks fast down the massive hallways, each step forceful and calculated. Because she's taller than me, her stride is so quick I have to practically run to catch up.

But I don't mind. I need to see the Queen Mother and ask her about Cally, and I'd run to beg for her freedom if I could.

After multiple long hallways and what seems like dozens of twists and turns, we approach another set of double doors. The carvings on these seem to depict women and children, which is fitting for the mother of the king's chambers.

The woman knocks lightly, and I hear a voice like music from the other side, allowing our entry. I lower my eyes and prepare to show my respect as we enter.

"Esmerelda, my dear," that same melodic voice chimes out. "It's lovely to see you."

I brave a quick gaze toward the woman I'd been following, and my jaw drops involuntarily. She has a name, a lovely one— Esmerelda, and every cell of cold-hearted indifference she'd given me is gone, replaced by a bright smile that doesn't quite reach her eyes.

But the Queen Mother is clearly not surprised, walking up to her cheerfully. I shift my eyes back down to the floor but catch Esmerelda's bow and strange movements with her hands, a signal of respect for the wolves, I'm guessing.

"This must be her," the Queen Mother sings, placing a finger on my chin and forcing my head up. She releases it and smiles when I meet her eyes.

I greet her with a deeply respectful curtsey as I've been trained in my Father's court.

"Oh, how charming." The Queen Mother claps her hands together. "Humans have such lovely customs. Have a seat, dear."

She gestures toward a padded lounge chair nearby, but instead, I drop to my knees where I stand. "Your Majesty," I say, desperation in my voice. "I beg for the release of my lady's maiden, still held in the dungeon. I fear for her health and wellbeing."

"Goodness," the Queen Mother says, lifting a hand to her chest. "Rise, dear. There's no need for that." She turns to Esmerelda. "Did they not release her girl?"

"I-I don't know, Your Majesty," Esmerelda says, her voice honeyed, with a sharp edge. "I didn't know of her existence."

I shoot her a glare. I've mentioned my lady's maid to her several times when she was washing me. *Why is she lying?*

"Perhaps an oversight on the part of the guards," the Queen Mother suggests. "Go seek out the Beta and have her release arranged. Take her to the princess's chambers. She can stay in the servant's room."

"Thank you, Your Majesty," I say, offering another deep curtsey. Despite Esmerelda's strange behavior, my heart soars at the thought of Cally being set free.

"Right away, Your Majesty." Esmerelda makes the unfamiliar hand gesture to the queen again and steps out, but not before her eyes graze me, all the softness instantly gone in them.

The look is... evil.

A chill rushes up the back of my neck.

But the Queen Mother is already speaking in her pleasant voice, gesturing toward the chair again. I oblige this time, shaking off the strange encounter with Esmerelda and sitting where she requested.

"I'm terribly sorry about your girl," she continues. "We'll have that righted immediately."

"Thank you." I give her a genuine smile, and she smiles back.

"Tea, Calendia," she says louder, and instantly, a servant woman appears, wheeling over a tray that was across the room. "Do you like tea?" the Queen Mother asks me.

"Very much so." I nod as I answer, still thrilled about the thought of seeing Cally again and having her rested, clean and well-fed, in a proper bed.

Once the tea is poured and small finger breads and pastries offered, the Queen Mother turns to me again. "I'd also like to apologize for your treatment. I hope your time in the dungeon wasn't too unpleasant."

Her smile persists, and her tone is light and cheerful, as though months in a dungeon is nothing more than a stint in a slightly substandard hotel room.

"With my lady's maiden's release, I won't think of it anymore, Your Majesty," I tell her.

She smiles and hums to herself as we continue eating, and an uncomfortable silence passes between us, though it seems one-sided. The Queen Mother is perfectly content eating and drinking her tea, almost singing to herself as the moments tick away.

Something is strange about the Queen Mother, and the way Esmerelda acted around her. I hope she obeys the orders, regardless.

"Oh, these are so wonderful," she says, fingering another frosting-covered triangle of pastry. "Mm, once we're done here, let's go see my son. Would that be okay?"

The question unbalances me, my heart suddenly pounding in my chest. "Yes, that would be nice," I manage to say politely, my nerves standing at attention.

"Oh, splendid," she says, pushing away the cart suddenly and standing. "Let's go now."

I keep my surprise to myself, nodding. I give a lighter curtsey again and follow her as we exit her chambers. Something is definitely wrong with this woman. She's nice enough, but she doesn't seem quite stable.

And I'm about to be face-to-face with the Sea-King Alpha himself.

That steel rock forms in my stomach again, churning against the butterflies.

I don't think I can do this.

THE WILL OF THE GODDESS

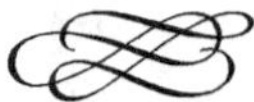

CASSIAN

'I SMELL IT TOO.'

Though I haven't said a word, Turgan senses my thoughts and confirms my suspicions in a private mind-link. The foul scent of forest wolves grows stronger as we approach the outskirts of our boundaries.

Assanan's warriors have already breached the perimeter of our lands.

And this means war.

'I'm beginning to think he and Cobour are working together,' I tell my Beta. "The Mountain-King Alpha is pathetic. He would only be emboldened by such a partnership—'

'To make our warriors tire before Assanan's attack,' he finishes for me.

'Exactly.' I test the air with my keen wolf's sense, closing my eyes to focus on their numbers. 'I have at least a hundred different wolf scents.'

'At least,' he agrees. 'What's our move?'

'Triple the guards on this line,' I tell him. 'For now, let's see if we can catch any of them on our side of the border and teach them a lesson.'

'Aye.'

To the rest of our scout party, I add, 'Kill any mountain or forest wolves encroaching on our territory. Zero tolerance.'

'Aye, Alpha,' they all say in unison.

I lead the pack, my white wolf guiding our twenty strongest warriors, along with Turgan, toward the outermost stretches of our territory. We make no play at stealth, the dead leaves and dried twigs snapping noisily beneath us as we make our way toward the border.

Though Assanan claims the bulk of the forest, trees line our territory toward its outskirts, blocking the strong ocean winds from reaching this far inland. Few plants hold their ground against the harsh salt sprays near the coast, as is evident by the efforts to keep the castle maintained, despite its natural rock construction.

Though wolves aren't normally seafaring, uncountable centuries ago, our ancestors chose coastal lands as their own, wisely understanding the importance of sea trade for future generations.

As I run forward, my mother's voice chimes through a private mind-link. Concerned, I engage with her. 'Mother, are you well?'

'I'm fine, son, just fine,' she insists. 'Lyra and I are awaiting your arrival in the tearoom.'

Lyra—the name strikes a chord, electric tingles echoing through my wolf, yet I have no idea who Mother is talking about.

'Mother, I'm out on patrol,' I explain. 'I don't expect to return until sunset.'

'But we're waiting,' she argues. 'Do you not wish to meet your bride?'

The word rattles through me. Bride—she must mean the human girl. I hadn't even considered what her name might be. I'd hoped allowing the girl topside would have appeased my mother for the time being.

But Mother's mind is so hollow now, she's gaining some sort of pleasure from pretending I'll wed a human female. Losing her mate has truly made her come undone.

'I'll be home at sunset,' I repeat. 'I don't doubt you'll be able to entertain each other until then.'

'We'll be waiting!' Her tone is enthusiastic, hopeful, like a child.

'Are we stopping here?'

Turgan's question floods into my mind, and I realize I'd nearly slowed to a stop. 'My mother called,' I explain.

'Has she had another attack?' he asks. 'Do we need to return?'

'No,' I tell him. 'She is well, just wanting me to entertain company.'

'The girl?'

I let out a sigh, or one somewhat resembling one coming out of my wolf's muzzle. 'It keeps her busy, entertaining thoughts of my marriage, so I allow it.'

'Surely you'll tell her the truth before you're standing at the altar.'

I very nearly clamp down on his carotid for the snide joke. 'It won't go that far,' I say instead.

He goes silent, knowing better than to test me further, and as we pick up speed, the others following unquestioningly. I need to focus, to take out any forest wolves who dare step foot in my territory.

Yet something in my wolf, something deep in its primal being, stirs me, calling me to return to the castle.

I'll do no such thing. I shall return at sunset as planned.

"GATHER THE UNIT COMMANDERS," I TELL TURGAN ONCE WE'VE returned and shifted to human form. "The dead we've left today will only be the beginning."

"Aye, Sea-King Alpha Cassian," he replies.

I turn to him, wrinkles forming in my brow. "You never call me by my full title."

"I may as well get used to it," he explains, a smile playing at the edges of his lips. "Once you have a Luna, we'll need to be more formal."

"I will have no Luna," I snap. "Well, I know not what the future brings, but this human girl certainly wouldn't be worthy of the title even if I did plan to marry her." I give him a dangerous scowl. "Which I do not," I add.

He holds up his hands in mock surrender. "Understood."

But I can practically hear his smirk as he walks away. Few other men would escape a death sentence for such behavior.

Having dressed, I make my way toward my mother's quarters. 'I'm on my way,' I tell her.

'Oh, lovely,' she replies. 'We're here in my suite, dear. Please hurry. We've been waiting so long.'

A groan escapes me, and a nearby guard jumps to attention at his post. But I pass him, ignoring him, cursing my father internally for getting himself killed and leaving me with a shell of a mother.

The guards outside her quarters give me the sign of respect and open the large double doors. Inside, my mother smiles broadly as she catches sight of me. I see the human girl facing away in the chair opposite her, catching only the dusting of crimson hair over the silk chair back.

My wolf shudders inside me. *Why?*

"Oh, there you are," Mother says, her face filled with nothing but hollow, infantile emotion. "You need to meet your future bride, Lyra."

She gestures toward the woman, who stands, keeping her eyes toward the ground yet not quite in a submissive stance, no doubt thinking herself a royal because she belongs to the human family currently in power in their small enclave.

She's lovely, I'll give her that, as I had also noticed when she was first brought to the castle. But she's not a Luna, not even a half-wolf, as I can clearly catch from her scent, pleasant as it might be.

The woman—Lyra, I suppose, is her name—makes a strange move, bending down low and giving me a nod of her head. It must be a human custom.

Silly and useless, just as they are.

"Well, aren't you going to say hello?" My mother grins and looks at me expectantly.

I have no intention of playing at a wedding to this pathetic human. My wolf growls at the thought, and I push him back. Why he reacts this way, I can't imagine. The Goddess surely has greater gifts awaiting our future than a pretty face with no substance.

"Greetings," I say coldly. "I'll say this from the start. What arrangements your father made are void here. I agreed simply as a courtesy. You may live in this castle in comfort, but there will be no wedding."

The girl lowers her eyes to the floor.

"Cassian?" Mother asks, her head tilted.

"I'm sorry, Mother," I tell her. "I won't marry a human. I will keep my word and give her father's kingdom access to the sea, and that is all."

"But—" Mother begins.

"No, Mother," I insist.

Her expression falters, and she sinks backward, too far away to return to her chair, her lips contorting in that all-too-familiar pattern.

Another attack.

'Get here now,' I tell the healer, stepping forward to break my mother's fall.

The human girl does the same, almost on the same level of instinct, catching my mother's arms and weakly assisting as we get her back into the chair.

I steady Mother's back, and my hand brushes across Lyra's as I pull it away.

Sparks of molten fire rush through my veins, my heart thumping wildly against my ribcage. I step back from the shock of it, turning my head toward Lyra.

Our eyes meet, hers wide, confused as they bore into my own. We stand there, our gazes unbroken, as the healer bursts through my mother's doors and rushes to her side.

I step away, finally getting my bearings and forcing myself to break that gaze.

'This one was strong.'

Blinking, my head shakes as I sort out the healer's words in the mind-link. 'But she will be fine,' she adds. 'She just needs rest.'

'See to what she needs,' I snap, turning away.

I cannot even stay by my mother at this time of need. My feet quicken as I storm down the hallway, bracing against the desperate whines of my wolf inside me.

How the fuck can this be?

How... and why, did the Goddess mate me to a weak, pathetic human?

I'M ONLY HUMAN

Lyra

Confusion overwhelms me, and I don't know what to do.

My entire body erupted in warm, electric shivers when the Alpha King's hand brushed against mine. That, and the way his gaze penetrated straight into my soul, had my heart thumping so hard I could almost hear it.

Then, he ran out as soon as his mother was in the hands of the doctor, which I suppose they call a healer here.

I'm not sure how I managed to stand back out of the way, but I can barely feel my legs now the way those strange trembles are still rumbling through my body.

There's another feeling that I just don't understand, the burning ache coiled around every nerve as he sprinted out the door. The sensation has calmed now, but only slightly, still lingering and causing my hands to quiver.

Flexing my fingers at my sides, I try to quell the emotion and remember to breathe. More people hurry in, circling around the Queen Mother and ensuring her comfort.

The maiden who had been serving refreshments all day, who like me had been frozen in place as the medical team worked on her superior, finally notices me and steps over, gently placing a warm hand on my shoulder. "The Queen Mother will need to rest now," she says softly. "It's probably best if you go back to your room."

I nod but look hopelessly toward the now-open door and the expansive hallways beyond. "I don't think I know the way," I tell her.

She turns back to the Queen Mother, who is still unconscious. The medical team is moving her into another room in the back of the suite, which I assume is her bedroom. She turns back to me. "I won't be needed here for a few minutes," she says. "I can show you the way."

"Thank you," I tell her.

Her steps are fast and light, and I'm beginning to think wolf shifters have some sort of innate speed about them, even when they're in human form. But I keep up, anxious to get back to my room, excited that I'll find Cally there waiting.

I'll be so glad she's no longer in that horrible dungeon, I'll help her bathe and brush out her hair—gently—myself. Hopefully, they've provided some clean dresses for her.

The labyrinth of hallways is still impossible to understand, especially while I'm practically jogging next to the woman. But finally, she stops at the familiar set of double doors outside my suite.

"Here we are," she says. "Please stay in your room until the Queen Mother calls for you again. Esmerelda will handle your meals."

I can't help the expression that pours over my face at the mention of Esmerelda's name. I'm in no hurry to see that woman again.

She giggles. "I understand your hesitation," she says. "Esmerelda is a bit harsh at first, but once you get to know her, I'm sure you'll become friends."

I don't see how that's possible, but I'm willing to try it.

"I'd better get back," she continues. "Esmerelda will check in periodically."

"Thank you," I say. "What's your name?"

Her face brightens at the request. "Oh, I'm Lizzy."

"I hope to see you again soon, Lizzy," I tell her. "Thank you for being so kind."

"My pleasure." She gives a wave and disappears around a corner before I can say anything else.

The large, ornate double doors are heavier than I expect, but then again, I'm likely still weak from my time in the dungeon, which only ended this morning. I guess it'll take some time before I feel close to normal.

Will my life ever be normal again? I suppose not.

With a strong push, I manage to get past those large doors and into the entryway, where I happily turn the knob and step in. "Cally?" I call out.

But I'm greeted with nothing but my own echo.

"Cally?"

It's been all day. She has to be here.

A heaviness sets into my chest as I run toward the bathing room, even checking behind the curtain to see if she's already in the tub.

Nothing.

I hurry down the inner hallway toward the servant's room, choking on my breath. No, I have to stay calm. She must be here. She probably just didn't hear me.

But as I turn the knob, I already know she's not there.

The servant's room is dark, but I grab a lantern from the hallway table and step inside. Cally definitely isn't here. In fact, it doesn't look like anyone's lived in this room for a while. Furnishings are covered in plastic, and the bed is completely stripped. Even the washroom is quiet, dark, untouched.

Why isn't Cally here?

Back in my main room, I pace the floor, my stomach churning with a mix of fear, confusion, and guilt. I remember clearly that the Queen Mother ordered Esmerelda to have Cally released. She has to obey, right?

But then, there was that look in her eye when she passed me on the way out. Did she intend to ignore her superior's orders just to spite me? Why?

Is it my fault Cally is still suffering in the dungeon?

Finally, I decide to try to find Esmerelda, or someone, anyone who can tell me what's going on. I rush out the entryway door and push my way past the double doors into the massive hallway, looking in both directions.

There's no one around.

I try to remember how many turns Lizzy and I made coming back from the Queen Mother's quarters. Could I find my way back? I don't want to bother the regent, but maybe Lizzy could help me find someone to release Cally as ordered.

Holding back the burning sense of dread washing over me, I attempt to trace my steps—I think in the right direction—back down the hallway.

I risk a turn I'm not sure about, and then another, and things look familiar for a moment until I make another turn. The hall I'm in now looks the same, but something tells me I haven't been this way before.

But as soon as I step back into the last hall, I'm confused again. Now, it doesn't seem quite right. Maybe I came from the other direction.

And now, I don't know how to get back to my room.

Eventually, I break into a sprint, hurrying down one hallway and another, turning and twisting down corridors that look exactly the same as the last one, never once running into anyone, not a servant, not even Esmerelda.

I'm lost.

I have to stop, struggling to regain my breath as I lean against the wall. I haven't regained enough strength for this much exercise. The churning in my stomach turns into a famished growl, and I realize I'd only eaten a dainty meal in the presence of the Queen Mother, and that was hours ago now.

Sinking to the floor, I wrap my arms around my knees, the tears forming heavy in my eyes.

Cally isn't up here, and I don't know how ill she is from being in that awful, musty dungeon. I can't get back to my room, and there's no one to help me.

And not only that, but I can't explain the strange feeling I had when the Alpha King touched me. Echoes of it still reverberate through me, like an outstretched ribbon reaching across time and space, intertwining with him. Somehow, I even feel like he's nearby.

But that's impossible… ridiculous, really. I have no connection to a wolf shifter Alpha I've barely met. I'm not powerful like these people here who can turn into wolves at will. I can't sense anything I can't see with my own eyes. I can't read minds.

I'm only human.

Powerful footsteps approach from around the corner, and I rise, hopeful.

Maybe this is someone who can help me.

A HUMAN MATE?

CASSIAN

'Meet me in the council room,' I tell Turgan in the mind-link. 'Summon the others.'

Assanan's warriors have been spotted again on our side of the border. A deep growl escapes my throat, and my wolf inside salivates at the thought of ending the Forest Alpha with its sharp canines.

My warriors know better than to take him down in battle.

His death is mine.

Plans for his elimination surge through my mind, until my wolf lets loose another sensation that ripples through my veins with the strength of the tide. I quicken my steps, now fully understanding this ache is from my mate.

My Goddess-damn human mate.

How can fate be so cruel?

Now that I am aware of its cause, I realize I've felt the sensation since the girl first arrived. Though we were too far apart to touch, my wolf let out a distressed cry as she passed into the castle below my terrace upon her first arrival.

I dismissed it then, explaining it away as just a lustful wail. I have to admit, the woman is fair, and I certainly noticed it as she passed that day. Her hair, the color of the amber crystals the healer uses for pain relief, flowed in waves as the ocean crashes into the southern beaches. Her eyes, bold like emeralds, gleamed in the glistening sunbeams of the morning light.

Just noticing such detail befuddled me at the time. There are legions of beautiful wolf shifters in my kingdom and those of our allies. I dismissed it as harmless lust.

In the months the human girl was held protectively in the dungeon, tiny shards of emotion plagued my dreams. It all lacked clarity. I had no truth crystal as the witches use to identify the source of these feelings. So, I again dismissed the disturbance in my mind.

But now, I know.

And since I touched her, I've sensed her presence in my mind. She and I have our own private mind-link—I feel it—but I dare not disturb it and consummate any part of this blasphemous connection.

I doubt the human girl knows what it is or how to use it.

As I hurry toward the council room, I want only to think of war, of paying back that son of a bitch Assanan for ripping my father from his throne.

But that ribbon of connection reverberates through my nerves. She's close, but how is the human girl in my wing of the castle? She was told to stay near Mother.

Ugh, another problem I will save for another day—how to cure my mother's ailment. The attacks have come swifter now, and more frequently. The healer is adept at bringing her back physically, but she has told me clearly the prognosis is not a good one.

Her mind is gone without her mate.

These thoughts disappear in an instant, and my heart thuds in my chest when I turn the next corner and nearly collide with the bright emerald eyes gazing back at me. "Lyra."

Her name exits my lips with no effort, with no will of my own. My wolf hums with blissful pleasure at the sight of her, the proximity, the second near-touch of this day.

Her emerald eyes glisten with moisture, and though shock fills them in this instant, I see the pain she blinked away just moments ago. My wolf howls in agony at the sight.

But then Lyra breaks our gaze, her eyes meeting the floor.

Such an act is proof that I cannot accept this strange pairing brought me by the Goddess. No mate of mine cowers in my presence. We will be equals, once I accept a true mate.

And this girl is not her.

"Y-Your Majesty, I'm lost," she says softly, meekly.

I clear my throat, steeling myself against the way her pathetic whispers enchant me. "I'll have a servant escort you to your quarters," I tell her. "You do not belong in this wing."

She nods, and I notice a single tear beginning to form in the corner of her eye. My wolf rages inside, begging me to wipe it away and never let another form in those precious windows of her soul.

Instead, I clear my throat again, summoning one of the servants from the ladies' wing through the mind-link, one of my mother's favorites, Esmerelda. "One of the women is coming for you," I explain.

She nods softly, daring to raise her gaze. The tear forms now, threatening to drip down her ivory cheek.

My hand moves without my permission, my thumb gently grazing her tender skin. Thunderbolts rage through my blood at the touch, the effect elevated by the moisture—her moisture—left on my hand though I had quickly pulled it away, leaving behind a delightful sizzle that reverberates through my veins.

I see her reaction as her body trembles, and the muscles of her throat as she swallows thickly, the milky white skin on her begging for my touch.

I refrain, though holding back causes my wolf to scream in agony.

The moment passes when I hear the tender footsteps of a woman running toward us. She rounds the corner, and I gesture toward the servant. "Esmerelda will show you back to your room," I tell Lyra.

Lyra breaks our gaze and stares at her, and my wolf growls.

There's something amiss between the two women, and my wolf demands to know what.

Lyra turns back to me, quickly falling to her knees.

The sight shocks and repulses me, and my wolf tries to take over, but I refuse it.

"Your Majesty, the Queen Mother requested that my lady's maiden be released from the dungeon, but upon return to my room, she was not there," she says quickly. "I beg for her release, for her safety. She grows ill in the stale, sour dungeon's air."

My brow gathers into a deep furrow as I turn to the woman servant. "Is this true?"

Esmerelda's eyes go wide. "Your Majesty," she begins, falling into a deep sign of respect. "I made the request of the guards. I did not know they hadn't obeyed. Only now I have returned to the human woman's room to find her and her servant missing."

I catch a glimpse of Lyra's eyes in my periphery. They burn with anger.

"See to it personally, immediately," I order the servant. "The lady's maiden is to be in her quarters within the half hour."

"Yes, Your Majesty," Esmerelda says, offering another sign of respect. She turns to leave, but I stop her with my voice. An order of the Queen Mother *will not* be ignored.

"You'll be reassigned from our guests' quarters, effective immediately," I demand. I feel the relief flow from my human mate immediately.

Esmerelda nods without turning, breaking into a run down the hallway. Once out of earshot, I turn to Lyra.

"Thank you, Your Majesty," she says, and this time her voice is firmer, but not quite confident. She looks at me again, and the corners of her lips tilt up in a smile.

My wolf rejoices, and I am intrigued.

"I will escort you back to your room myself," I tell her, offering my elbow, my errand in the council room forgotten.

REJECTION

Lyra

MY EYES WIDEN AS THE ALPHA KING OFFERS HIS MUSCULAR ARM TO ME, bent at the elbow. It's a familiar gesture, one I accepted from many of my father's courtiers. I never felt a sense of hesitation to take a man's arm offered in escort.

But now, sharp emotions wash over me and cause me pause, and many of these feelings I simply do not understand. Just a brush of the Alpha King's hand caused a jolt of electric pleasure to wash through me, back in his mother's quarters.

What will happen when I actually hold his arm?

Not only that, but I am meant to be this man's bride. My status as a princess shielded me against any untoward suggestions before, especially since all the courtiers escorted me in the presence of my father.

But here, the empty hallways echo every unsteady shuffle of my feet. We are alone, and I am completely at his mercy for any advances he would make. The one chaperone I've been assigned—awful as she is—has run away under the Alpha King's threatening commands.

And what was that exactly? If I didn't know him to be a brute, a cruel and unjust ruler who locked me in his dungeon for unknown weeks, months… I would have thought he had defended me.

But regardless, this man, beast… whatever he is, I belong to him. Vows spoken or not, I am already his bride, his property. And so, obediently, I slip my arm around his firm bicep.

The sharp sensations that weave through my body unsteady me the moment I touch him, and despite his being the cause, I tighten my grip on his elbow to remain on my feet. He assists with his other arm, catching me as I misstep, his strong, powerful hand reaching over to hold me up by the shoulder.

That extra touch causes the sparks to flare even stronger. "What's happening to me?" I ask, though I hadn't intended to trouble the king with any questions, certainly not that one.

"You're human, so it probably is too much for you," he says without explanation.

I feel a blush rise in my cheeks, though I don't know why. Am I supposed to know what "it" is? The silent moment between us lingers, and soon it's too late to ask what he means.

Now that I'm steady, he has begun walking, assumingly to lead me to my room. Will he expect to come in when he gets there? I can't refuse him, and I won't, but the idea sends a chill to the back of my neck.

Maybe I don't want to go back to my room just yet, though Cally should be there by the time I get there, and she probably needs me.

Though, what if she's there and he wants to….

My free hand trembles, and I clutch the side of my dress to steady it.

We've gone through five or six hallways now silently, the only sound our footsteps, the etched glass lanterns flickering as we pass. They bathe the hallways in an amber glow, and I notice it adds depth to the portraits as we pass.

The entire length of this hall is filled with them. One is the Alpha King.

He stands looking off into the distance, his strong jaw jutted out in the decisive pose of a military leader. His silver eyes are haunting, as bright as well-polished armor, glistening from a far-off light source that adds wisdom to his gaze. I stare at it longer than I mean to, even turning my head toward it as we pass.

"It was dreadful, posing for that," he comments casually.

I almost jump at the sound of his voice, and once again, my face is awash with a rosy blush, so I don't dare look up at him. "Why is that?" I somehow manage to ask.

"I had better things to do."

I certainly don't doubt that. And I have no idea what brings the next words out of my mouth. "Maybe you had an army to quash, or some pesky humans overstepping their bounds who needed their heads chewed off." I regret speaking instantly, but his response is unexpected.

The pure, authentic chuckle that escapes his lips is immediate and joyful. And it awakens yet another strange sensation deep within me.

I can only describe it as a voice, or maybe just a spark of a voice, it's so small, unexplored. It's me, but seems to be another side of me, something more carnal, sensual.

I wonder for a moment whether it's my inner desire. It frightens me, but this man is going to be my husband. Unless he completely rejects me outright, we will one day share a bed. Is this what people experience when they feel such a yearning? Is it safe to feel this way about a wolf shifter Alpha King?

I have no more time to consider these thoughts because we've reached the doors to my suite. Fear envelops me as I wonder whether he will expect to step inside with me.

I don't think I'm ready for this.

"Here are your quarters," he says distantly, dropping my arm. I feel a rush of cold air between us, and a thickness of separation. That little spark inside seems to cry out, almost painfully. "The lady servant will be along shortly."

Without a goodbye, he spins on his heel and strides off.

My heart feels hollow, and it churns with some effort as I watch him disappear around the hallway corner. That spark inside I felt before—I can't explain it, but it's crying, calling out in agony, more so, the further the Alpha King is away from me.

What just happened? I'd braced myself to invite this man into my bed, but his steps moved so quickly, it was as though I'd doused him in fire.

What did I do?

And why do I ache so badly for his return?

CASSIAN

'I HAD A DETOUR,' I EXPLAIN TO TURGAN CURTLY IN THE MIND-LINK AS I hurry away from the human girl's suite. 'I'll arrive shortly.'

He does not dare question me, but I shut off the private channel before he has a chance to respond anyway. I need a few moments with my own thoughts.

I don't know what possessed me to offer to escort the woman—Lyra—back to her quarters. But my arm very nearly acted of its own accord, offering an elbow for her soft body to lean against as we walked along.

As her slender arm wrapped around mine, my tunic adjusted up, leaving a small portion of our arms skin-to-skin.

I forced myself to hold it together as passion echoed through my veins, but the reaction seemed to have been overwhelming to the human. I don't know what her kind knows about the mate bond, or whether they have a similar mate's connection. Perhaps not, because Lyra seemed overcome and confused by the sensation.

So much so, I very nearly revealed to her that she is my mate. As a human, perhaps she doesn't know this already. If I withhold this knowledge, perhaps I can spare her some grief.

After all, I'm going to reject her. It's inevitable. I can't spend my life attached to a human female when there must be a Luna out there for me somewhere.

The Goddess would not refuse me such joy as a proper Luna and pure wolf offspring to carry on my lineage.

Perhaps Lyra won't feel any pain at all. Ignorance is bliss, after all.

It's too bad the rejection will tear my wolf's soul to shreds.

MY NEW FUTURE

Lyra

I DON'T KNOW WHAT I DID TO ANGER THE ALPHA KING. A DEEP shudder runs through me as I close the huge entrance doors with a light thud. Whatever happened, it's clear he's not coming back.

I have no idea why that bothers me so much.

That strange feeling inside me, that voice, I suppose it is, seems to have gotten stronger since I took the king's arm. Right now, it's screaming at me to run after him.

I'm certainly *not* going to do that.

I step through the common area to the entrance to my suite, these confusing thoughts and emotions running through my head so wildly that I barely notice the voice that greets me.

"Lyra?"

Frozen with surprise, it takes me a moment before I react, but when I do, it's pure joy. "Cally!"

I sprint toward her, and she meets me halfway. We wrap our arms around each other as I squeeze her tight. But she pulls back quickly.

"Goodness, Lyra," she says. "I can't get that gorgeous gown dirty."

I shake my head. "I don't care. I'm just so glad you're out of that place!" Only now do I examine her, looking for bruises or sores. "Are you okay? Did they hurt you?"

She shakes her own head briskly. "No, I'm fine. No one really paid any attention to me after they took you. They brought me food as usual, though." She looks down at her tattered, grimy dress. "Oh, I must look horrible."

"You look beautiful to me, as always," I insist. "How long have you been up here?"

"They just brought me a minute ago," she explains. "I haven't had time to wash off. I'll go do that."

She turns to walk back to the servant's quarters, but I reach out an arm to stop her. "No. You'll wash up in here, and I'll help."

"Are you sure?"

"Of course I am," I insist. "Come on."

She follows as I lead her into the bathing room, where she looks around with awe. "This isn't quite like your castle, is it?"

"No." I can't help but let out a little smile. "The décor is different here. It's simple, classy, not so over-the-top like everything in my father's castle."

"I was going to say something like that, but I didn't want to insult you or the royal family," she says quietly.

I shake my head briskly, turning the knobs on the tub faucet to fill it the way Esmerelda had before. "You don't have to worry about that," I insist. "Here, our old titles don't mean much anymore. I still refer to you as my lady's maiden whenever I'm with the people here, but that's just so they'll treat you better, like getting you out of the dungeon."

A cold shiver rushes up my spine when I mention the place, and Cally's reaction seems about the same, understandably. I turn to her and smile, patting her arm reassuringly before continuing. "But really, we're equals here as far as I'm concerned. You're my friend, and I hope I'm yours as well."

"Of course you are!"

It's good to see a smile returning to her face. "Anyway, I do like the way they've decorated this castle. I've always thought it was silly to insist everything be gold like Father does."

She giggles at the thought, putting a hand over her mouth out of habit. My father never liked the servants showing emotion around him, so she always had to hide her feelings. Come to think of it, that's a horrible way to treat someone who takes care of your needs. If I ever have a chance to lead people, I will never be that way.

But right now, I need to focus on Cally, who looks pretty anxious to get all that grime off her. "Let's get you cleaned up," I tell her, gesturing toward the tub.

"Don't we need to send for boiled water?" she asks.

"No, they have some strange way of making it warm," I explain. "It comes out of the pipes that way. Here, feel."

I giggle lightly at the expression on her face when her hand touches the warm bath water.

"How is that possible?" she asks.

All I can do is shrug. "Apparently, the wolf shifters know some tricks we do not. Maybe it's magic. I mean, these are people who turn into wolves."

Her brows raise at the thought. "I guess anything is possible."

She takes off her filthy dress, which I carefully put into the trash, just as I had my once beautiful purple lace gown. We're about the same size, so I'm sure the staff can bring something she can wear.

I'll ask the new lady they send down here. I'm sure glad Esmerelda is out of the picture, though I might still see her in the castle. I shudder at the thought.

"Are you okay?" Cally asks, now in the tub, which is already turning brown from the grime lifting off her.

"I'm fine," I insist. I'll have to tell her about Esmerelda later. "Here, let's get you some soap."

There's a fantastic supply of differently scented soaps and oils, some of which I've never smelled before. There must be different flowers in the Alpha King's realm, or maybe these wolf shifters know more about scent variety than we did back home.

Home—I feel the ache in my gut thinking about my mother and

Aisla. I miss them so terribly. But I suppose this is my new home, so I shouldn't be thinking of Maelie. That's my old kingdom, but I need to set my focus to the future… my future here in Oceana.

I help Cally as much as I can with the cleaning. As with my bath, we have to empty it and refill it a few times before she's able to soak in clean, warm water. Then, I add some of the oils to give it a lovely scent.

"Relax here for a while," I tell her. "I'll go figure out something for you to wear."

She nods, sinking back down so the water hits her chin, her eyes closing softly as she inhales the sweet scent. It feels so good to see her this way instead of cold and sickly as she was in the dungeon. She hasn't coughed at all since she's been here, so for that, I'm also grateful.

I make my way into the dressing area, where there's a huge walk-in closet I've yet to explore. It's probably empty, but maybe the robe I wore earlier has been cleaned and returned at least.

My brows lift as I open the double doors to find the entire closet filled to the brim. Colorful gowns line the wall to the left, some in luxurious materials I've never seen before. Looking closer, I see they are all my size.

Running my hands over a lovely pink one with an embroidered skirt, I know instantly this is the one for Cally.

The other side of the closet is mostly drawers and shoe racks, all of which are also full. I gather some shoes and undergarments for Cally and take them back to her.

When she's finished dressing, I help with her hair. "I've always loved your beautiful hair. Now, it's back to normal again."

"It feels so good to be clean," she agrees. Her countenance darkens. "It was awful down there," she says softly.

I meet her eyes in our reflection. "I know. I'm sorry that happened to you."

"It happened to you, too," she says. "We're in this together, right?"

I crack a smile. "Right."

"How did you talk them into freeing me?" she asks.

"The Alpha King ordered it after the lady's servant disobeyed the Queen Mother," I explain.

Her eyes go wide. "You spoke to the Alpha King?"

I nod, feeling the pink rising in my cheeks. "He escorted me back to this room."

She spins around in the vanity chair. "He's that handsome man we saw that day on the terrace, isn't he?"

I simply nod in response, my cheeks flashing hotter.

"And he personally escorted you?" she asks. "Did you take his arm?"

"I did."

She gasps, her lips rising in a smile. "Tell me everything," she insists.

As I open my mouth to explain, I don't know how to describe the feeling I have when I'm around the Alpha King, or that strange voice inside me that feels like another part of my being.

Maybe someday I'll understand it myself.

DINNER PLANS

"I've called up everyone on leave, as ordered," Turgan tells the council. "We'll be organized and ready to attack by morning if needed."

Darragh, the eldest of the council members, turns to me. His once-black hair is fully gray now, though he is still as spry as he was when he fought alongside my father. I remember watching his moves as they sparred on the training grounds, hoping one day I could be as swift and cunning as he was.

"As always, this is your call," he says. "But Assanan's actions have moved beyond a threat, and you have the blessing of this council to take preemptive action."

I nod, appreciative of his support.

"I agree, but I have another concern." All eyes turn to Nolan, another of the council members, as his voice rings out across the table.

"Speak it," I tell him.

"It's rumored that the human girl is now running about the castle," he says. "Is this true?"

My wolf sparks with a low growl inside, but I show no hesitation in my words. "My mother requested that she join the others in the ladies' wing." I owe no explanation about this matter to anyone on the council, yet, like my father, I have made a strong commitment to answering all the council's inquiries.

No matter how foolish.

I turn back to Turgan, ready to deliver my orders to attack, but Nolan speaks again.

"Do we have a Queen Mother running this kingdom or an Alpha King?" he asks, his voice tilted with accusation.

Silence hangs thick in the air as I turn and answer his challenge. "You know that my mother is ill, Nolan. It gives her pleasure to believe she is preparing a wedding."

"But you have no intention of wedding this girl, I presume?" It's more of a statement than a question.

"I do not." My wolf cries in agony within, but I ignore it. "But I see no harm in allowing the ladies the pleasure of selecting fabrics and whatever long-term preparations are necessary. Such will be required when I find a true Luna. Arrangements may as well be in place." Again, my wolf rallies against my words, but I maintain a calm exterior.

Nolan shakes his head. "I still don't approve of making deals with the humans."

"We make deals with humans all the time," I state. "We've all agreed numerous times to appease their belief that their offers buy them favors."

"Yes, Nolan," Darragh adds firmly. "We need nothing from the humans, but they must believe we are in trade agreements. We can't simply allow them use of the sea with no sacrifice."

Nolan shakes his head. "I'll never understand why we don't just kill the humans and be done with it. They offer us nothing. We could use those lands."

"I disagree, and we will not commit genocide to acquire lands we do not need." I've used the Alpha voice, and Nolan shudders, almost undetectably, before he regains his composure.

"Very well," he says.

My eyes fix on Nolan's as I add, "I appreciate the council maintaining confidentiality in the matters involving my mother and the ladies."

He raises his hands in mock surrender. "Oh, you certainly have mine."

Something in his eyes sits wrong with me. Though I usually rely on my wolf's instincts to interpret such things, he has retreated inside me and lies silent, raging against my denial of the mate bond with Lyra.

"If there are no other questions—" I meet the eyes of each man in the room, all of whom shake their heads respectfully. "Very well. Turgan, have the warriors ready by dawn. We will answer Assanan's invasion of our lands firmly."

"Aye, Alpha," Turgan answers.

We rise, and the men give the sign of respect before moving toward the exits and engaging in their own conversations.

"Turgan, a word," I say, and he nods and walks out another exit with me.

'That was awkward.' He keeps it in a private mind-link until we are well clear of the others.

'It was infuriating,' I correct him. 'Nolan has been bold lately.'

'He's still upset he wasn't chosen as your father's Beta,' he tells me.

'Yes, but that was years ago, and my father is long gone.' By now, we've taken a few turns through the hallways and are out of earshot, so I speak out loud. "Is he planning to join the attack?"

"He's a little old for that." Turgan chuckles.

But I'm in no mood for levity. My blood boils at Nolan's suggestion to murder the humans. I destroy only those who transgress our sovereignty, not innocents.

"Yet he's likely to try something if he's given a chance," I insist. "There's something odd about his sudden boldness. It's not like him."

"You don't trust him," Turgan states.

"I do not." I turn, suddenly wishing to be on the other side of my castle. "Watch him closely. I'll meet the warriors in the morning before the sun rises."

"We'll be there," he assures me.

"CASSIAN," MOTHER GREETS ME AS I STEP INTO HER QUARTERS. "I WAS just about to send for you. I'm planning a dinner party tonight, and you must be there."

A sigh escapes me as I consider a response that will not send her into another attack of her illness. "Mother, this is the eve of battle," I explain, straining to keep my words controlled. "I was just in the council chambers. We're set to attack tomorrow to keep Assanan's forces at bay."

"Assanan?" she asks. "Oh, yes. Your father spoke of him often. They were good friends, I believe."

My brow lifts as I consider my mother's mental state. "Mother, they were sworn enemies. Assanan killed my father with his own hand."

"Oh?" Confusion clouds her face. "Hmm. Anyway, I've arranged for the young lady to sit with you at the king's table. It's going to be so lovely."

A warm tingle erupts inside me at the thought of being near my mate. "Mother, I said we are going to war in the morning," I remind her, ignoring the feeling as much as possible.

In a private mind-link to the healer, I say, 'I need an assessment of my mother's mental health immediately.'

'Yes, Alpha,' the healer answers. But before I end the connection, she adds, 'She has been struggling lately.'

'Thank you.'

I look up to see Mother gazing at me expectantly. "So, you'll be there? It's in the ladies' wing. It's nothing special. I haven't invited any dignitaries. I just thought it would be nice." Hope fills her eyes, and I cannot refuse her in this state.

"I'll be there," I say decisively, regretting the words the moment they come out.

I don't know if I'll be able to keep our mate bond a secret when I'm sitting right next to the human girl.

My wolf sings joyously inside, and he does not wish to keep any secrets.

And so, I take my leave of Mother to prepare for more than one war.

A DATE WITH THE ALPHA KING?

Lyra

"I'm going to pass out," I tell Cally. "I can't do this. Is this like… a date? Why would the Queen Mother ask for a special dinner with the Alpha King present?"

I stare into the mirror, trying to focus on the delicate lace of the emerald-green gown I've chosen, but it's not helping. My heart is racing so fast, I feel like I'm going to throw up.

She smiles at me in my reflection, far too calmly, twisting my hair high in the air so she can wrap it around in an updo. "You've done hundreds of these dinners, Lyra."

I raise my brow at her. "You're kidding, right?" She's not exactly the type to remain calm at a time like this.

She drops my hair, joining me on the vanity bench and scooting close, her eyes bright with excitement. "Of course I am. If I were having a dinner date with an Alpha King—especially one who looks like him—I'd die right here, right now."

There's my Cally.

"Thanks for your support," I say.

But I can't even be sarcastic now without laughing. We both giggle, and it helps calm my nerves—a little.

Very little.

"It'll be fine," she says after we've stopped. "The Queen Mother will be there, and you said she's very nice. I doubt the Alpha King would make a scene in front of everyone."

My eyes go wide at her in the mirror. "You think he'll make a scene over me?"

Goodness, I can see it now. He has decided he hates me, and he wants me back in the dungeon immediately. He'll order his guards to take me there right away, pretty green dress and all.

Oh, no. *What if he sends Cally back down there too?*

"You're shaking," she says, grasping my hand to steady it. "No, I don't think he'll make a scene. I think he'll eat dinner. And I think he'll be admiring how beautiful you are."

More anxiety shoots through my nerves. "He's going to be looking at me?"

She pauses, turning back to the mirror. "Of course he is," she insists. "But not with that hair," she adds with a giggle.

She grabs the brush as she stands and gets behind me again, doing her magic with my hair in a way I'd never be able to do myself. She's an artist when it comes to things like that.

"Hmm," she hums, looking around the room. "Let's give you a touch of the wolf shifter style." Walking over to a nearby floral arrangement, she selects a small sprig of lilac and comes back to weave it into my curls. "There. Now you're ready to go!"

My reflection in the mirror looks ready, but fear washes over every nerve ending in my body.

I think I'm going to pass out.

MY FINGERS TWITCH NERVOUSLY AS ORLA, THE WOMAN WHO REPLACED Esmerelda to assist me in the castle, leads me toward the ladies' wing dining hall.

"Does the Alpha King usually dine here?" I ask her.

She nods and smiles politely. She's been very helpful to me so far and is much nicer than Esmerelda. "Yes, about once a week," she explains. "The Queen Mother isn't always up to a full formal event in the main hall."

I nod but don't ask any more questions. It was horrible seeing the Queen Mother collapse like that, and it's not polite to ask health questions about royalty, at least in my kingdom. I assume it's the same here.

The scent of broiled meat and garlic wafts thick in the air as we step into the dining hall. Like the other rooms of the castle, its décor is simple and elegant, though there is more of a flower motif here than I've seen elsewhere. Several ladies are already seated, and Orla quickly introduces me.

I turn at the sound of a familiar voice.

"Oh, my dear, there you are!" The Queen Mother comes toward me with her arms extended. Orla makes what she has explained to me is the sign of respect, crossing her arms against her chest, and she backs away.

The Queen Mother's gown is embroidered with silk threads in the shape of daffodils, the stark yellow a lovely contrast to the deep purple velvet of her skirt. She looks much healthier than she did last I saw her, her cheeks bright pink.

"Greetings, Queen Mother," I tell her, extending a full curtsey before she reaches me and takes my hands.

"Oh, I'll never get over how charming that is," she says, her pearl-white teeth glistening. "And, I'd love it if you'd call me Alyssa."

I open my mouth to object to that, but she shakes her head.

"I insist that you do," she says. "Come. Your seat is over here. My son has not yet arrived."

The mention of the Alpha King leaves a startled tingle down my back, but I force myself to hide the effect. "Thank you... Alyssa. Everything smells wonderful."

"The chefs here are quite talented," she explains, guiding me to my seat. Surprisingly, her chair—and that of the Alpha King—are like all the others in the room, just situated at the head table. My father always insisted on throne-like seating for himself in his dining hall.

"I'm excited to try their dishes." I take my seat, eyeing the conspicuously empty chair beside me and feeling a strange ache form in my gut. It feels a bit like longing. But how can I miss a man I barely know?

Ahead of us, the kitchen staff members are laying out the dishes on a table opposite us. It's a fantastic spread, with roasted vegetables lining the trays of different types of meats. The garlic scent I've been enjoying, I find comes from the cheesy dish near the center, and a colorful tower of sliced and whole fruits includes some I've never seen before.

My breath hitches when the door opens again and everyone rises. I stand with them all, shocked by the electric tingle running up the nape of my neck.

What are all these strange sensations I'm having when I'm near the Alpha King?

"Be seated," he says as he walks toward us—toward me—his voice clear and commanding, yet surprisingly kind. I suppose he calms his cruelty around his mother.

I'm not sure how I feel about that.

"Mother." He sets his hand gently on her shoulder and bends to kiss her cheek.

He's very kind to her, apparently.

As he brushes by me to make his way to his seat, a powerful wave of energy, a hundred times greater than that tingle I felt before, shoots through me. I grasp the table involuntarily, and for a moment, it feels like all my breath is trapped in my lungs.

The Alpha King reaches over to steady me, and his touch is both comforting and adds to the strange feeling. As soon as he pulls away, I hear that little voice inside of me practically wailing in agony.

What in the world is going on with me?

"Are you well, dear?"

I blink a few times, recognizing the Queen Mother's voice and finally finding my own. "Yes," I lie. "I'm fine. I just slipped; that's all."

"You slipped while seated?" she asks.

All I can do is shrug and shake my head. "I suppose. I'm not sure how it happened."

"Well, all's fine now, it seems," she says. "And since Cassian is here, we might as well get started with our meal." Her smile is broad as she instructs the staff to begin serving the food.

By now, the Alpha King is seated next to me, with a bit of a larger gap than what's between me and the Queen Mother.

I don't blame him for not wanting to sit by me. He probably thinks I'm crazy.

I'm beginning to wonder about that myself.

MATE PULL

CASSIAN

My wolf is on fire, and it's taking every ounce of self-control to keep from grabbing Lyra and carrying her off to my bed. Her porcelain white skin begs for my touch. Even brushing by the sleeve of her gown moments before caused a jolt of lightning to snake up my veins, and I felt her have the same reaction.

I have to scoot my chair a bit to the side as I sit, but even that doesn't calm the craving inside me.

But it's my mother's dinner party, and carrying off my mate to savor our passions isn't appropriate, and neither is revealing in front of all these ladies and staff that my mate is a human.

I can't even stand the fact myself.

It doesn't mean I wouldn't enjoy a taste of her, though.

Shoving the thought down, I turn my attention to my mother, who is busy introducing Lyra as my bride.

"Through an agreement with her father—" She pauses, turning to Lyra. "I'm sorry, dear. What is your father's name, and the area he controls?"

"King Chez of Maelie," Lyra answers politely, though I detect a slight squeak in her voice, a lingering reaction from our mate pull.

I can't even imagine what it feels like from a human point of view. The mate bond is very nearly uncontrollable by a wolf of my lineage. A weak human would certainly be overwhelmed.

"Oh, yes," Mother continues. "King Chez of Maelie and my son, Alpha King Cassian of Oceana, have entered an agreement to make her his bride. She's a lovely girl, and I'm so excited for the ceremony."

The discomfort in the crowd is palpable, though I'm sure most of these ladies have been informed of the arrangement already. Even so, having a human marry the Alpha King is a horror story for some of them.

But before I can ease their minds, my mother is already reading the room. "Oh, I don't doubt you're all a bit concerned because she's a human. Please don't worry. The chances of her producing a shifter heir are quite high."

I can feel Lyra sinking into her seat, though the reassurance does seem to keep half the crowd happy.

My mother continues to appease the other half. "And I have no doubt my son will meet his Goddess-given mate soon," she says. "When that occurs, of course, she will be the Luna Queen. We'll go ahead and reclassify Lyra here as a concubine in that case."

I see Lyra's eyes go wide despite her obvious struggle to control herself. Considering my mother just said another woman would replace her with her own true mate, she's doing remarkably well at holding in her emotion, no doubt the result of years of training as a king's daughter. But she soon lowers her eyes in only slightly veiled despair, staring at the empty plate in front of her.

"So, today should be an exciting day," my mother continues, oblivious to Lyra's pain. "We get to plan a wedding!"

Cheers echo across the hall, as I'd expected. If there's one thing the ladies of the court enjoy, it's planning an event.

Still, I can't help but feel the aching cry of my wolf at my mate's distress.

To ignore it, I address the crowd myself. "Thank you for your excitement. Please, let's enjoy the meal now." I mind-link the staff to have them begin serving the meal.

It's a good distraction, and I avoid eye contact with Lyra throughout dinner to keep my wolf in check.

After the staff clears the plates, I turn to my mother. It requires looking at Lyra since Mother is on the other side of her, and once again, the sight of Lyra's smooth skin, shimmering in the lighting like silk, and her incredible scent—a mix of floral with a hint of sweet maple—drives my wolf to madness inside again.

'I'd better get back to the war room,' I tell Mother in a private mind-link, shoving my wolf's longing howls deep inside me.

'Oh, Cassian,' Mother replies with an outward sigh. 'This is to celebrate your bride! Surely, the warriors can wait for one dance.'

The thought of touching Lyra ignites my wolf again. 'One dance, Mother,' I insist, not sure whether I'm answering out of respect for Mother or in response to the begs of my wolf.

Mother smiles broadly, claps her hands together, and speaks out loud. "Begin the music!"

The band plays a soft melody fitting for most wedding announcement dances with true mates, and I can feel my blood heat up as I turn to Lyra and offer her my hand.

She smiles in a way that seems genuine for the first time tonight and accepts my gesture. Electric tingles rush over me, and I feel them flowing through both of us.

Her eyes close somewhat in response, and I take my other arm to steady her, the now all-encompassing fire between us drawing us together.

In front of the crowd and my mother, I control myself, but the urge to rip off Lyra's dress, throw her on the table, and take her right here and now is stronger than the will of my fiercest enemy combatant.

Bloody battles are easy compared to this.

I lead her to the dance floor, where I tighten my arm around her slender waist and take her hand in mine, struggling to keep a respectable distance between us as I move her across the floor.

She spins gently with my lead, obviously very familiar with the act, no doubt from years of practice with similar dances as a princess.

The thought makes it occur to me that other men have touched her this way—surely, she's had dance partners with which to practice, likely from hundreds of dinner parties just like this one.

My wolf's blood boils.

How dare another man touch my mate?

I vow to kill every one of them as soon as I know their names, but I keep a polite smile on my face as I spin Lyra around again.

When she comes out of the spin, she is closer to me, her warm, soft breath wafting across my neck to meet my ear. There, it strikes a chord of desire, erupting a powerful need that's almost impossible for me to control in this room full of people.

So, I choose to let it go.

Her scent responds by intensifying, drawing me closer to her until our faces are within millimeters of touching.

She licks her lips, and my cock stiffens beneath my kingly robes.

The audience fades from my mind.

WHAT IS THIS FEELING?

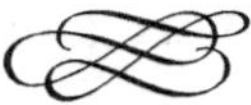

Lyra

I SUPPOSE I'D DESCRIBE MYSELF AS GETTING DIZZY IN THE ALPHA KING'S arms, but not in a way I've ever felt before. It feels… exhilarating, like simply the touch of his hand is awakening every nerve inside me.

My head buzzes with this tingling feeling all over, and it is pure pleasure that runs down my spine and straight to my core.

I've never had this reaction at a man's touch before, and I've danced with nearly everyone in my father's court in just the past year.

This is different.

Everything is different, like all my senses are experiencing something for the first time. His scent, which I remember enjoying before, is even more intense, and I wonder whether he's added more cologne for the dinner, though I didn't notice it this much when he first walked into the dining hall.

Pine, I think it is, like a thick forest just after a light rain, mixed with some kind of candy I've had before but I can't place.

It doesn't matter because all I can do is inhale it as deep as possible to savor the moment.

But then... he pulls back. Cold air rushes between us, cutting off every pleasurable sensation. Deep inside, it feels like I'm crying.

What an odd feeling.

"Ladies, please continue with your celebrations," he says to the crowd. "My future bride and I need a moment to discuss some aspects of the nuptials."

The room goes silent for a moment. My brow crinkles in the same way Queen Mother Alyssa's does, but understanding soon rises in her face, and she smiles broadly.

"Everyone, please, continue to enjoy the music," she says.

I wish I knew what's going on as much as she does.

Apparently, everyone else in the room gets the message because they're all laughing and chatting again, and a group of them are forming a line for some type of dance I've never seen before. Servants jump into action serving dessert to those ladies who are still seated.

I'm so confused.

Seconds later, it doesn't matter anymore because he has slipped his hand back into mine, and the pleasurable sensations return. But instead of dancing, he pulls me gently off the dance floor and toward the door.

I happily follow, confused or not, as he leads me out the door and down the hallways, turning a few times in the confusing labyrinth until the sounds of the party disappear into a silent echo.

Then, he pulls me into a room, alone, and I suddenly realize he expects much more than dancing.

Does he want to do... that... before we're married? I've certainly never been with a man before. I suppose I already belong to him through my father's arrangement, so it may not matter whether we've technically had a wedding.

But I don't know what to do or how to do it, and what if I do something wrong, and he throws me back into the dungeon... and Cally along with me?

All those worries disappear the moment he puts his lips on mine.

Sparks of pleasure echo through me, and I let out an involuntary moan into his mouth. He responds by wrapping his arms around me, and immediately, I can't get close enough to this man.

My arms find their way around his firm, well-defined muscles in a way I've never dared do—I've never wanted to do with anyone else—before.

But I don't have time to be surprised at myself. My feet leave the floor the next instant as he carries me away, whisking me over to some piece of furniture—a sofa, I assume—but who cares when his hands caress my body in places I've never let anyone touch before.

There's not a hint of shame or embarrassment I would have otherwise expected, just pure pleasure.

And the moans keep escaping my lips, until his are on mine again, and his tongue softly encourages them to part.

It doesn't take much convincing.

I've never done it before, but it feels so natural to explore his tongue with mine. One of his hands reaches up, his large palm covering my entire cheek as he somehow pulls me even closer.

I feel wetness pool between my legs and notice his hardness rubbing against my thigh.

Are we going to do this right here?

I hope so.

Though I'm on my back, he takes his hand off my cheek and reaches under me, undoing the buttons on the back of my dress. The moment he loosens the first one, I realize how much cloth is between, and all I want to do is rip my dress off, rip his clothes off, and lay here naked in his arms so I can feel every inch of his skin against mine.

If his hands feel this good, I can only imagine what the rest of him feels like.

And I don't want to imagine anymore.

I try to sit up and help him, but he shakes his head and gently pushes me back down. The buttons come loose painfully slow, almost as if he's expecting me to savor it, which I do. But impatience fills me, especially since I can clearly feel the ache in my core now as the heat builds up between us.

Finally, he gets enough loose to pull the top of my dress down, and

I slip out of my sleeves, leaving nothing but my undergarments beneath.

He doesn't bother taking those off, just pulling them aside to expose my left breast. My nipple hardens against the cool air, but the chill doesn't last long until he pulls his mouth away from my lips and envelops it around half my breast.

I cry out, not in words but in raw emotion as the feeling of his warm, moist mouth against one of my most intimate parts of my body shoots across me like a lightning bolt.

I don't know what this feeling is, but I know I want more.

My other breast begs for him, as does my now drenched core, but he takes his time savoring this one for several minutes.

He lifts up finally, pulling the fabric off my other breast and playing with my other nipple with his tongue.

And then he stops dead, his eyes wide.

Shock rushes over me as he stands abruptly and adjusts his robes.

What did I do wrong?

"I have to go," he says. "War has begun."

"What? War?" Inside, the deepest part of me is screaming to run after him, but my legs are so weak from the sudden shock, it's all I can do just to sit up straight on the sofa. "How do you know that it's—"

"I have to go—now," he repeats, his expression unreadable.

"Um, okay," I say, my voice meek. Cloth pools around my waist. "I can't do my dress myself. And I don't know where I am."

"I'll send in Orla," he says gruffly. "Wait for her."

"When will you be—"

But he's out the door before I can finish my question. I adjust my undergarments, slip my arms back into my dress, and slump back into my chair, hoping he remembers to go get Orla before he runs off to whatever war he's fighting.

What just happened? How did he know the war had started? And what war is he talking about? Did my father attack?

My heart is still racing from all the new sensations I've felt over the past few minutes, not to mention being suddenly cut off from all of them when he stood up.

The ache inside me is different now. But still, it's like there's a separate voice inside me, one that hurts more the farther away the Alpha King gets from me. Somehow, I can almost feel his footsteps and the distance between us.

And it's almost agony to know that he's going to war.

Will he die when we've barely had a moment together?

My mind tries to keep up with all the sensations I felt with his hands and warm lips on me. Why did it feel so good, and why does it hurt so much now?

All I can do is sit here by the soft light of the lantern in this strange room and wait to be rescued.

If Orla even comes for me.

WAR CRY

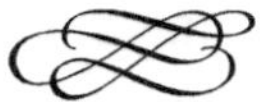

CASSIAN

'ASSANAN HAS HIS WARRIORS WELL INTO OUR TERRITORY,' TURGAN TELLS me in a private mind-link.

I'm already crossing the castle at a fast pace, but I break into a run, feeling the lag of the mate pull that doesn't want me to leave Lyra.

Dammit. Giving into it has made it stronger. I should have kept my distance from the woman.

'Activate everyone,' I tell him.

'Already done.'

I crack a grin, having expected as much from my Beta. 'What are we hearing from the front lines?' I ask him.

'That every wolf there is an easy kill.'

'The bastard is sacrificing his own warriors to wear us out.' The mate pull tugs at me again, but I curse it down. I don't fucking have time for this. 'Shorten the fight times and double the rest periods. Keep everyone fresh.'

'Aye, Alpha,' he says.

'I'm headed to the front.'

'Aye.'

I close the mind-link and quicken my steps again, knowing they'll lag more the farther I get from the castle. Memories of my mother's words flood my mind. I was an adolescent when she described these strange sensations.

She was lucid then, when Father was alive. She was experiencing the mate pull firsthand and trying to explain the feeling to me.

"It's a very powerful force," she told me then.

Now I understand why that was such a difficult task. It's not easily explained, the feeling of one's whole body overcome with need for another, as though life itself cannot go on without them.

But she did give me some valuable insights I've only appreciated at this very moment, like how distance between mates makes their feet feel like weights of pure lead when trying to walk away, and how the pull turns into an ache when those steps become miles.

It's a hundred miles to that border.

"Open the walls!" I holler at the guards, who quickly obey, the large stone gates rumbling as the mechanism pulls them apart. It doesn't take much to open just enough to slip out, and I shift right in the courtyard before barreling through and running at top speed toward the fighting.

I've always trained on my pacing, as it's difficult for most wolves to sustain a strong pace over miles of distance. Now, the mate pull is a new complication, but I don't let it slow my speed. Instead, I use the ache as anger to push myself even farther.

Miles later, the mind-link opens again. 'They've sent in the real warriors, ones that actually know how to fight back,' Turgan reports.

I quicken my pace even more. 'I'm there in five minutes.'

'Aye.'

I hear the battle before I reach it, wolves growling and howling, many screeching in the pain of death. I only hope those aren't our own warriors meeting death, though I know it to be possible.

Turgan's voice echoes through my mind again. 'I can go in when you get here to give you a rest.'

'I need no rest,' I insist.

'After running a hundred miles?'

I don't answer. He knows better than to question me. And in those hundred miles, I've turned every ounce of mate pull into a deadly ferocity so intense that I almost pity any wolf in my path who dared cross our border.

Almost.

I reach the battle and jump right into the fray, ripping through the neck of every enemy wolf in sight. One by one, I sink my teeth into their carotid arteries, the metallic taste of their blood further fueling my rage.

I keep going, noticing some of my warriors stepping back and letting me dispatch the wolves they were fighting just moments ago.

My rage doesn't disappear until every wolf that bastard Assanan sent over my border is lying dead on the ground.

Silence covers the battlefield as I pant with exhaustion and force my heartbeat to calm before shifting back into human form. An assistant runs forward with clothes.

"Throw their bodies back over the border," I order.

For the first time, I notice the look on Turgan's face. He's also back to human form, his eyes as wide as all my warriors around him.

"Aye," he nearly whispers.

I turn and walk back toward my castle, my wolf howling joyously inside at the thought of returning to my mate.

Mother was right. The mate pull is powerful.

LYRA

I DON'T KNOW HOW I KNOW THIS, BUT THE ALPHA KING IS FAR AWAY from me now, and he's in danger. And the ache in my gut is too much to bear.

Could it be that wolves have powerful connections between people? But then, why am I experiencing this? I'm only human.

Maybe the magic they use to turn into wolves also includes some sort of bewitching power over emotions.

Whatever it is, it hurts.

And I can't even pull myself off the sofa, not even when the door-knob turns. Here I lie, my clothes unfastened, my undergarments still soaked from the pleasure that was ripped from me, but I can't move a muscle.

So, I guess all I can do is just apologize and hope whoever it is understands.

"Milady."

Relief washes over me at the sound of Orla's voice. But the pain is still there, and I still can't move.

"We need to get you back to your room," she says. "Can you walk?"

I shake my head. "No. I mean, I don't know. I haven't tried. I'm having some pain, and I can't get up."

She nods without another word, scooping her arms under my back and pulling me up. Surprisingly, I can stand, even with the weird pain, though it doesn't subside one bit.

"Let's get your dress settled."

I take a few deep breaths as Aisla taught me to calm my worries about Anastasia. But memories of my sister just cause a different kind of pain, one that stacks over the agony I'm already experiencing.

The tears come easily.

"Milady," Orla says, patting my arm reassuringly. She moves around me, having secured all the buttons on the back of my dress. "Let's save that for your room. I'm sure your lady, Cally, can help comfort you. I know this... experience... can be emotional. But we have some distance to cross before you're secure in your own quarters. Let's get your hair straightened."

I nod, wiping away the tears and trying those deep breaths again, this time forcing myself not to think of my family and my old home, just focusing on making the tears calm, at least until I get back to my room.

At least I have Cally here. And Orla is nice, too.

She whips out a brush and does a few quick swipes through my hair, then she pulls a moist cloth out of her pocket and gives it to me to wipe my face. She holds a small mirror up to me. Other than a blush of pink under my eyes, I look okay, but I sure don't feel the part.

"You can bathe and change once you get back," she says. "Are you ready?"

All I can do is nod again, and that's all she needs. She peeks around the door first to make sure no one is in the hallway and then waves me over. I follow her, hurrying down several hallways through multiple twists and turns, and I'm so glad she's guiding me.

I'd be completely lost without her.

I'm almost feeling better, knowing I'm close to my room where I can cry all I want, when we make another turn.

This hallway isn't empty.

In fact, we almost crash right into her.

Esmerelda stands in front of us like a brick wall, folding her arms as she sniffs the air.

My breath catches in my lungs.

WOLF SHIFTER 101

Lyra

"Disgusting."

The tone in Esmerelda's voice is gruff and frightening, and it's the last thing I want to hear right now.

"Are you seriously parading this... bitch in heat... around our castle?" she continues.

I slink back a little behind Orla, happy she's the one Esmerelda is addressing. I should have known she'd call me names. In heat... wait.

Oh, no.

I guess she can smell me and what we were just doing. And I admit, that is gross. I'm glad I'm not a wolf, and I don't have to smell that on someone.

"I'll ignore that," Orla says, her voice strong and steady. "The Alpha King will be furious that you've disparaged his bride. Now, move aside. We need to get back to the lady's room."

"Lady?" Esmerelda turns and sneers. "You certainly have a loose definition of the word."

This time, Orla ignores her, and I'm surprised Esmerelda actually does step aside so we can go through. I quicken my pace while passing her and look the other way. I'm already half crying. I don't need her judgement to add to the mess I'm in.

"Ignore her," Orla says. We're still within earshot, especially for wolves, which I understand have much better hearing than I do. "She's not even supposed to be around you, much less interact with you."

I nod and wait a few minutes while we make a few more turns through different hallways before I dare to speak up. "You handled that so well. I'm terrified of that woman."

"And she knows that," Orla says. She turns to me, patting me on the arm as we walk. "But you don't need to be afraid. The Alpha King is clearly interested in you, and that puts your status so far above hers, she could be thrown in the dungeon just for speaking to you in that way. I'll be sure to inform the Alpha King as soon as he returns. I doubt he will stand for any of that behavior."

I only caught one sentence of that, and it makes my heart race. "He's interested in me?"

She stops walking and turns to me. "Of course, milady. Were you not just—" She looks around. "Perhaps we'll finish this conversation back at your room."

"Yes, please."

She starts moving again, and I'm walking even faster now. He's interested in me? He pulled away right in the middle of... what we were doing. Is that normal? I wouldn't know.

After what feels like forever, we get back to my room. As soon as we close the door, Cally runs over. "How did dinner go?"

"I'll run you a warm bath, milady," Orla says before disappearing into the bathing room.

I thank her and turn back to Cally. "It went... well, um... really well, I suppose."

"Tell me everything!" She plops into a chair, her eyes wide.

But I still feel disheveled, and I don't really want to have this conversation right now. I will fill Cally in on what happened, but what I want to do is ask Orla more about what she means by the

Alpha King being interested in me. And all that can wait until I feel a little more comfortable.

"I think I'd better bathe first," I tell Cally.

She stares at me for a moment, tilting her head and softening her eyes until they grow wide again. "You… did you—"

"Not entirely."

She frowns, and I know that doesn't make any sense to her since she doesn't have any more experience with men than I do. I open my mouth to start to explain just as Orla walks back in.

"Your bath is ready, milady," she says. "Would you like assistance?"

At this point, I don't even want Cally to help me since I feel so… untidy. But I want both Orla and Cally to be here when I get out.

"No, thank you," I tell Orla. "But I would like to discuss things when I'm finished. I won't be long."

"Yes, milady."

I turn to Cally. "I'll be back soon and will explain it all."

Cally nods, her eyes still wide. "I'm not going anywhere!" She gestures toward my dress. "Here. I'll get that."

Once she's undone the buttons, I hurry to the bathroom, my half-falling dress reminding me of the state I was in just a few moments ago when he walked out on me.

The scent of lavender overpowers the room when I get to the bath, and I'm more than happy to soak in something with a strong scent to get rid of whatever smell it was that Esmerelda turned her nose up at. The bubbles reach my neck when I slide into the tub and grab the soap.

I love baths and usually like to soak as long as the water is still warm, but right now, I want to just feel clean again so I can talk to the ladies about what just happened. It felt so incredible, his lips against mine and the way he gently sucked on my breasts.

Just the thought of it awakens that feeling in my core again, so I try to focus on the soap.

It only takes a few minutes to finish up, and I dry off, wrap my hair up in the towel, and throw the soft cotton robe over me before stepping back out into the sitting area of my suite.

Orla and Cally are still waiting there patiently. "You look tired," Cally says immediately. "I think you need to go rest for a while."

She knows me well, better than myself sometimes, because suddenly, I feel exhausted.

"I'll turn down the bed," Orla says. "Get some rest, and I'll bring you some warm tea and snacks later."

They both make sure I get settled into bed. Maybe it was the intimacy. Maybe it's just everything I've been through. But I drift off quickly with memories of his lips on mine.

SUNLIGHT IS FILTERING THROUGH THE CURTAINS BY THE TIME I AWAKEN. I can't believe I slept so long. Cally tiptoes in. "Good, you're awake," she says. "I was worried."

"I guess I was really tired." I stretch and yawn, and Cally brings me the robe I wore before.

We head out to the sitting area of my suite, where Orla is waiting with tea as promised, but the rest is breakfast, not snacks.

"Thank you," I tell her. I turn to Cally, immediately feeling like I need to explain things, so I jump right into it. "Last night, the Alpha King and I... we got sort of intimate."

She sucks in a quick breath. "How do you get 'sort of' intimate?"

I don't know how to explain. "Well, we started, but all of a sudden, he just sort of finished... well, he stopped and got up and said he had to go to war."

Only now I realize that those actions had brought me to tears, and talking about it again, the same thing is happening. Did he hate touching me?

"I don't understand," Cally says. "How would he suddenly know he's at war? Did someone come in and tell him?"

I shake my head. "No. He just suddenly said he knew. I don't get it."

Cally steps over and puts her arm around me. "I'm so sorry, Lyra."

"I think I can explain," Orla chimes in. She points to the chair next to me. "May I, milady?"

"Of course," I tell her. "And please, call me Lyra."

"It's unusual, but if you'd like me to, I'll call you your given name when we're in private," she says, gathering her dress and sitting next to me. "I'm afraid that around others in the castle, it wouldn't be appropriate to call you anything but milady."

"I understand." I wipe away a tear that threatens to drift down my cheek.

"Okay, Lyra," she begins, smiling a little at the familiarity. I have to admit, I like it, too. "You both are fully human. Is that correct?"

"Yes," Cally answers for us.

Orla nods. "We wolf shifters don't often mingle with humans. Oh… I don't mean that as an insult!" she adds quickly. "There are just a few things about our community that we don't share with yours. You should probably know these things."

"It's okay," I tell her. "I do appreciate you telling me anything you think I should know."

"We have a thing called the mind-link," she begins. "I understand you don't have such a thing."

"Mind-link?" Cally and I ask together.

"It's how we communicate without words," Orla continues. "I'm not sure how it even works. We all just do it–somehow. But we can talk to one person or a specific group of people at the same time. Alphas can speak to their entire kingdom at once if needed."

"So, you're saying he got a message from someone saying the kingdom had been attacked?" I ask.

She nods. "Exactly."

"Well, that explains a lot. I don't feel as sad now." At least it wasn't something I did that sent him away, if that's the case. Or, it probably wasn't.

Maybe.

"He must really like you," Cally says. "I mean, with what you two were doing before he had to leave." Before the words are even out of her mouth, she turns beet red.

"I hope so," I say, not pointing out her blush because I know it'll make it worse, and she hates it when she blushes. "It was strange, though," I continue. "I barely know the man, but it feels like this powerful magnet draws me to him. Even just touching his hand sends something like a shockwave through me. No, it's not that, because that would hurt. This is a pleasant sensation, like the best thing I've ever felt."

Orla gasps, holding her hand over her mouth.

"What?" I ask her. "What's wrong?"

"If it feels that way with him, then maybe—" She pauses and takes a deep breath. "Maybe I'd better tell you about the mate bond."

THE MOON GODDESS IS NEVER WRONG

CASSIAN

BEING BACK IN THE CASTLE HAS CALMED MY WOLF, AND MY MIND FEELS clear without the ache of mate distance clouding my thoughts.

I should never have given in to the pull. I don't know what evil trick the Moon Goddess has played on me to give me a human mate, but the idea is completely untenable.

If anyone finds out, they'll find me weak as an Alpha. That would be the perfect opportunity for Assanan to move in and take over control the way he's wanted to all this time.

I can't let that happen.

But my wolf cries in agony at just the thought of rejecting Lyra. It's something I'm going to have to do regardless, but I'll need time to research ways to bypass the mate bond. I don't wish for my mind to rot like my mother's has.

Dealing with a mate bond is something I've never had to think about before.

'Do you have a moment?'

Turgan's voice in the mind-link pulls me from those thoughts. 'I'm in my suite,' I tell him. I've been expecting him. My performance on the battlefield was strange, to say the least.

He steps in after a quick mind-link announcement. "The border is quiet," he reports, "other than those picking up their dead, and the undertakers are sticking to their own territory."

"Good." I nod, leaning back in my chair.

"So, are we going to talk about what happened out there?" he asks, plopping into a chair next to me and putting his feet up on my coffee table. I glare at him, and he lowers them.

"We fought a battle," I say. "We won."

"You won," he corrects me.

I raise a brow. "I saw a large contingency of our warriors out there. They'd been fighting long before I showed up."

"You know what I mean, Cassian." He puts an emphasis on my name as he usually does when he's speaking as my friend and not my Beta. "I've never seen you like that, and neither have the warriors. They're starting to ask questions."

"Tell them to mind their own fucking business," I quip.

"That's not what I mean, and I think you know that."

I raise my brow again, wondering how far he'll dare push me. Not many men can be this insolent with me.

"They're not asking anything out loud, but I can tell they're all wondering," he explains, though he was right. I already knew that. "And the only thing that has changed recently is the girl. I'm pretty sure they'll put two and two together."

"You sure say a lot of words," I point out. "Since when have you had any trouble being direct with me?"

"Since you discovered your mate is a human."

I say nothing and push up out of the chair, heading toward my bar. Not that alcohol has any effect on me, but I've always used its bitter taste to bite back thoughts I'd rather not explore.

I can tell Turgan won't shut up about this, so I pour him a whiskey as well.

He stands and takes the second glass from me. "It's not a horrible thing, you know," he continues. "An Alpha needs a Luna."

"A human is no Luna," I say quickly, narrowing my eyes at him.

But he just shrugs. "How do you know for sure? The Moon Goddess is never wrong."

"She is this time."

"I disagree," he says, "respectfully." But the smirk on his face as he takes a sip from his glass is hardly respectful, and I'd punch it right off him if it weren't for my wolf inside agreeing with him.

Even my wolf is betraying me.

"A human might have the qualities we're missing in the kingdom," he adds.

I shake my head, but he holds up his hand. "Hear me out. We have everything here—strong warriors, plentiful resources, good leadership."

"Don't try to kiss my ass."

He chuckles at that. "I just mean that there's not much anyone could add to this kingdom to make it better. But an Alpha needs a Luna."

"You're repeating yourself in all your babbling."

"Maybe, but it's true," he asserts. "So, what could the Moon Goddess possibly give us when granting our Alpha King a mate? It's probably a new perspective, something we don't even know we need yet."

"That's a stretch."

"But it's possible," he says. "You have to admit that."

He's smirking again because he knows he's right, and once again, I feel like punching him. But I don't.

"Just because humans can't do what we can doesn't mean they're useless," he continues. "There must be something about her. It'll take time to figure out what that is, but in the meantime, it can't hurt to just let it happen. I mean, she is quite a looker."

My wolf growls inside. "I thought you were fond of your face," I tell him.

He snickers in response but then holds up his hands in mock surrender. "I am, so don't break it."

"You know I won't," I say. "I can't have my Beta running around looking like a broken-up fool."

"And for that, I'm grateful." But he's still laughing. "Seriously, though, the Moon Goddess gave you a beautiful mate who probably has a lot of other good qualities."

"Like what?"

"She's strong for one," he says. "She lasted in the dungeon longer than some male wolves manage to do."

"There's another problem," I say. "I locked my Goddess-given mate in the dungeon."

He at least attempts to hold back his smirk this time. "You didn't know who she was then."

"I should have," I correct him. "There was something about her when they brought her in. I thought she was just attractive, and that's why she caught my attention. But now I know it's something more."

"You also thought Assanan's warriors were planning to storm the castle," he reminds me. "It was prudent to keep her safe. I'm sure that now that she's out, she won't mind anymore."

"I wouldn't forget," I insist.

"Well, she's not you, thank the Goddess." He lets out a laugh again. "By that I mean she's your complement, someone to fill in the blanks where you have weaknesses."

I practically growl at him.

"Everyone has weaknesses," he quickly explains, "even Alpha King Cassian of Oceana. Maybe she's better at the softer side of things, which is exactly what a Luna needs to be."

"Maybe." I hate when he has a point.

"Anyway, I'd better get back to the warriors," he says, setting down his glass. "Helmswood is getting fresh troops to watch the border, and I should lead that group back."

I nod. "Make it happen."

"Aye, Alpha," he says, emphasizing the word before another smirk covers his face.

I pour another drink after he leaves, his words still lingering in my mind. I can't deny I want to finish what I started with Lyra. But the fact that she's a human still troubles me, no matter what Turgan says.

I'm not sure the Moon Goddess hasn't made a mistake.

CRY OF THE MATE BOND

Lyra

"I've never heard of such a thing," Cally says as Orla describes the mate bond.

Neither have I, but I can't really speak right now from the shock of it. Two people destined for each other sounds romantic in a way, but it also feels strange. Don't wolf shifters get to choose?

Well, I guess I don't either way.

"It's common in our shifter community," Orla explains. "Not everyone has a fated mate, but most do, especially royalty like the Alpha King. Our citizens have been wondering for a long time whether Alpha King Cassian would find his fated mate."

"But that's for wolf shifters," Cally says. "Lyra is human like me. How could she possibly have a fated mate, especially one who's a wolf shifter?"

I've been wondering the same thing, but my breath feels heavy in my lungs, and I can't even talk right now to ask the question.

Thank goodness for Cally.

Orla shrugs and shakes her head at the same time. "I really have no idea," she says. "It's not something I've ever heard of. But the Moon Goddess is all-knowing, so She does things we don't understand all the time."

"Moon Goddess." Cally says it as though it's a question, but her tone is more like a statement.

"Yes, the deity who watches over us, the Moon Goddess," Orla explains, though it's really not explaining much.

Cally shakes her head. "I've never heard of a Moon Goddess," she says. "Our people worship the gods of old, those who make the crops grow when we please them or flood the land when we don't."

I finally find my voice. "Most human royals have stopped any kind of worship other than using the priests for ceremonies."

"It's much different here," Orla says. "The Moon Goddess is revered by all. She has cared for our people for generations, and Her mate bond is one of her most treasured gifts." She looks straight at me. "You're fortunate to receive it."

I'm not sure I feel fortunate, but I can't ignore that strange feeling of connection I have with the Alpha King. Somehow, I could tell when he was gone—and it hurt like crazy—and it was a huge relief when he came back.

"But what if you don't like the person?" Cally asked. "I'd hate to be stuck with a jerk."

Orla giggles a little, but then she turns serious. "Many mates find some disagreement at first," she explains. "But over time, they come to realize why the Goddess mated them. There will usually be characteristics that complement each other, such as one person lacking something where the other is strong."

"I can't imagine the Alpha King needing anything from someone like me," I say. "I'm only a lower princess of a human kingdom."

"I'm sure you will find those things the longer you are together," Orla assures me. "But to answer your question," she adds, turning to Cally, "there is no choice if you don't think you like the person at first. You must follow the path the Moon Goddess has laid out for you."

"What if you don't?" Cally asks.

"There are only two options." It may be my imagination, but Orla seems to shudder when she thinks of those things. "Either you reject the mate, or one of you dies."

"Well, that's good then," Cally says. "You can just reject him if he's a jerk."

Orla takes a sharp breath in. "You can, but you will be abandoning that person to a life of torture. To be rejected by one's mate is painful, and you feel its effects every day. Usually, that person is slowly driven mad. Life becomes more than unbearable."

"Well, if he was a jerk, maybe he deserves it," Cally says.

Orla shakes her head. "It's not that easy to be the one who rejects the mate, either. As a mate, you often aren't able to harm your fated mate in that way, not to mention that you'll feel the effects of ignoring the Moon Goddess's plan as well."

"Well, that sounds miserable," Cally says.

"It is," Orla agrees. She looks back at me. "But you've been blessed as the mate of Alpha King Cassian. You'll have no need to reject someone of his stature."

I wasn't planning on it, especially since my father gave me to the man anyway.

"Though—" Orla hesitates.

"What is it?" I ask.

"Well, to have a human mate is unheard of for anyone, much less the Alpha King," she explains. She seems to be trying to choose her words carefully. "So far, no one knows about it but you, the Alpha King, Cally here, and myself. Should others find out... this might become a problem for him."

I feel a rock instantly form in my gut. "How would it be a problem?"

"I don't know exactly," she says. "But... perhaps they may question the Alpha King's power for having a human as a mate. Please know that I won't betray his or your trust by revealing it to anyone. But these things are difficult to hide since our kind is very perceptive."

"What would those people do?" I ask.

"They may try to usurp his throne," she says gravely. "It may leave him no choice."

"Choice about what?" Cally asks.

Orla inhales deeply and lets it out slowly before blurting out, "He may have no choice but to reject you as a mate."

Something deep inside me screams in pain at the idea, and I clutch my chest. I feel agony shooting through every nerve in my body, and I can't even sit up anymore.

I feel myself falling forward as the world goes pitch black.

CASSIAN

THE DRINK DOESN'T CALM THE ACHE FOR MY MATE. I'VE ALWAYS BEEN able to control myself, but now I cannot think of anything but running to Lyra's room and stripping her down, finishing what we started before I had to run off the battle.

I suppose I've already given into the feeling. It can't hurt to follow through.

I feel a rare smile cross my face as I leave my chambers and head toward the ladies' wing of my castle. The woman is supposed to be my bride anyway. Maybe after a good round of pleasure, I'll stop craving it so much.

Turgan pops into my head again as I walk. 'We're heading out,' he says in a private mind-link. 'I'll tell you right away if we have any trouble.'

'Prepare a line of message runners as well,' I tell him. 'That border is on the outer rim of the mind-link radius. It's always possible I won't get the message.'

'Aye, Alpha.'

We begin speaking of other things, such as which warriors he's taking with him and what my orders are upon conflict. But then a tiny voice rings in through another private mind-link.

I ignore it at first. It's a female servant, and I don't have time to choose silver patterns for the wedding I probably won't ever have.

But eventually, I can't ignore the pleading and open the link. 'Alpha King!' the woman is practically screaming, something we can somehow do through the mind-link. 'Please, come quickly! Something has happened to Miss Lyra!'

I say nothing, but I break into a run, racing toward Lyra's suite.

My wolf howls in agony within me.

A NEW SENSATION

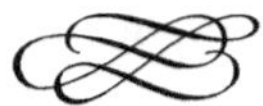

CASSIAN

THE GUARD OPENS THE DOOR FOR ME AS SOON AS I TURN THE CORNER. I'll reward him later.

I don't understand why I didn't sense my mate was in danger before. But now, I feel it–an empty ache of confusion and despair. Is this what she's feeling now?

When I get to her side, the lady's maidens are there, holding Lyra's hand, her body limp and sagging in the chair.

"Why isn't the healer attending to my… to this woman?" I demand.

"She's delivering a pup in the infirmary," one of the women, Orla, I believe her name is, says. "An assistant is on her way."

My wolf growls inside me. "And yet, I arrived first."

The women, wisely, say nothing.

I reach around Lyra, and tingles of fire alight on my skin. My mother did not exaggerate the bliss of a mate's touch.

Lyra is breathing in a soft, even pattern. She's still alive, thank the Goddess. My wolf howls with gratitude, yet Lyra is clearly unconscious for some reason.

A new sensation washes over me, and I struggle to identify it. It's a mix of terror, concern, and… maybe empathy. As if hit by a lightning bolt, now all I can think about is Lyra… her comfort, her health, her safety.

She is mine, and I am hers.

To hell with what anyone else thinks.

And I won't leave her slumped over in a chair. Clearly, the women are too small to move her. Lifting her light frame, I gently carry her to the bed and set her down, her long, soft red hair curling around the silk pillow.

"What happened?" I demand.

The women look at each other, and Orla addresses me in a private mind-link. 'We were discussing the mate bond. These women were unfamiliar with it. I'm afraid I… well, I explained about rejection and suggested this could happen since she's human."

Mixed reactions rush over me. I'm furious that Orla suggested I might reject my mate. But then, it's a thought that has crossed my mind several times since I discovered the Goddess had matched me with this human woman.

At the same time, I'm grateful Orla is helping Lyra understand our concepts. I don't believe humans have fated mates. The Goddess has not blessed them with shifting, after all.

'I will not reveal that she is your mate, Alpha King,' she adds.

Only now I look into Orla's eyes, and I see she is telling the truth, though she's clearly terrified.

"Fetch some cool, wet towels," I tell her out loud.

She moves quickly to do so just as the healer's assistant hurries in. "What happened?" she asks immediately.

I back up slightly to let her examine Lyra but keep my hand on my mate's. "It was an emotional shock," I explain.

The healer's assistant nods, listening to Lyra's heartbeat and forcing her eyes open to examine them. "In that case, it's just fainting," she deduces. "I'll give her some smelling herbs."

She pulls the medicine from her healer's bag and holds the herbs under Lyra's nostrils. My mate's eyes blink open only moments later.

"I—" Lyra begins to say.

I pat her hand. "Relax," I tell her. "You just had a fainting spell. You'll be fine." I look toward the healer's assistant to confirm.

"Yes, Alpha King," she says. She turns to Lyra. "Do you feel any dizziness?"

Lyra shakes her head. "No."

"Good," the healer says. "But please, rest for the rest of the day. Have a good meal and plenty of water. And be sure to avoid any further stress."

Lyra nods.

"Thank you," I tell the healer. "You may go." To Orla, I say in the mind-link, 'I need a moment with my mate.'

'Yes, Alpha King,' she answers. To the other woman, Lyra's human lady's maiden, she speaks out loud. "Come. I'll show you the kitchen. We'll get some food and drinks for your lady."

The woman looks reluctant to leave, but Orla coaxes her, and soon I'm alone with my mate.

"I'm so embarrassed," Lyra tells me. "I've never fainted like that before."

I pat her hand again. Inside, my wolf whines for more physical contact, begging me to put my lips on hers and hold her body next to mine. But I hold it back.

"You had a shock," I say instead. "Orla explained your discussion."

"Oh." Her eyes turn from mine for a moment. "I've never even heard of a mate bond before." She looks back into my eyes. "Is that what we have?"

"Yes," I tell her.

"How can that be if I'm a human?" she asks.

I shake my head. "I don't know. I haven't had time to research this to see if it's ever happened before. But you feel it, don't you?"

"Yes," she says quickly.

A warm feeling rushes through my chest.

"It's... strange," she adds.

"I suppose it would be." She starts to sit up, but I stop her gently with a hand to her shoulder. "You need to rest. You should keep lying there until the women bring your food."

"I am hungry," she says.

"Good." I let go of her hand for a moment, feeling the absence of her touch immediately, and emptiness with our parting.

I can only imagine what my mother went through when my father was killed. No wonder her mind is gone.

Pulling over a chair, I sit close to my mate and take her hand again. The all-encompassing warmth returns.

We're silent for a moment, but then she speaks again, her voice meek and soft. "Are you going to reject me?" she asks.

My wolf panics inside. "No," I tell her quickly.

"No?" she asks. "But what if the people try to take power away from you for being mated to a human? Orla says that could be a problem."

I stroke her cheek with my palm, her skin soft as silk. "I don't give a fuck about…. Sorry. I don't care about what others think. Let them try to take my power. The Goddess gave me you for a reason, and they'll just have to accept that."

She smiles, and it sends thrilling sparks through me. "You don't mind having a human mate?"

"No, not when that mate is you." Moments ago, I didn't think that, but now, I feel it with every fiber of my being.

'Is it too soon to return with her tray?' Orla asks in the mind-link.

'Give me five minutes,' I tell her.

I stroke Lyra's cheek more and bring my lips to hers. Our bond sets fire the moment we kiss, and though I want to look into those jewel-like eyes, I close mine so I can feel every moment of it more intensely.

My cock stiffens with the sensation, but I have to force myself to pull back. My mate needs to recover, and I will give her that space.

My wolf cries when we part, but I ignore him. "I'll never reject you, Lyra," I tell her. "And you'll never be in any dungeon again. I regret that choice, and I will make it up to you every day forward."

She giggles a little, and the effect tingles all over. "It's already forgotten," she says.

I stand, squeezing her hand one more time before letting go. "The ladies are coming with your food and drink. Please relax for the day. Tomorrow, please join me for breakfast."

"I'd love that," she says with a smile.

I kiss her again on the forehead before pulling myself away and out of the room.

Orla and Lyra's ladies pass me in the hall with the cart. I nod to them and move quickly away, pushing all my wolf's desires down inside me, for now.

Something just changed in me... in her.

If any shifter even suggests I reject my mate, I'll rip their fucking head off.

BOTH SIDES OF HIM

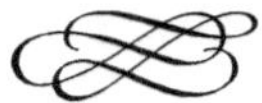

Lyra

HE'S SO... NICE TO ME. THAT'S STRANGE FOR A COLD-HEARTED ALPHA King who threw me in the dungeon for months. But he even apologized for that. It seems so sudden, but something inside me says that he's being genuine.

It's strange that things seem so clear now, guided by whatever this voice is inside me.

I don't want the Alpha King to leave, but I'm lying here helplessly watching the door close behind him. I'm not even embarrassed that I fainted now. He's been so kind and considerate.

I hope I'm not dreaming.

The door opens again, and I'm hopeful that he decided to come back, but I already know it's not him. I feel him widening the distance between us, though I know it's not far this time. He's still in the castle.

"Are you okay?" Cally asks as she runs toward me.

I nod, giving her an easy smile. "I'm just fine."

"You do look better," she says, relaxing into the chair the Alpha King has just left. "You have to tell us what happened!"

"What happened where?" I ask.

"With the Alpha King, of course!"

"Oh. He was very nice."

Her eyes widen, and I see a gentle smile spread on Orla's face behind Cally as she uncovers the food dishes on the cart she brought in.

"The Alpha King who threw you in the dungeon for... I don't even know how long... was nice?" Cally asks.

"Well, yes." My stomach growls with the scent of the fresh biscuits. I push myself up, and Cally stands to help me arrange the pillows behind me so I can sit up. "I don't understand it, either," I add. "But it's like something changed just in those few moments he was here in the room."

"The Alpha King recognizes the mate bond," Orla says quietly, placing a tray across my lap. "You are his mate. The connection is already there. The rest will happen naturally."

I don't say it out loud, but it's a relief to feel this way about Alpha King Cassian.

Back in my kingdom when my father announced his decision, I was so terrified. To be sold to a wolf... a cruel-hearted ruler at that... felt like the end of the world.

Now, it just feels like the beginning.

"I'M GLAD YOU'RE FEELING BETTER." THE ALPHA KING PULLS OUT MY chair the next morning in the private sunroom, and as he pushes it in, his hand brushes lightly over my back.

The sensation tingles all over me.

Our plates are already full of breakfast food–fried potatoes, a variety of meats, and eggs seasoned with fragrant herbs.

"I guess some of this is just... sudden, Alpha King," I tell him, picking up my fork.

He sits by me and lets out a light chuckle, his handsome features relaxed and warm. It still seems so strange to see this man like that, the one who terrifies my father so much that he has given up one of his daughters.

"You don't have to keep calling me that," he says. "We're mates. We're equals."

My heart skips a beat. Never in all my life has my father or anyone in my kingdom considered me an equal, even as a princess. And now this man—the Sea-King Alpha with power over every human kingdom in his realm—tells me I'm his equal.

Is it true?

"What should I call you?" I ask.

"Cassian."

I nod softly. "Okay… Cassian." A warm feeling passes over me when I say his name. "But what about when other people are around? Won't that be strange? They might think that—"

"I don't give a—" He pauses before continuing. "It doesn't matter what other people think. You're my mate, and that's it."

I nod again, but I'm still worried about that. It sounds like people in this kingdom don't like humans, and they sure won't want their Alpha King marrying one.

Cassian radiates power, but I'm so new, I have no idea what politics are like here in Oceana. If he loses power, maybe we'll both end up in the dungeon.

He finishes the bite of food he took. "You look worried," he says.

"That's because I am," I tell him. "This is all so new to me. I don't know what to think."

He reaches over and pats my hand gently. "There is a lot to adjust to. Take your time. Maybe my mother could help. Her mind is gone since my father died, but I think she still remembers the workings of the court from a ladies' perspective. She can help you work out some things."

I can feel the sadness in his heart as though it's my own. "How long has he been gone?"

He looks blankly at his plate as he answers. "Two years." His gaze turns to me. "They were true mates. It's tearing her apart."

"I'm sorry."

"That has nothing to do with you," he assures me.

"Is that why you're... we're at war?"

He nods. "Assanan, the man who killed my father, has designs on my... our kingdom. He hopes I'm weak, and unfortunately, I need to show him otherwise."

His tone tells me he's willing to go to any lengths to do so. The idea of him dying on the battlefield has a twinge of panic rising up in me. What if I lose my mate like his mother did? She seems so ill, and now I understand why.

"War is dangerous," I tell him. "Please be careful."

He lets a smirk rise at the corner of his lips. "You have nothing to worry about. Now, eat your breakfast. You need your strength."

"For what?" I ask.

Something changes in his eyes. They turn hungry... and not for breakfast. "For the wedding night."

My breath catches in my throat, and I can barely speak, much less eat. "Oh," is all I can manage to say. I feel heat rising in my core, like it did when we were kissing and... other things... before.

Is this how it will be from now on?

I'm not sure how I feel about that. I've never even... been with a man. Yet, I feel like I crave it with Cassian.

I take a bite of my eggs, trying to get those thoughts out of my mind. And the food is delicious. We both eat quietly for a while, and I occasionally steal a glance at him.

I find that I do enjoy spending time with him like this, especially with how nice he's treating me now. I feel like there's a connection growing stronger.

And I like it.

The next time I look up, he meets my gaze for a moment, and a rush of electric tingles dances across my chest. He smiles, disconnecting our gaze and turning to his food, and I try to do the same.

Once again, I'm suddenly very hungry. If there's one thing that's certain in the Oceana castle, it's that the chefs are amazing.

I'm enjoying another bite of seasoned fried potatoes when I look up again. This time, I notice his expression has darkened.

"What is it?" I ask.

"There's been another attack on our border," he says, setting down his fork.

"They've told you in the mind-link," I say.

"Yes," he confirms. "I have to go, Lyra."

Something inside me screams. He's leaving again for another dangerous battle. "Can't the army handle it? Do you have to go personally?"

"I do," he says, standing and putting his hand on my shoulder. "It demonstrates strength that encourages the other warriors. Participating in battles is part of my responsibility as king."

"And you have to keep being strong to be around me," I say.

He shakes his head. "This is just how it is."

Leaning down, he kisses me softly, his lips lingering for a moment. My body erupts with his touch, like the exploding fireworks my kingdom always lights during celebrations. I put my hand on his cheek instinctively, trying to pull him closer, to keep him here with me.

I know it's futile.

As expected, he pulls back. "I need to go," he says.

I nod, trying to ignore the terror growing in my heart. "Be careful."

"I will," he assures me.

The moment he steps outside the door, his voice changes as he addresses his men. "Send everyone to the border," he barks out. "But no one is to touch Assanan. He's mine. I'll personally rip his heart out and force-feed it to anyone who dared invade my lands."

It's cold, cruel, and nothing like the man I just shared breakfast with. A frightened shudder runs down my spine.

This man really is the cruel killer I've been told of.

And he's my mate? I'm going to marry this man?

I wonder if that other part of him, the Cassian he showed me, is real. I think it is. But this side of him is real, too.

Will he ever unleash it on me?

Suddenly, I'm not hungry anymore.

A TERRIBLE LOSS

CASSIAN

ONCE AGAIN, I'M PULLED AWAY FROM MY MATE, AND IT IS AGONY.

But an incursion by Assanan must be answered swiftly. The bastard has the balls to send more warriors over the border after we just killed dozens and delivered their bodies to them. Striking again this fast is a statement.

I'll make one of my own.

So, I've shifted again, barreling past the gates held open for me and sprinting toward the border, another long run.

But it's cathartic to feel my paws beat against the warm ground, the scents of the land awakening in my nostrils once again.

The clarity opens my mind to thoughts of Lyra. I no longer question the choice of the Goddess. The exhilaration of Lyra's touch, the warmth of the connection... these are enough to throw all my doubts aside.

Rejection is no longer an option, and regret washes over me knowing that I ever had the thought. No, I will marry my mate and consummate the mate bond. The people will come to accept my human mate as Luna soon enough.

It's the Goddess's will.

Eventually, the sounds of battle reach my ears, though I'm several miles away from the borderlands.

Has Assanan dared to come so far?

I open a channel to Turgan and await his response, knowing he is mid-battle.

'We're dealing with them, though this time, he sent some better warriors,' Turgan tells me eventually.

'How many are left?' I ask.

'About a hundred, but it's not a problem holding our own.'

'I'll be there soon.' I close the mind-link, picking up my pace.

When I arrive, I can see it's true. I dispatch several enemies myself, the salty-sweet taste of their blood dripping across my teeth.

Once again, my warriors are successful, and the battle ends with blood and bodies strewn across the forest floor. My warriors begin to shift back into their human forms to recover, their assistants running forward with clothes and supplies.

"No!"

The anguished cry erupts through the trees, a horrid screech of despair. Unable to immediately determine its source, I open the mind-link to all my warriors. None answer, until one of them opens a private mind-link.

'It's Hera,' the warrior explains. 'Her mate has been killed.'

The words ring through my mind with horror. I cannot count the many times I've heard the statement before. But only now I feel its true consequence.

Only now, I feel the bond of a mate myself.

Hera is one of my best warriors, a woman whose mate was also in my army. Though at first many questioned having a woman among the ranks, all went silent when they witnessed her skill. It opened the door for many other brave women to become warriors. Hera and her mate had been fighting side-by-side for years.

'Where is she?' I ask the warrior who delivered the news.

'Near the front lines,' he answers. 'They were among the first to strike into battle.'

Without another word, I rush forward, leaping over the bodies and navigating through the trees to reach the front. 'Casualty count?' I ask Turgan in a private mind-link as I move.

'Roughly twenty,' he replies, 'though we're still working through this.'

I don't reply because I've reached the front, and the scene is brutal. Hera, her long blonde hair curtaining her face, kneels over her deceased mate, her forehead buried in his chest.

She has shifted back to her human form, and her mate shifted with the final blow.

I stand back, allowing her the time with her mate. But an angry voice echoes behind me.

"Perhaps we wouldn't have lost so many warriors had you not been lounging with the human girl," Nolan says.

I spin toward him, closing the distance between us and grabbing his shirt with my fist. "Who the fuck do you think you are, accusing me?" I demand.

A slight blink of terror alights in his eyes, but he quickly shoves it down, moving to stand a little taller, though he still can't match my frame. "I am a member of the council, if you'll remember," he bites back. "I'll thank you to unhand me."

"Be thankful you didn't meet the grip of my jaw," I say, though I do release his shirt. "This—" I gesture around the battlefield. "This was a surprise attack. I'd only recently returned to the castle after the first one."

"Where you did, I must admit, make an impressive showing," he says.

His eyes meet mine, and I see laughter in them, laughter and insight.

He knows.

"Normally, one would only have such strength in battle with the connection of a mate bond," he says, his eyes dancing with glee. He knows he will deliver news the others will not accept.

"Perhaps the Goddess has provided Her gift to you in the form of a human?"

Gasps rip across the forest at the news, and my wolf growls internally. Acknowledging the bond places my mate in danger, should anyone object and form a coalition against me. My wolf wants to sink his teeth into the man's neck.

But my rational mind wins over. It's better to announce the pairing now before rumors get it wrong. "The human princess is indeed my mate," I say, using my Alpha voice loud enough to be heard by all.

No one dares to speak.

"I don't question the Goddess's infinite knowledge," I continue before meeting Nolan's eyes as mine go narrow. "Do you?"

He chuckles in response. "Oh, no," he says. "Of course not." It's clear by his eyes that he, in fact, does object to the Goddess this time.

Turgan joins me, his expression steady.

"Then all is well," I say. Louder, I add, "Though not customary, this bond will add strength to our kingdom. The Goddess has given your Alpha King a mate."

An uncertain hush hangs heavy in the air for a moment before one warrior stands and holds his fist in the air.

"Our Alpha King has a Luna!" he calls. "Praise the Moon Goddess!"

He repeats the phrase, and others join in the chant, some sooner than others, but none so enthusiastically as Turgan beside me.

After a time, I wave my arms to quiet them. "While this news is a joy, the time for celebrating is not now," I say. "Some of our warriors have perished here. We will have a period of mourning of these deaths, and their families shall be rewarded for their brave service to our kingdom. And we will have no mercy for Assanan and his warriors from this day forward."

I turn to Turgan. "Burn these bodies."

"Aye," he answers simply.

I turn and walk away without another word, but I first step over to Hera and place an understanding palm on her shoulder for a moment. Her tears do not lighten, and I don't expect them to.

It's a loss for which I now have the strongest empathy.

After a private discussion with Turgan, I turn back in the direction of my castle to make the long run home, this time pacing even faster than I did running toward the battle.

It's obvious that Nolan deduced that Lyra is my mate some time ago. Goddess knows what he has been planning.

As soon as I'm clearly within mind-link range of the castle, I alert my guards to protect Lyra. Then, I open a private mind-link with my mother.

'Cassian,' she says happily, in a voice showing escape from her own mate loss. 'Will you be joining me for dinner?'

'Yes, Mother,' I tell her. 'But before that, I need you to do something for me.'

'Oh?' she asks. 'What's that?'

'Arrange for my wedding to Lyra as soon as possible.'

SOMETHING ISN'T RIGHT

Lyra

ORLA MEETS ME IN THE SUNROOM TO ESCORT ME BACK TO MY ROOM. I'D be so lost without this woman. I feel like I have a new friend here in her.

I follow her back to my room feeling a bit more confused than before, but on the whole, I'm happier about being here in the castle now.

The rumors about Cassian are probably true. He is cold and ruthless, ruling his kingdom and all the human kingdoms inside it with an iron fist.

But he's not that way with me. He was kind and considerate at breakfast, and he told me I was his equal, even though I've never been more than a lower princess, and most people back in my kingdom, except Mother and Aisla, reminded me of that constantly.

So, maybe Maelie just isn't my kingdom anymore.

Oceana is.

"How was your breakfast?"

Orla's question kicks me out of my thoughts. "It was nice, really nice," I tell her. "But—"

"But?"

"But Cassian is a lot different around me, I think," I say.

She smiles. "Yes, and that's to be expected," she explains. "You're his mate. There is no other person in the world who shares a closer bond with him, not even his own mother."

"Does that mean I'm more bonded to him than my mother?" I ask.

She stops us in the hall and turns to me. "Yes, though I don't imagine you feel that way quite yet. You're human, so I'm not sure how things work on you. But you will need to consummate the bond for it to be fully secure."

I immediately feel the blush rise on my cheeks. "Consummate?" Just saying the word makes me even more embarrassed, though Orla is easy to talk to.

She giggles a little as though she's embarrassed with the concept too. "Yes, it's what you think it is."

"Oh." My cheeks burn even hotter.

We go silent and start walking again while I think about that. My mother had spoken to me a few times about sex and marriage, but the concepts seemed so distant back then. Now, after having done… some of that… with Cassian, I understand it more.

And I'm looking forward to the rest of it, though it's still a bit scary.

"I think I'd like to learn some more about the mate bond," I tell her after a while.

"That's a great idea," she says. "I can tell you some things, but I think the ideal way is to read some of our books. You can get familiar with our community while also learning about what you're feeling for the Alpha King right now. There's a library just up this hallway." She points to the next turn.

"I'd love that." I guess I'm not in any real hurry to get back to my room, and I'd rather learn something about my new kingdom.

So, we head down that hallway. She opens two large carved wooden doors, and my eyes go wide. I didn't expect such an incredible selection of books here. I don't know what I thought wolf shifters did with their time, but I never considered they'd be avid readers or historians.

But this room shows me they are, with its walls stacked to the ceiling with mahogany bookshelves, their ends carved just as intricately as the doors coming in. The temperature is different in here, so I can tell it's regulated for optimum book storage, just like my father's grand libraries back home. The earthy scent of paper fills the air, along with some hints of vanilla and almond, which I know come from the wood pulp in the paper.

She sets me down at a table and brings over a few books.

"You can get started with these," she says. "If you'd like, you can read them here. I have a few things I've wanted to look up myself, if you don't mind."

"That sounds great," I say, lifting the cover of the first huge tome, its cover crackling slightly at the movement. "I hope I don't ruin this one."

"It's fine," she says. "Most of us don't read those often since our history is such a part of everyday life since childhood."

"That makes sense."

I go silent and dive into the book, which tells ancient stories about the Moon Goddess and the wars between humans and wolf shifters. The mate bond, apparently, is a gift from her, a way to ensure that all the shifters are properly mated for happiness and a stronger community. Though, there's nothing about any humans mated to shifters.

I keep reading, hoping I find that. The rest of the world seems to disappear while I read.

"You can take some of these back to your room if you'd like," Orla says after a while, snapping me out of my reading trance.

"Oh, yes," I say. "What time is it?"

"Well after lunch," she answers. "But I didn't want to disturb you."

"I'd better get back then," I tell her. "Cally might be worried."

She nods and helps me choose a couple of smaller books that are more suitable for carrying back to my room. If Cassian doesn't come back for dinner, I certainly won't be bored. I want to know every-thing I can about this place.

I am worried about how the battle went. I suppose I'd feel some-thing if it hadn't gone well.

A light shudder runs through me at the thought.

When we reach my suite with my armful of books, Cally looks like she wants to jump up and down, she's so excited about something.

"Lyra, I've been waiting for you!" she says, and I can tell she's about bursting at the seams with some sort of news.

"Well?" I ask. "What is it?"

"The Queen Mother was here!" she exclaims. "They're preparing for your wedding! It's going to happen soon!"

My heart races at the news. He didn't say anything at breakfast about the wedding, but I think I'm ready.

And it means we'll consummate this bond sooner than I expected. That little voice inside me practically screams for joy.

"And this came, too!" Cally adds, pointing across the room.

"My trunk!" I run over to it, running my fingers over the floral decorations on the outside. "I thought it was thrown into the ocean!"

Cally shrugs. "I guess not. I got mine back, too. See?"

Her smaller case, already unpacked, is on the other side of the room.

"I didn't want to touch yours until you'd seen it," she adds.

"This is amazing." I crack open the lid, and sure enough, there are all my lovely gowns and other possessions.

He didn't throw away my things… or Cally's.

I'm going through my trunk and had just held my yellow gown with beautiful lace trim up to me when the door opens, and a woman I've never seen comes in.

Orla turns to me. "This is Raylynn," she says. "She works with the Queen Mother."

"Hello," I greet her, holding out my hand to shake hers.

She takes it tentatively. I'd forgotten this isn't a custom here.

"The Queen Mother would like to have you fitted for your wedding gown," she says with a polite smile. "Will you follow me?"

Excited tingles race through my heart, and I put the yellow gown back in the trunk. "Absolutely!" I look at Orla and Cally. "Are you two coming?"

They both nod and turn toward the door.

"The Queen Mother has requested that only I accompany the princess," Raylynn says quickly.

"Oh," Orla says. She frowns a little but then nods, and Cally stops in her tracks. "I'll help Miss Cally put away your things while you're gone," Orla says, nodding toward the trunk.

"Thank you," I tell her, giving Cally an excited look, which she returns, before following Raylynn out the door.

I can barely contain myself. I'm doing a fitting for my wedding gown! And I've just found out that Cassian is more considerate than I ever imagined.

What a fantastic day!

I'm practically skipping as she leads me down the hallways. Eventually, I get the feeling I've never been in this part of the castle before, even though it's still pretty impossible for me to tell one hall from the other.

"Here we are," she says finally. "Step into this room, please." Her voice is a little higher pitched now, a little too sweet. Something about that strikes me as odd, but I step inside the room anyway.

And I'm immediately face-to-face with Esmerelda, who laughs like a cackling hen.

"What are you—"

I haven't even had time to finish the sentence when something hard hits me on the back of the head.

The ground is suddenly approaching fast, just as the world goes dark.

KIDNAPPED

CASSIAN

SOMETHING'S WRONG.

Something feels off about Lyra. She doesn't register with consciousness. I'm not sure how I know that, but it's no doubt the mate bond.

It's probably just a mid-afternoon nap.

But somehow, I don't think so.

I approach the gate and notify the guards in the mind-link, who promptly crank the great walls open as I run through. I shift, and my assistant approaches with clothing, but I barely have time to put on the pants before dashing upstairs to my mate's quarters.

Mid-run, I connect with Orla in the mind-link. 'Where is Lyra? Is she well?'

'Yes,' she answers. 'Though she's been gone for quite a while. She went with Raylynn for a wedding dress fitting quite some time ago.'

I can't place the name, but then again, there are hundreds of servants in the castle. 'Why didn't you accompany her?'

'I tried, but Raylynn insisted that the Queen Mother wanted milady to go alone,' she answers.

A low growl forms inside me, and I connect with my mother. 'Mother, is Lyra with you?'

'Oh, hello, Cassian,' she answers, her tone gleeful. 'Not yet, but I was about to send my lady's maiden to ask her to tea.'

'Isn't she trying on her wedding dress?' I ask.

'No. Why do you ask?'

'Because her lady Orla told me she went to do that,' I explain.

'Oh,' Mother says. 'Well, I don't have that planned until after dinner this evening. But you can't be there anyway. You know the groom can't see the bride in her dress before the wedding!'

I ignore that. 'Who is Raylynn?' I quicken my pace, taking two steps at a time on the last stairwell before I reach Lyra's floor of the ladies' wing.

'Raylynn? Oh, you know her, Cassian. She's been with me for about a week now.'

'A week.' I repeat the phrase as a rock of lead forms in the pit of my stomach. Flinging open the doors into Lyra's suite, I find Orla and Lyra's human maid standing near the entrance.

'Cassian, be sure you come by later,' Mother continues. 'I need you to help choose colors for the hall decorations.'

'Not now, Mother. Goodbye.'

'Goodbye, son!'

"How long has she been gone?" I ask Orla and the other woman out loud.

"Since one o'clock this afternoon, Your Majesty," Orla answers, her eyes wide with worry. "She didn't even have lunch yet. We assumed it would take a few minutes at the most."

"Which way did they go?"

She shakes her head. "I'm not sure, Your Majesty. Cally?" She looks at the other woman, who also shakes her head briskly.

"I don't know either," that woman says. "It's hard to hear past these large doors."

"Next time, one of you is to follow her everywhere," I order, my tone harsh.

"Yes, Your Majesty," they say together.

But I'm already out the door, trying to get a hint of Lyra's scent in the hallways. It's strong by her suite and seems to fade down the westward hall, so I start there.

It's too damn faint for me to track it in my human form, so I shift, my heightened senses instantly picking up her scent down the hall that leads out of the ladies' wing and toward the utility area.

No wedding dress fittings could have been happening down here.

I race down the scent trail.

But soon, the smell of bleach and lemon cleaners overpowers Lyra's scent, and I can't follow it anymore.

Fuck. They've cleaned up after themselves.

I can't connect with her in the mind-link. I curse myself for not consummating our bond when I had the chance. It didn't matter that Assanan started attacking the border. I could have pulled Lyra out of the fucking dungeon months earlier.

If I had, we'd be married and properly mated, and I'd be able to speak to her now, to find where the hell they've taken her.

I have no one to blame but myself for that.

As to Lyra's disappearance, I have an idea of where I can start the blame. I do a quick about-face and tear toward the one man who can tell me where the fuck they took my mate. I know he's a part of this.

I'm going to rip Nolan into a thousand pieces. He'll regret the day he dared touch my mate.

Lyra

My head pounds and throbs at the same time as I try to open my eyes. I see nothing but black, and my heart races with panic.

I try to lift my arm to hold it against my painful head, but I can't move it.

What is this weird dream?

It takes me a minute to realize it's not a dream. I'm awake, and the groggy feeling is leaving me, though the ache in my head only sharpens.

And I still can't see.

I shake my head, and scratchy fabric rubs against my cheeks and nose. There's something covering my head!

Again, I try to move my arm, but now I can feel the rope burning against my wrists, both of them, behind my back. That same sensation binds my ankles together.

I'm tied up!

Every ounce of air seems to leave my lungs, and for a moment, I'm suffocating. My heart beats so hard and fast, it feels like it's pushing against my chest, and my nerves shatter from the pain of my head, my arms, my legs, and a complete lack of oxygen.

I'm dying.

I don't think I'm going to make it.

"Ah, looky.. Our li'l princess here is awake."

I startle at the sound, forgetting my lungs for a moment. The man's voice is gruff, raspy, unfamiliar, with a lilt of laughter in it that makes me want to throw up.

"I'll have a look at 'er."

I feel him approaching, but I'm dizzy, in pain, frightened. And I'm tied up, so even though I try to wiggle away, it's impossible.

Then I feel his hands close to my chest, and I close my eyes even though I can't see anyway and brace myself for whatever horrible thing he has planned for me.

But then the scratchy cloth comes off, and breath returns to me in the form of choking gasps. I open my eyes between them and see the man.

His face is full of wrinkles, dark and rough from too much time in the sun. A scar covers his left eye all the way from his forehead to his cheek, and that eye is almost completely white, the remnants of his once-functioning iris faded into a gloopy, pale yellow in the center.

"What's t'matter, missy? Ye donna like what ye see?"

I don't answer, still choking. Lowering my gaze, I see the black felt bag they'd had over my head.

Now that I can breathe, I sense there's something strange about the air in here, about the whole room. It's moving, and though the stench of this man in my face is nearly overwhelming, I catch a whiff of saltiness in the air.

Then I catch sight of another man in the room, leaning against what looks to be the only door out of here, his face twisted in a frightening smile through missing teeth.

I recognize their style of dress—sailors, like the ones my father sends out fishing on the vast ocean.

Now, the gentle rocking of the room makes sense. I'm on a ship, and we're already at sea.

Icy terror shivers up my spine. I'm alone at sea with these evil men.

No one knows I'm here.

But my mate is the Sea-King Alpha....

He can find me, right?

BETRAYAL

FURY ENVELOPS ME AS I RACE TOWARD THE COUNCIL CHAMBER, WHERE I know that asshole Nolan has joined the others for war strategy.

I'm going to tear each of his limbs off one by one until he tells me where Lyra is.

My paws hit the smooth stone floor with colossal strides, and I make my way across my castle in mere moments.

I don't bother to shift as I burst through the chamber door and catch his scent.

The others rise instinctively and step out of the way as I leap toward Nolan, his eyes wide with fear and surprise.

In an instant, my claws sink into his chest just as he shifts in response.

'You have five seconds to tell me where she is,' I say in the mind-link, opening the channel to all in the room.

'Who are you talking about?' he asks innocently.

'Five.'

'Cassian—'

'Four.' I'm not fucking around with this asshole.

'He's attacking me for no reason!' he pleads to the others. 'Please stop him!'

'Three.'

No one dares interfere.

'Two.'

When he realizes no one is coming to his defense, he shifts back to human form, holding up his hands in surrender. "Okay, okay," he begs. "I can't tell you anything if I'm dead!"

I growl in response, my teeth bared.

He cowers against the wall, and his assistant throws him a pair of pants, the man wisely keeping his distance from me. Nolan lowers his hands just long enough to move the clothes over his midsection but raises them again instead of putting them on.

'One.'

"No!" he shouts desperately. "I did it for the good of the kingdom! Assanan will hear immediately if we've installed a human Luna."

'*We* have done nothing,' I say, my Alpha voice thundering in the minds of everyone in the room. '*I* choose my Luna, and it shall be my mate, Lyra!'

Involuntary gasps ring out across the room, but every one of them quickly contain themselves.

'Now, where the fuck is she!'

"She's... she's safe!" he hollers, his voice coming out with a squeak. "I paid good money to ensure her safety in the Winter Realm."

I bring my fangs in closer to his face. 'You dared touch my mate... and ship her across the sea to another realm?'

"Cassian, please listen to reason."

My head snaps sideways, and my fury grows stronger. 'Gideon... you'd better tell me you're not a part of this.' I've known Councilman Gideon since I was a child. He was always kind, though known to be easily fooled.

"We saw the way the mate bond was affecting you, Cassian," Gideon begins, attempting to soothe my rage. It's not. "Assanan has already assaulted our borders. News like this would only embolden him. I thought the distance might solve things."

Darragh rises, tapping his cane on the floor as he faces Gideon. "Gideon, what have you done?"

"Th-the men assured me the princess would be safe," Gideon argues, his voice cracking. "The princess's sister is betrothed to the king in that realm. She'll be with loved ones."

I cross the room in an instant, growling at Gideon. 'Her loved one is *her mate!*' I address the others. 'Who the fuck do you think you are going against the will of the Goddess in my kingdom?' I don't have time for this. 'Darragh, straighten this the fuck out. Anyone involved is off the council.'

"But—" Gideon is terrified, but he's not important right now.

'Anyone!' I holler before turning on my paws and tearing out of the council chamber.

She has been gone for hours already. It may be too late to overtake them. If it is, I'll follow them to landfall, and I'll burn that fucking Winter Realm to the ground to find her.

'Kabir!' I call in the mind-link.

My ship's captain answers immediately, as always. 'Yes, Your Majesty?'

'Ready my fucking ship,' I order. 'We leave now.'

I'm coming, Lyra.

LYRA

THE TERRIFYING MAN IS STANDING CLOSE, HOVERING OVER ME WHILE his friend behind him just laughs.

I was never trained to defend myself. There were always guards around, warriors to handle all the fighting, to protect me, to keep me safe while my father decided the best way to use me as a pawn.

I'm not weak, though. I've always exercised regularly, and I've tried to keep myself strong, despite everyone but Mother and Aisla telling me it's a waste of time. I just don't know if I can fend off two grown men… strong sailor men at that.

Scanning the room, I look for anything I can grab to use as a weapon, but there's really nothing here, and my hands are still tied behind my back anyway. I'll just have to knee him where it counts as many times as I can if he gets any closer.

I ready myself, trying to find something inside me to give me the courage to do it.

And far down in my heart, that little voice that's called for me since I first met Cassian fires up. I swear it's almost growling. Good. That's the strength I need.

But then… the man doesn't come any closer, because another man bursts into the room, knocking the man who'd been leaning against the door practically off his feet.

"What are you men doing here?" the new man demands angrily. "Get out!"

Surprisingly, the two scary men who have been bothering me seem to respond. They even appear frightened of this man.

Oh, great. He's going to be even worse.

As the other two pile out the door, he yells after them. "Stay away from here! If I catch you within ten yards of this room again, I'll throw you overboard!"

Their feet shuffle in response, and they leave the room quickly.

He turns to me now, and all the air in my lungs is held in by a huge lump in my throat.

"Did they hurt you, miss?" he asks.

I furrow my brow, distrusting. "N-no."

"I apologize for my men," he says. "I'm afraid the likes of them are far too unsophisticated. But I'll ensure they never come into your room again."

"Um, thank you." I don't know what to think.

"I'm Captain Elias," he says next. He nods toward my feet. "I apologize for the rough treatment. I would have untied you earlier, but I didn't want anyone to come that near you before you were awake. May I?"

He has to get pretty close to me to untie me, and I'm not comfortable with that, but I can't exactly do it myself. "Sure," I say quietly.

I'm nervous as he approaches with his knife, but he's actually very gentlemanly about it while he cuts me loose. I stand when he frees my feet, then turn around so he can get my wrists. He cuts those free quickly, and I rub my red, chaffed wrists once I have them in front of me.

He steps back a few feet, and I sit back down. Maybe I can reason with this man and get him to turn the ship around.

"I'm the mate of the Sea-King Alpha," I tell him quickly. "Please, take me back to him."

He shakes his head. "I'm afraid I've already made a deal with some very powerful people."

"More powerful than the Sea-King Alpha?" I ask. "You're a ship's captain. You depend on the sea routes."

"I do," he confirms. "But I also need my trading partners to know that my word is solid. I've been paid a lot of money to take you to the port city, and I have to keep my word."

"Port city?"

"Icehaven," he says.

That's in the Winter Realm. Anastasia....

Is my sister involved in this?

"Why there?" I ask.

He shrugs and turns around to open the door. "I just take 'em where I'm paid to, miss," he says. "I'll send someone more trustworthy in with some refreshments for you. Please make yourself comfortable. And of course, don't leave this room."

"But, can't you—"

"My word, miss," he says. "I've got to keep my word to my paying customers."

With that, he slips out, and I hear the hard metal lock click securely on the door.

THE CHASE

CASSIAN

'HELMSWOOD HAS THIS HANDLED,' TURGAN INSISTS. 'YOU KNOW HOW HE is in battle. He loves the slaughter. I should go with you.'

My Beta is already half home, so we have a clear signal in the mind-link, but I can't allow him to continue back to the castle. It's bad enough that I'm leaving during a war.

'I need you there,' I tell him. 'I'm taking my guard and am leaving two hundred warriors to guard my mother and the castle, and I'm sending the rest to you.'

He answers next as my friend, not my Beta. 'Are you sure, Cassian?'

'I trust Helmswood,' I tell him, 'But he's an enforcer, not a strategist.'

'Aye.' I can tell by his tone he can see my point, but he's not happy. 'I'll handle things here. Just go get her back.'

'I will.'

I want to shift and run to my ship as fast as I can, but I know the crew needs at least as much time as it takes me to walk to the port to get the ship ready for launch.

My guards follow as I race toward the port.

I round the corner into the massive wharf, where the salt air hits harder than it does in the castle. The port is alive with seamen and deckhands scurrying along the hardwood decking, loading cargo, and barking orders as they ready my ship.

Hundreds of vessels are moored here. Fishing boats, private yachts, and speedboats line the docks, though most of the activity has stopped now to allow for my ship's preparations. Every available man has been redirected to the task.

The longest pier stretches far out into the distance, and at its end sits the *Ironhawk*, her massive hull gleaming in the warm sun, gentle waves lapping against her sides, the battleship's black cannons jutting out in stark contrast to the ship's smooth white finish.

"Alpha." Captain Kabir approaches me and gives the sign of respect. "We'll be ready to launch in twenty minutes."

I give him a firm nod. "Excellent. Speed is of the utmost importance. We're already trailing behind the kidnappers."

"Understood," he says. "The winds are in our favor. However, they also favor the criminals."

"We'll catch the bastards."

"Yes, Alpha King," he says.

"I'll be in my quarters."

"Aye, Alpha King."

I turn away and step up the gangway into the vessel, the crew stepping aside as I stride toward my stateroom. A crewman stands by a cupboard when I enter. He turns to me with the sign of respect.

"Alpha King," he says. "I am Silon. Your closet, toiletries, pantry, and bar are all stocked for the journey. Should you need anything else, please summon me."

"I will," I say with a nod, thankful that he quickly leaves because my mind is overrun with thoughts of Lyra, her soft cheek against my hands, her warm lips, her strawberry blonde hair enveloping me as we join in a deep, delicious kiss.

But all pleasant thoughts fall away as her absence eats at me. I could have done more to prevent this.

She was well guarded, but the threat came from within. I should have insisted that her lady's maidens and four guards accompany her every move, even within the castle.

I left her in the dungeon for months to keep her from Assanan's grasp only to lose her to one of my mother's ladies.

My anger seethes as I realize that in my hurry to leave, I have not dealt with the woman.

'Reinhart,' I call in a private mind-link to my castle guard commander.

'Yes, Alpha King,' he answers promptly.

'Find my mother's servant Raylynn,' I order him. 'Take her to the dungeon immediately. No privileges.'

'Aye, Alpha King.'

'Also, get her to talk,' I add. 'Detain anyone who assisted her in this kidnapping. I'll deal with them all when I get back.'

'Aye, Alpha King.'

I disconnect the mind-link, pouring a strong brandy into a wide-mouthed glass. The liquid swirls, and my mind churns. Nolan should be in the dungeon now under torture orders, but I know Darragh will be more lenient. Even expelled from the council, Nolan is no doubt relaxing in his own quarters, where he can do more damage.

I reconnect with Reinhart. 'Send the sorceress to Nolan's suite. Have her install containment glyphs to suppress the mind-link. And post guards. Nolan Bandlant does not have permission to walk freely about my castle.'

'Aye,' Reinhart answers simply, and I know it's as good as done.

I consider my next move. Gideon is not a problem. Darragh has already spoken to him, no doubt. Gideon is not disloyal, but his mind is simplistic and can be easily bent. Nolan, on the other hand, though he put on a show of innocence, is sharp and daring.

He's dangerous.

My mother could be in danger, but I trust Phelan with her protection. As my father's Beta, he was always loyal to our family, especially when it came to her after my father's death. I've left her care to him.

The clock on the wall ticks away as I sit with my drink, closing my eyes to picture Lyra. Again, anger rises in me that I did not complete a consummation of our bond. Our connection would have been deeper, and I could console her through the mind-link as we come within range of the kidnappers' ship.

But it's too late for that.

That captain's voice comes to me in the mind-link. 'We're setting sail, Alpha King,' he tells me.

I don't answer, just set down what's left of my drink and close my eyes, listening to the anguished cry of my wolf inside me.

Lyra isn't far enough away that the pain has started, the kind my mother always described to me as sharp and biting whenever my father was far from her. Yet, our distance still aches, scraping against my nerves as my wolf reaches out to her and finds nothing but emptiness.

I feel the ship move, the familiar rocking that normally energizes me now overshadowed by the rush of anxiety growing a bitter knot in my stomach. My mind starts to wander, coming up with dark images of what those bastards could be doing to Lyra at this very moment.

But that fury is too much to bear. Until I reach her, I'm helpless to protect her from them.

I force myself to temper those thoughts with the knowledge that any ship's captain who dares cross me knows he endangers his very right to sail this ocean. I believe that alone is enough to ensure no one puts a hand on her.

But I'll kill them all anyway as soon as we overtake them.

All I can do now is wait.

A NEW FRIEND?

Lyra

IT'S A GOOD THING I DON'T GET SEASICK. I'VE HAD NO IDEA WHETHER I do or not until now, because I've never been sailing on the ocean before.

But the rocking back and forth is getting tiring. A couple of times, it got so rough I thought the bed would slide across the floor. Thankfully, there's not much else in this room to move around.

I definitely wouldn't want to live my life on a ship.

At least I'm untied. Either the men tied me up tight, or I fought too hard against the ropes, because I see purple bruises rising in the red, inflamed lines around my wrists. My ankles aren't as bad. I guess I was more worried about my hands than my legs.

But now, I'm worried about everything. Will Cassian ever find me? Why would I be going to the Winter Realm? There's nothing but humans there, as far as I know.

Come to think of it, I don't know whether the men on this ship are humans or wolves. If they're humans, it's pretty gutsy to do something to make the Sea-King Alpha mad. If they're wolves, I don't know what they'd do. Maybe these are Cassian's enemies.

A cold shudder runs up my back.

I sit on the bed for the fifth time, the only piece of furniture in the room. It seems relatively clean, which surprises me since those men in here before are so filthy, they stink like skunks. No, that's not quite it. More like skunks that had rolled in cow dung. Well, maybe not the captain. But those other two... definitely cow dung skunks.

A giggle escapes me at the thought. I guess it's either laugh or cry at this point.

It's not very comfortable to sit on this lumpy mattress, so I lie down again, for the hundredth time. But lying down just makes me think, and right now, my thoughts aren't that great.

I don't have any food or even water in here. If they forget about me, I'll lie on this bed and die. I don't think I could stand the rocking waves if my stomach were empty and growling. Just the thought of that makes me feel sick.

Maybe I do get seasick.

The lock clicks on the door, and I jump to my feet and run across the room. There's no way I'm letting myself get caught on the bed if one of those creepy men comes back in here.

I plaster my back against the wall, glaring at the door across the room as it cracks open.

I smell it before the person walks in wearing a hooded cape and carrying a tray—the scent of toasted bread and garlic. Now, my stomach erupts in muted growls, but I ignore them for now, watching closely as the person sets the tray down on the bed and turns to me.

She reaches her slender hands up and swipes off her hood. *She?* There are women on this ship? She appears to be not much older than me, with straight blonde hair trailing down her shoulders and bright blue eyes.

"Hello," I tell her, hoping to show her that I'm just like her and that I really shouldn't be locked up in this room on this ship.

I shouldn't be on this ship at all, but first thing's first.

She nods but doesn't speak, her azure eyes cutting back to the still-ajar door. She opens her mouth like she wants to say something, but then she doesn't. With one more glance at me, she slinks out the door and closes it behind her, the clank of the cold steel lock echoing through the room.

"Wait!" I cry out, running toward the door and throwing my palms against it. But there's no window, not even a tiny peephole to help me see if she's walking away.

But then I hear a voice, deep and gruff—a man—but I can't make out what he's saying. It doesn't sound very kind, whatever it is.

The scent of food draws me away from the door for now. It's not like I can go after the woman or anything. Hopefully, she'll come back.

The tray is surprisingly full of food. There's fresh bread toasted with a topping of cheese and garlic, a bowl of sweet peas, and some drinks, both orange juice and water.

I sure hope this isn't poisoned or anything because I'm starving, and I'm already halfway through the first slice of bread. It's delicious.

Eventually, I finish everything on the plate, though I save the water, which is in a glass with a lid. The juice satisfies my thirst for now. I just hope no one takes the water away from me when they come to get the tray.

Once again, I'm stuck either pacing the room or staring into space. There's not much to do here. I recall the books I'd borrowed from the castle library just before that awful woman led me away to get captured. I'd give anything to have those books right now.

Without them, all I can do is think about where I am, captive on a ship going somewhere I don't want to go with people I don't want to be with. I guess I was in a similar situation when I first arrived at Cassian's castle.

But this is different. Now, I know he wants to be with me. And I want to be with him. And I don't know what these people want with me, or if I'll ever get back to Cassian.

I don't know why they'd take me so far if they're just going to kill me, but I have a feeling that these people aren't thinking logically.

There's no way to know what time it is, so after eating, I set my tray on the floor and put the water to the side, then lie back and close my eyes.

Maybe I can dream my way back to him.

MY NERVES JERK ME AWAKE WITH ANOTHER SOUND AT THE DOOR. LIKE before, I jump away from the bed as quickly as I can so I'm not near the bed when whoever it is comes in.

The scent of food again has me hopeful. I guess I've been asleep longer than I thought, and it's time for another meal. Maybe it's the woman again, and maybe this time, I can talk to her.

My breath hitches when I see that it is.

"Hello," I say to her. "Thank you for the tray last time."

The corner of her mouth curves up, but she still looks scared as she glances at the door.

"Is someone following you here?" I ask in a whisper.

She nods, setting down the tray and tiptoeing back to the door. She opens it, looks both ways down the hallway, then clicks it shut quietly before turning to me again.

"I'm not supposed to talk to you," she says, her voice a quiet whisper I can barely hear.

"Why not?" I ask, still keeping my voice low. I don't want to get her in trouble.

She shrugs. "I don't know. But since you don't seem to be here by choice...."

I nod. "You're not supposed to talk to the prisoner. Maybe they think you'll help me escape."

She leans back gracefully, sitting on the end of the bed, a long sigh escaping her lips. "There's no escape from here."

My heart sinks, dejected, though I already know there's no way out of here. "I suppose not, not out in the middle of the ocean like this," I say, walking over to sit by her. I keep my distance so she's not uncomfortable. "What's your name?"

"Maggie," she says quickly. "Yours?"

"I'm Lyra."

"That's a beautiful name," she says.

"Thank you."

She startles at the sound of footsteps, standing as quickly as I've been every time my door opens. She's just as scared as I am, I guess.

Is she a prisoner too?

I want to ask her, but she's already shuffling toward the door. "I have to go," she whispers.

The next question on my lips melts away as she disappears and locks the door behind her.

I guess I've made a friend. I'm still alive, so she didn't poison me. But it doesn't seem like she can help me.

Maybe there's a way I can help her.

IN HOT PURSUIT

CASSIAN

I̲t̲'s̲ b̲e̲e̲n̲ d̲a̲y̲s̲, a̲n̲d̲ I̲'m̲ p̲i̲s̲s̲e̲d̲.

The more I think about Lyra being stuck in a ship full of horny asshole pirates, the more my wolf howls in agony inside me. Once I get her off there, I'm burning that ship to the ground with all aboard.

Those fuckers better not dare touch her.

I lost contact with Turgan long ago since he headed back to the border hundreds of miles away, and recently, we sailed out of mind-link range for anyone back at the castle.

I trust those I've left behind to protect my mother, but it's infuriating that I have to split my anger between the assholes threatening my mate and those threatening my own castle and kingdom.

They're all going to pay.

I long to shift and charge through the grasslands. This ship isn't long enough to run off all this anger.

My knuckles turn white with my grip on the cold steel railing as I gaze out into the rippling ocean waves. The sunlight shoots off them like reflective mirrors, and I have to squint to cut through the glare.

But then I see it—a tiny dot on the horizon. I snag a pair of binoculars from the first crew member I see.

And clearly, what I'm seeing is a ship.

'Kabir! We're gaining on them!' I holler in the mind-link.

'They are within sight?' he asks.

'Yes! Go faster!'

Within seconds, every man on the ship is mobilized. The riggers grab the ropes and work to move the sail into a more optimal position, other crew scurry downstairs to relieve the exhausted oarsmen, and I abandon my position at the bow to race up to the helm.

Kabir is still barking orders when I arrive, and he addresses me without taking his eyes off the vast ocean ahead of us. "I have my spotters on it, Alpha King," he explains quickly, "and we've set a course to intercept."

"Any way to tell for sure that it's them?"

"No one has left our port since the kidnapping," he replies. "I don't have the ship's logs from every kingdom, of course, but not many trade with the Winter Realm. It's unlikely to be anyone but them."

"Can we overtake them?"

"Aye, all men are working toward full speed," he explains. "I imagine that their captain feels safe this close to port, so I doubt they are focused on speed."

I nod.

"Until they spot us," he adds.

My wolf writhes in agony. We can't let them make port.

"We will catch them, Alpha King," he insists. The confidence in his eyes almost convinces me that he's sure of it.

"I'll be at the bow," I tell him. "Fire on them when we are close enough, but only as a warning. We have no idea where they're holding her."

"Aye," he says. "We're readying the light cannon for the first shots, and the others for when we're sure of the target."

"Thank you, Kabir."

He raises both brows and meets my eye for a beat before saying, "My pleasure, Alpha King. We will get our Luna back."

A crack in my anger holds me in his gaze for a moment before I break it, saying no more. Sprinting for the bow, I take up the binoculars again, but I don't need them anymore. The ship ahead is in plain sight.

And that means they can see us, too.

I sense a change on the deck with the efforts on speed well in place. Now, they're getting ready to fire at the kidnappers.

And I'm getting ready to climb aboard and rip off some heads.

Lyra

I'm so glad it's Maggie bringing my food instead of those awful men. She seems to be as sweet as Cally, and I can tell she doesn't want to be on this ship any more than I do.

I just need to figure out why. We haven't had much time to chat since there's always a guard making her hurry up, but last time, she whispered to me that she was going to try to come alone. I hope she manages it. Then I can find out what she's doing here.

So, I'm counting the minutes until she gets here again. Or I'm trying to, at least. I wish I had a clock in here because I can't count time at all without one.

It's not long before the lock turns. Just in case, I move to the back of the room. I'm sure that eventually, one of those men will come in here to make sure I'm still here.

Not like I can go anywhere.

To my delight, it's Maggie again. "Hi!" I greet her.

She smiles but puts the tray down and checks the door before returning the greeting. Popping her head out, she checks the hallway both ways before closing the door behind her.

"Hi," she says then. "I think we have a few minutes. I told them I have to help you with some female things, and I'm pretty sure that horrified all the men."

We both sit on the bed, my tray of food between us. This time, there's a small bowl of fried potatoes along with the bread and vegetable. They look so good, I can't help but dig in. "Mm, this is heavenly."

"I was hoping you'd like that," she says. "I'm sorry they're not as hot as they should be. It took some doing to sneak them in."

I swallow the bite and meet her eyes. "Maggie, don't do anything for me to get yourself in trouble. I enjoy these, but not if it's going to be a problem for you."

"It's no problem," she says, waving the thought away. "No one sees me put the tray together but the cook, and he'll just think I'm eating them myself. I don't think he'll even mind, but I'm not completely sure, so I sneak it in."

"Okay," I say, taking another grateful bite. "How much time do we have?"

"Maybe five minutes, tops," she explains. "I'm sorry. I wish we could talk longer."

"It's not your fault," I tell her. "But I do want to ask why you're here on this ship. You don't seem to belong here with all these rough men."

Her smile fades.

"I hope I'm not prying," I add. "But we seem to both be stuck here against our will. Maybe we can help each other."

She nods slowly. "You're not prying. I just… I haven't had anyone to talk to about this since it happened."

"What happened?"

I can see the moisture pooling in her eyes as she begins. "My home is in Bellthan."

Crinkling my forehead, I try to remember where that is from my geography studies, though my tutor didn't exactly teach much about the shifter kingdoms.

"It's in the Forest Kingdom," she continues, reading my confusion. "Things are very… bad there. My family members are poor farmers. I have six brothers, so we barely had enough to eat."

"I'm sorry, Maggie."

She nods. "It's okay. Well, I'm the only girl. And one day, this man came and—" She stops a moment and holds a hand to her chest as if trying to steady herself. "Anyway, my parents cried hard, but they said I had to go with him and to do as he says, that I belong to him now."

I gasp, bringing my hands to my mouth. Her parents sold her! "Maggie—"

She shakes her head. "It's not your fault. And I mean, no one has really hurt me or anything. I just have to work for them. For a while, I cleaned a family's house, but then another man took me away to this ship. So now I do the cleaning here, you know, cleaning the rooms, doing dishes, that sort of stuff."

Standing, I pull her hand so that she is up next to me, then I wrap my arms around her. She erupts into sobs, and I just hold her, feeling the moisture of her tears dripping on my shoulder.

This is... appalling, horrible. Those words don't even cover it. When we make landfall, I'm escaping this place and taking her with me.

We are just pulling apart from the hug when the entire ship seems to jerk, and a thunderous boom shatters the silence.

"What was that?!" she hollers.

Something in my heart knows exactly what it is. "This is our ticket out of here," I tell her. "Come on."

I take her hand and pull her out the door, encouraging her to run down the hall.

This is it. We're saved!

ESCAPE ROUTE

CASSIAN

'FUCK'S SAKE, KABIR!' I HOLLER IN THE MIND-LINK. IT TAKES EVERY ounce of control to keep from running up to the helm and slamming him against the wheel. 'That was too close!'

'It's only a cargo hold,' he explains. 'I know those vessels well. Sailed on one myself.'

'Did it not fucking occur to you that they may be holding her down in cargo?' The man is usually a lot smarter than this.

'I—a lady?' he stammers. 'Alpha King, I seriously doubt that.'

'Make no assumptions about the assholes who would dare touch my mate!' I answer. 'Go for the fucking sail so they can't get away!'

'Aye.'

Moments later, another volley flies through the air, this time a chain shot, its two cannonballs stretching the chain between them mid-air before they crash against the ship's mast, twisting around the rigging and causing half the sail to collapse.

The other half goes down with the six more shots we fire, and there's not much they can do about it. Theirs is a cargo vessel, not equipped for combat and barely satisfactory for light defense.

Their crew runs in circles around the deck, attempting to salvage the mast and rigging, but more shots have them scrambling away to avoid getting hit by the flying balls of iron.

There is no hope for them to sail away now. They're immobilized.

'Get me closer, Kabir!' I order him in the mind-link.

'Aye.'

Moving toward the other ship is painfully slow. I hop over the railing, clutching onto it behind me while the wild ocean slams our vessel with sprays of saltwater. Tightening my grip, I assess the enemy ship.

Most of the crew members have abandoned their efforts to save the mast and have already gone below deck. Those who haven't stand frozen, their eyes wide with terror as our battleship approaches.

For a moment, I tap down the rage burning inside me. These men are innocents, obeying orders. They don't deserve to die for this, but they won't go free, not easily, not until I learn which of them is responsible for my mate's capture.

Those men will be the ones I'll rip to shreds.

I decide that shifting is not ideal. It'll be no problem taking these men prisoner in my human form. If Lyra is unconscious, I'll need to quickly carry her off the ship.

The thought ignites the fire of fury again.

But I don't sense that she's injured, and though I can't speak with her in the mind-link yet, I'm sure I would feel her pain. Tapping into the thread of our connection, I do feel her fear, and with it, elation.

She knows I'm here.

The ship is still a few yards too far away, but I take the risk and jump.

❀

LYRA

. . .

"Hurry!" I whisper as we make our way down the hall. We reach a split, and I have no idea which way to run.

"The kitchen is this way, toward the stern," Maggie tells me, waving for me to follow her, her words breathless as we run. "We can make it through there and up onto the deck. What's our plan when we get there?"

I shake my head. "I don't know. But I think the Alpha King is here. I'll jump in the water if I have to. He'll save us."

Her eyes go wide as she leans against a wall by a door and catches her breath. "Jump into the ocean?"

"Don't worry," I assure her. "It'll work."

Her hair flops in her eyes as she shakes her head briskly. "I can't swim."

Okay, that's a problem. "I'll hold you, I promise. But we might not need to do that. With all this noise, Cassian may be on the deck already."

"Goddess, I hope so," she whispers quietly. Scooting toward the door, she peeps through the round window. "I think it's clear," she tells me.

"You think?"

"There are a lot of shelves and things in there," she explains. "It's hard to see."

Footfalls… and a lot of yelling, erupt behind us. "Well, we can't stay here. We'll have to chance it."

She nods, opening the door and motioning me in, where we plaster ourselves against the wall on either side of the door while men rush by in the hall outside.

"That was close," she whispers.

I nod, following her as she motions in the direction we should go. She's right. It's crowded in here with shelves stacked high with dry goods and cookware, all secure within cages, I suppose so they don't fall in rough seas.

Maggie guides us through the labyrinth of shelves and stacked boxes until the door on the other side is in sight. Through its window, I can see a set of stairs leading up.

We're almost there.

But then my breath falls out of my chest when a man appears in front of us, a filthy white apron around his middle and his blue eyes narrowing at the sight of us.

Maggie gasps and steps back. "Cookie...."

He turns his gaze to me, then back to Maggie. "You two'd best get outta here," he says. "I dunno what's going on upstairs, but it sure ain't good."

My heart thumps with relief. This guy is on our side. I guess Maggie was right about him not minding the extra food for me. He's been helping her all along, and that's good enough for me to trust him.

"Come with us," I tell him. "I'm sure the Alpha King will be lenient on you if you help us."

He nods once and beckons us forward, stepping toward the door.

But we don't get far, because as quickly as I can blink, chaos erupts. Steel pans crash as a blur of a man jumps at the cook, and in an instant, all I see is blood gushing out of the cook's neck before he collapses on the floor.

"Cookie!" Maggie screams, diving toward him.

But the man who just killed him steps into his way. My heart thumps against my ribcage as the evil man with the eye scar laughs.

"Ah, lassies, did ya think ya could get away?"

He laughs again and reaches for Maggie, but I pull her back toward me.

"Eh, c'mon now, lassies," the creepy man says. "You and I are gonna have a bit 'o fun, that's all."

"Don't you dare touch us," I sneer.

But that just makes him laugh again. "Oh? What ya gonna do, little princess lassie? Gimme a paper cut?"

This sends him into a fit of amusement, and he steps back a little.

But then I see movement.

The cook raises the knife the awful man had cut him with, and with what must be his last bit of strength, plunges the knife right into the horrible man's chest.

He immediately doubles over. Maggie and I back up a little as he staggers toward us, then he leans over to the side on one of the counters, looks at us with wide, terrified eyes, and collapses onto the floor.

Maggie runs over to the cook, and I follow with several glances back at the awful man. I think he's dead, but I can't be sure.

When I turn back, the pool of bright crimson blood under the cook is creeping even further across the floor.

He's not going to make it.

Maggie takes his hand. "Hold on, Cookie," she pleads. "We'll get you some help! Just hold on!"

But he doesn't answer. He can't.

I put a gentle hand on Maggie's shoulder and reach forward, closing the lids of the cook's kind eyes with my fingers.

"He's gone," I whisper, rubbing her shoulder. "I'm sorry, Maggie."

"He… he was the only one who was good to me."

I wrap my arm all the way around her and pull her close. "I know. He was a good man. I'm sorry."

Tears start streaming down her eyes, but some pans crashing in the back of the kitchen tells me we have no time for mourning. "We have to get out of here," I whisper.

She's too distracted by her own grief to listen, so I pull her up as gently as I can. Luckily, she follows, but she keeps turning her head back to the cook, and I have to pull her forward.

I open the door, and the stairs are clear. We have to go now.

Wrapping my fingers around her hand, I lead her up, her steps heavy as I drag her away from her friend.

As we reach the top of the stairs that lead to the fresh, salty air, I whirl around to assess our position.

And my breath catches in my lungs.

RESCUE

CASSIAN

THERE SHE IS.

I see her from across the ship, coming up from below deck near the stern. We lock eyes, even at this distance, and I can instantly feel her joy and elation, though it's troubled with sorrowful grief.

I need to know why. I take the asshole I'm grappling with and throw him one-handed toward one of Kabir's men and bolt toward her, pushing everyone else out of my way.

There's another woman with her, no doubt also a prisoner on this ship for some reason, and Lyra is holding her hand. The woman looks beyond distraught.

But as I get closer, a man comes up behind Lyra and scoops her in his arms, holding a knife to her throat.

She gasps.

My wolf howls in terror and anger, and I want to jump on him not and tear his head off, but one slip of that knife could harm Lyra.

That's not going to happen.

I slow to a walk as I approach, my palms forward so he doesn't get nervous and move that damn knife. The closer I get, the more I recognize the man.

"Captain Elias," I say as calmly as I can. "Let her go."

"Alpha King," he says with a nod. "With all due respect, Your Majesty, this human girl was given to me by one of my best clients to transport to the Winter Realm. They paid a handsome sum."

I can't believe he had the nerve to say that to me. "Are you out of your fu—" It takes everything within me not to curse in front of the ladies. "Have you lost your mind? You have your hands on *my mate!*"

His eyes widen and fill with terror as he processes this. He loosens his grip on her shoulder, then pulls the other hand away, the knife dropping with a light ping on the deck. He keeps his hands visible and up over his head while Kabir's men approach.

Lyra takes a moment to get the other woman away from the captain, then runs for me, leaping into my arms.

Everything fades away… the ship, the ocean, the men I want to kill for harming her.

There's nothing but us.

I hold her so close, and her racing heart beats into mine. My wolf comes alive with her floral, sweet maple scent. My hands drink in the feel of her body, her hair, every inch of her sending electric tingles through my nerves.

My wolf practically purrs with relief and begs me not to ever take my hands off her.

But the commotion around us grows louder. There is unfinished business here, as the men remind me.

"Your Majesty." Kabir is suddenly standing beside me, his rough sailor's voice as gentle as he can muster. "Your orders for the captain?"

I keep an arm wrapped around Lyra as my gaze searches Elias' face. By all rights, I should kill him myself right on the spot for daring to touch my mate, much less kidnap her and sail her across the ocean, yet the fear in his eyes the moment I identified Lyra as my mate was obviously genuine.

She's a human. He could not have known.

Still, he won't go unpunished. "Take him alive," I order Kabir. "I'll deal with him and the others later."

Immediately, the men tie Elias' wrists behind his back and shove him over toward the *Ironhawk*.

I turn to Lyra, her eyes welling with moisture. "I need to get you off this ship," I tell her gently, knowing she's been through a great ordeal. "We're going to burn it down to nothing."

"No!"

The sudden objection by the woman I don't know catches me off-guard. Lyra and I both turn toward her.

"Please," she pleads. "Cookie…."

My brow furrows as I look toward Lyra for explanation. Her smile fades, and she steps away from me, the cold ocean air suddenly between us chilling me through to my bones.

But the woman seems to need attention right now, and Lyra wraps her slender arms around her. She looks up at me. "Her name is Maggie," she explains. "She was also here against her will. She befriended the cook—"

She sends a sorrowful glance down the stairs from which she'd emerged earlier. "We were ambushed. He gave his life for ours. With his last ounce of strength, he killed the man attacking us so we could break free."

Horror rips through my veins, both at the thought of my mate nearly perishing only moments ago, and the fact that this man gave his life for hers. Maggie's quiet sobs carried on the breeze.

"Collect the man's body as you would a hero soldier," I tell the men. "We will prepare an appropriate funeral for him when we hit land."

Maggie nods gratefully.

"You need to come with us," Lyra tells her softly. "Cassian will be sure he's well taken care of."

Maggie looks up at Lyra through her tears as Lyra takes her hand again. I wrap my arms around Lyra and guide them toward the *Iron-hawk,* where the crew has set up a gangplank between the two ships.

'Help the girl over,' I tell Kabir in the mind-link. He nods in response and gently coaxes Maggie toward him, and Lyra finally releases her hand so I can safely guide her over the planks.

Once aboard, Kabir turns to me. "I'll take Miss Maggie to suitable quarters."

But the woman shakes her head, stepping back from him and taking a moment to watch as the crew brings the body of the cook over the plank and onto the *Ironhawk*. Her tears fall again, and Lyra wraps her arms around her in comfort.

I tell the men in the mind-link to hurry the body below deck, and they obey, disappearing down the bow stairwell. Kabir gives them a head start, then gently takes Maggie from Lyra, leading her downstairs.

My arms envelop my mate in seconds, and now, her soft lips meet mine through her salty tears. I wipe them as they fall, and as they dry up, my hands lower to feel her soft body as I pull her closer.

We stand for a moment, the crew respectfully looking away as they scurry around us preparing the ship for departure.

Kabir reappears from below deck as I pull back from our embrace. "Your Majesty," he says. "We're ready to sail. The enemy ship has been cleared, and we're ready to volley the fireball on your orders."

My gaze lowers to Lyra. "Would you like to wait below with Maggie?"

She shakes her head, firm and confident. "No," she tells me. "I want to watch that damn ship burn."

"Aye," Kabir says softly, the first man in my kingdom to accept my mate's orders as final.

We wait until the *Ironhawk* is clear of the enemy vessel, then I order the volley. The strange, glowing purple and gold ball, one of many onboard enchanted by the kingdom's lead mage, sails across the sky, landing squarely in the center of the enemy ship.

I feel Lyra's arm tighten around me. We stand at the rail, arm in arm, watching as the golden glow of fire erupts from the other ship's belly.

Magic fire burns hot, and the ship quickly collapses, board by board, until there is nothing seaworthy left of it, and it disappears violently under the rippling ocean waves.

"Our course, Your Majesty?" Kabir asks behind me when it is gone. "It would be prudent to refuel before returning to Oceana."

"On to the Winter Realm then," I order him. "We'll refuel there and perform the warrior funeral ritual."

"Aye."

He begins to step away. "And Kabir—" I say to stop him.

He freezes in his tracks. "Yes, Your Majesty?"

"Ready yourself to perform our wedding."

A wide grin spreads on his face. "Aye."

He nods at both of us and steps away, and I turn to be greeted with my mate's brilliant smile.

We say nothing. No words are needed, just our lips joined and our arms around each other, holding fast and tight.

THE PAST IS GONE

Lyra

IT FEELS SO GOOD TO BE IN CASSIAN'S ARMS AGAIN. IT'S LIKE I'M WHOLE again.

And now, I'm going to be his bride for real. It doesn't matter that it's not some grand ceremony with heads of state. In fact, it's kind of romantic, being married at sea.

I'll be his wife.

I never expected to feel like this as the bride of the Sea-King Alpha. It was my duty to come to his castle, the price I was willing to pay as a royal of Maelie so our people could continue to reap the bounty of the sea.

But now....

When I'm with him, I'm home.

I'd love to kiss him forever, but I feel pulled to go make sure Maggie is okay. Though she'd seemed unsure about the cook's loyalties when talking to me about the food she was sneaking out, there was no question in the end.

She must be devastated.

As though he could sense this, Cassian pulled back. "You're worried about the girl." It's a statement, not a question.

"Yes," I confirm. "He was the only one who was kind to her on that ship. Some of those men… like the one he killed to save us… were horrible. I can only imagine what she had to do to fight them off."

His eyes narrow with anger. "She will be safe now. Where is her home?"

"I'm not sure," I tell him, trying to remember what she told me. "Oh, it was Bellthan, or something like that, in the Forest Kingdom."

"Assanan," he growls.

"He's your enemy, right?"

"Yes," he confirms, and I can see the rage in his eyes. "He steals all his kingdom's resources for himself. It leaves families no choice but to offer their children into slavery."

"That's awful." It's forbidden to sell one's children in every kingdom I know of. And those who prey on others and to practice slavery are punished by death. I'm sure Maggie's parents did it out of desperation, but those evil men who came to get her need to be brought to justice. "Someone needs to pay for this."

"They will, believe me," he assures me. His eyes meet mine for a moment, then his voice softens. "Lyra, your father will need to answer to that crime as well."

I let out an involuntary gasp. I'd never thought of myself as being trafficked. But come to think about it, selling one's daughter as a bride in exchange for fishing rights isn't much different than selling her as a slave.

I break our gaze and stare out at the vast ocean. "I'm not sure how I feel about that."

"You have time to come to grips with it before anything is done," he assures me.

I turn back to him. "If what he did is wrong, then why did you take me?"

"Because when he offered, I knew he'd make the same deal with Assanan, or maybe someone worse," he explains. "You were safer in my castle."

"In the dungeon?"

The look in his eyes is an internal wince, as though I'd just slapped his heart. "Lyra—" He takes both my hands. "I will apologize for that forever. At the time, we had credible intel that Assanan was joining with allies to storm the castle. Had they had a large enough force, we may have been overwhelmed. They would have killed everyone who didn't make it to the safe zone. You're human, so you cannot shift and keep up. I didn't want to take the chance of them finding you running toward the others. In the dungeon, they would have assumed you were a common criminal and set you free."

I swallow back the thick lump in my throat.

"I should have checked on your condition," he adds, dropping one hand, reaching up to stroke my cheek with his palm. "I will never forgive myself for that."

I shake my head. "It's the past, and the past is gone. It was horrible being in the dungeon, but that's not my life anymore. All I care about is our future."

He smiles, a spark of fire lighting in his eyes as he brings his lips to mine again. We linger a moment, savoring the taste, the feel of it, before he pulls back again. "Go to her," he says. "You two are the only ladies aboard, and we need to plan a wedding."

I giggle at the thought and kiss him again quickly just as the captain walks up to us.

"She's one deck down, first cabin on the left," the captain tells me.

"Thank you." I grin at Cassian one more time before stepping away and heading down the stairs. The deck below smells like a mix of pine wood, linseed oil, and strangely, spices, which must be stored somewhere down here.

I knock on the first cabin door.

"Come in," Maggie says softly.

The door creaks a little as I open it and close it behind me. She looks up from an old wooden truck she's been rifling through and stands. "Lyra, I'm so glad you're here."

I close the distance between us and give her a tight hug. Pulling back from her, my gaze turns to the truck. "What's this?" I ask.

"It's Cookie's things," she explains. "Before they burned the ship, the crew members here asked about my room and where to get my belongings." She nods toward a couple of very old crates stacked in the corner. "I also asked them to get his things too and told them where to find his room."

I sit next to her on the cot while she handles each item delicately.

"This was his wife's," she says, holding up an embroidered handkerchief. "Sometimes he would hold it in his pocket when he missed her the most." She looks at me. "She passed away from an illness about five years ago."

I nod solemnly, touching the delicate lace around the edges. "Did they have children?"

She shakes her head briskly. "No, though they tried for many years. He said the Moon Goddess didn't want a father who sailed off away from his children all the time. I told him that was silly. Any child would have been lucky to have him as a father."

"I'm sure they would," I agree. "He gave his last ounce of energy to save you."

Her eyes well up with moisture. "I know. He also said once that he wished he had a daughter like me."

"I'm sure he thought of you as one since he couldn't have his own," I tell her.

She nods. "Maybe. I just wish I hadn't spent so much time being distrustful of him. I should have known by the way he talked to me that he was a kind man."

"You couldn't have known for sure." I pat her on the shoulder. "But I'm sure he loved you."

All she can do is nod as a tear escapes her eye and rolls down her cheek. I wrap my arm around her the rest of the way and pull her close while she cries.

"I'm sorry," she says after a while.

"You have nothing to apologize for," I insist.

She wipes her tears with the back of her hand and sits up straighter, changing the subject. "It must be nice being with your mate again," she says.

"It's wonderful, thank you," I tell her.

"I've always thought I'd never find a mate," she adds. "You know, trapped on a ship for so long. Definitely none of those bastards were my mate. But I always had hope."

"Well, now you're free," I tell her. "You can go wherever you want to. And if you'd like to stay with us, I'd love that as well. I'm sure there are plenty of young men in the royal court back in Oceana, and one of those might be your mate."

She brightens a little. "Do you think so?"

"I don't see why not," I say with a shrug. "Oh, and speaking of that, I came to ask you something. I hope it's not too soon after...." I gesture toward Cookie's things.

She shakes her head. "I'll always be sad about Cookie," she says. "But now I want to know what you were going to ask me."

"Well, I thought I'd ask if you'd stand up for me as my maiden of honor at my wedding."

She smiles. "Really?"

"Yes, really," I tell her. "The captain will be marrying us soon, and I'd love for you to be there with me."

"This is wonderful news," she says. "How romantic! You were kidnapped and rescued by him, and now it's time for a wedding!"

I giggle a little. "I think it's romantic, too! And I'm so glad you want to be there. Thank you!"

I hug her tight, then we pull back and she hops up, heading toward her crates. "Wait until you see this! I have the perfect thing!"

I cross the room with her, excited to see what it is.

I can't believe it.

Finally, it's almost time for my wedding!

BRIDE AND GROOM

CASSIAN

IT'S NOT IDEAL, WITHOUT MY MOTHER PRESENT AT THE EVENT TO welcome Lyra as my Luna, and without a proper wedding ceremony, but it will take well over a week to return by sea after refueling in the Winter Realm.

And I do not intend to sleep in separate rooms, as I know my mother would insist at home. It's taken every ounce of self-control just to make it through this night, knowing she is resting in the room down the hall with Maggie.

Desires aside, it's prudent that we seal the mate bond long before we return to Oceana. I'm not foolish enough to think that Nolan had no other accomplices.

No doubt, there is a coalition in my castle seeking to usurp my power simply because the Goddess gave me a human as a mate. I hate to admit that I felt uncertain about having a mate at first, but it is true.

Now, I know there is more to Lyra than being a simple human

princess. Something on the thread that ties us together tells me this, but I can't put a finger on what it is.

I roll off the bed, tossing off the blanket with a grin. I'd told Kabir a hundred times that I didn't need a real bed in this room. I'm perfectly fine with sleeping on the same cots the men have. But now… it's going to be my wedding night bed.

I'm glad the bastard didn't listen to me this time.

Last night, Lyra sent the woman, Maggie, with a message to inform me that she doesn't wish for me to see her before the ceremony, a tradition she deserves to be upheld, so I've honored her wishes.

I have a few ideas of my own about how to make this day special for her.

I hurry to get dressed and go find the captain.

LYRA

I DON'T KNOW WHAT'S KEEPING MAGGIE, BUT ALL I CAN DO IS PACE around the room. I don't want Cassian to see me today before the ceremony, so I can't leave. He could be anywhere on the ship.

She said she had a few surprises for me, and she left early this morning after we had a quick breakfast. I could barely eat with all the excitement.

Tonight, I'll be the Sea-King Alpha Cassian Oliver's wife.

I can't hold back the little squeal of excitement as I run my hands over my wedding dress again. I'm so happy that Maggie loaned me this gown to wear. She must have been up all night sewing on little pieces of lace she had in her crates and making it look like a real wedding dress.

She didn't have any white dresses, but she had a lot of cloth and managed to cover one of her pink dresses with a bright white tulle fabric. She's sewn the lace she had, along with some pretty embroidered flower appliqués, along the bodice and skirt hem. The effect is just lovely, essentially a blush of rose against a garden of color.

I love it!

Though, she has given up many of the few belongings she had left in the process. I'm sure Cassian will buy her a whole sewing room full of things if she wants them, once we get home.

Home... Oceana. Other than my mother and Aisla, who I wish were here to see my wedding, there's nothing about Maelie that feels like home for me.

I shudder a little, thinking of what Cassian said about my father. It was both illegal and immoral to send me away as a bride to a complete stranger, royal or not. I have mixed feelings about him being sent to the dungeon, a place that was so awful for me.

But I wouldn't have been there—or here, for that matter—if it weren't for my father's choices. And Cassian was protecting me from King Chez's greed, afraid he'd send me to an even worse place.

How terrifying.

The door opens, and Maggie comes in, her smile brightening the room. "Goodness, Lyra," she says. "What is all the doom and gloom in that look? It's your wedding day! Smile!"

That makes me laugh, though I feel the need to explain. "Sorry. I was thinking about my father. I can't believe what he did to me." I meet her eyes. "I guess your father did the same to you but for different reasons."

She nods, her smile dropping for a moment. "My parents did the only thing they could. There was no work in my village for a girl like me. I was just a burden. All my brothers could work the fields, but Alpha King Assanan doesn't allow girls to do that."

I shake my head in disbelief. "Why not?"

All she can do is shrug. "I really have no idea. I think he just wants to make things harder for us. He takes ninety percent of everything our farmers grow for himself. That leaves very little for the village."

"Well, Cassian will put a stop to that, I assure you," I say. "We'll help your family."

She smiles again, almost as bright as when she first walked into the room. "Thank you. But you need to be his wife first, so let's get you ready!"

I nod nervously and take the dress off the hanger, and she helps me fasten the back. There aren't any full-length mirrors on the ship, but she holds a handheld one in front of me and tilts it up and down.

"Maggie, this is the most beautiful dress I've ever seen," I tell her.

Her cheeks turn bright red. "You're a princess," she says. "I know your dresses were just incredible."

I walk over to her and take the mirror. "None of them were ever made with as much love as this one. It's the most perfect wedding dress I've ever seen in my life."

A stray tear falls from her right eye, and I'm about to let one go myself, so instead of standing here blubbering, I give her a tight hug. "Thank you, Maggie, for making this day perfect. You must have spent all night on this."

"It's absolutely my pleasure," she answers with a shrug. "And I can sleep once you're married."

We giggle and pull back, and she looks me over. "Let's get your hair done. I don't have much makeup, either, but I have a little blush and powder we can work with."

Several minutes later, she has my hair in a loose updo with tendrils of curls hanging down around my face and a perfect hint of blush across my cheeks.

"Here's the final part," she says, practically squealing as she turns around and pulls something else out of her crate.

I gasp when I see the beautiful lace veil she's fashioned out of her things, which also has some of the floral embroidered appliqués. Along with that, she has somehow folded silk cloth into flowers for a couple of makeshift bouquets, a large one for me and a modest one for her as my maiden of honor.

She fastens the veil on my head and holds up the mirror again, handing me my bouquet.

I'm definitely going to cry.

"No crying!" she says as though reading my mind. "It'll drip down and mess up that blush."

We both giggle again, and she goes toward the door and opens it just a crack, speaking to someone outside.

"They're ready!" she announces when she comes back. "Is our bride ready, too?"

"More than I can say," I answer, though my nerves are shaking a little. I want this more than anything in the world, but I can't help being a bit nervous about marrying the Alpha King. And something deep inside me longs for the first night I spend in bed with him. I've never done anything like that before, so I hope I don't suck at it.

Maggie's voice jolts me out of my thoughts. "Let's go!"

I nod, and she escorts me out the door, where some of the crew members are waiting to show us to the room where Cassian and the captain are waiting. It's down a long hall, and my nerves rattle even more with anticipation.

Once we finally reach it, one of the men opens the door with a big grin.

I gasp when I see my groom standing there waiting for me in his full dress regalia.

He's the most handsome man I've ever seen in my life.

WEDDING DAY

Cassian

I knew Lyra was beautiful from the moment I laid eyes on her, but I didn't expect to lose my breath at the goddess that just walked into this room.

Her eyes smile at me from across the galley, now a makeshift wedding chapel with all the tables pushed to the side and white napkins tied in bows along the aisle, as her maiden of honor—the artist behind those bows—escorts her toward me. She glimmers like a flower in full bloom, her strawberry hair glistening against her alabaster skin, turning this ship in the middle of nowhere into a palace.

My wolf howls with joy, and everyone else disappears from my mind—the first mate, Cathal, who stands beside me in place of Turgan, who would otherwise stand up as my best man, Maggie, Lyra's maiden of honor, and the small contingent of my Royal Guard and its officers who are aboard ship, as well as just as many crew members as would fit in the room.

As far as I'm concerned, it's just me and Lyra.

When she finally reaches me, I take her hand, and a shimmer of electric pleasure shoots through my nerves. My wolf moans, aching to join with her and mark her, but I suppress the urge to carry her off and do just that... for now.

We turn to face Kabir, who is fumbling with loose pages in an ancient book, its pages heavily dogeared and crinkled from moisture. I clear my throat and shoot him an impatient glare.

I want to marry this woman—now.

"Sorry," he says, laying his finger on a page. "We are gathered today... here... here today, to witness the marriage vows of Alpha King Cassian Oliver of Oceana and Princess Lyra—" He glances at my mate.

"Lyra Molliton of Maelie," Lyra tells him.

"We're witnessing the vows of Alpha King Cassian Oliver of Oceana and Princess Lyra Molliton of Maelie, as wedded mates, chosen by the Moon Goddess in Her infinite wisdom," he continues. He flips through a few pages, and several fall to the floor. "Oh, I—"

He bends over to pick them up, and Cathal quickly helps him reorganize them. A low growl forms inside me, but turning to Lyra, I see her giggle a little, and it instantly lightens my mood.

I suppose a gruff ship's captain isn't the greatest substitute for a full-fledged priestess of the Moon Goddess Temple. I can forgive a few slip-ups today.

Finally, Kabir gets it together. "Goddess of the tides, She brings Her spirit in the full moon...."

My ship's captain's gravelly voice isn't exactly suited for high poetry, but I appreciate his effort. I'd thought about forgoing the fluff part of the ceremony and saving it for the one my mother will insist on when we return.

But Lyra deserves to have a proper wedding blessed by the Moon Goddess, and that's what we will have, right now.

I catch a glimpse of Cathal trying his best not to burst out laughing at his captain, his lips pressed firmly together, though the corners are curved up in a grin. I shake my head at him and turn back to my mate.

I have better things to look at right now while Kabir continues the ceremony.

"And thus, to the Goddess we entrust the spirit of our lives." Kabir pauses to clear his throat after the twenty-minute-long passage. "So, now we come to the fun part."

Lyra smiles, and her eyes glisten.

"We'll start with you, Alpha King," Kabir says. "Alpha King Cassian Oliver of Oceana, do you take this woman, Princess Lyra Molliton of Maelie, as your lawfully wedded wife and Goddess-given mate, forsaking all others and remaining true to her regardless of sickness or health, riches or poverty, joyfulness or sorrow, for as long as you both shall live under the moon of the Goddess?"

"I absolutely do," I answer quickly.

Moisture sparkles in Lyra's eyes as the captain faces her. "And do you, Princess Lyra Molliton of Maelie, take this man, Alpha King Cassian Oliver of Oceana, as your lawfully wedded husband and Goddess-given mate, forsaking all others and remaining true to him regardless of sickness or health, riches or poverty, joyfulness or sorrow, for as long as you both shall live under the moon of the Goddess?"

"I definitely do," she answers with a smile.

"Good," Kabir says, and laughter rumbles through the room. "The rings, please," he adds when everyone settles down.

Lyra's eyes go wide, and I know now that Maggie didn't let her in on our little plan for the rings. With the royal wedding bands back in the Oceana castle vault, there's little choice but to use a substitute. The only thing the captain and Maggie could find aboard the *Iron-hawk* were rubber O-rings from the mechanic's closet, so those will have to do for now.

My bride laughs again when Maggie hands her the rubber circle to put on my hand, and Cathal hands over mine for Lyra, his expression even. I suppose he's figured out how to stop laughing at his Alpha King's wedding ceremony.

Frankly, I don't mind if he does, I'm so pleased right now. But he doesn't need to know that.

I look up at Kabir, who is thumbing through the tattered pages again. "Hmm," he says. "There's no priest to bless these rubber rings."

Laughter rumbles again, much of it from me and Lyra. "I think the Goddess has that taken care of for now," I suggest.

He nods. "Likely yes," he agrees. "You are mates, after all. Okay. Please repeat after me. With this ring, I wed thee, my mate and wife."

I slide it on her finger, and it fits perfectly. "With this ring, I wed thee, my mate and wife."

Lyra's eyes are practically glowing.

"Princess, please repeat after me," Kabir says. "With this ring, I wed thee, my mate and husband."

Lyra slides the ring on my finger, but she can't get it past my middle knuckle. I take my other hand and roll it up a little more, though it's far too tight to make it all the way. I don't care. It'll do for now.

"With this ring, I wed thee, my mate and husband," she says, her eyes glistening.

"Well, there's just one more thing left," Kabir says. "By the authority given by the laws of Oceana and with the blessing of the Goddess, I now pronounce you husband and wife, bound mates forever. You may kiss your bride."

"About damn time," I grumble, and Lyra and the whole room erupt into laughter. That melts into joyous cheers when I wrap my arms around my mate and pull her close, putting my lips to hers.

My wolf howls in ecstasy as I deepen the kiss, pulling her into me as the crowd disappears from my mind again.

She's mine now.

My wife, my mate.

WEDDED MATES

Lyra

WHAT A KISS—MY ENTIRE BODY TREMBLES, PRICKLES OF WARMTH spreading across my nerves as we kiss. I'm vaguely aware of the cheering and whistling echoing through the room, but right now, I only want one thing.

More of him, more of my husband.

Strangely, it feels almost painful when he backs away, even though his lips still linger on mine for a few last breaths. But he doesn't take his hand off mine, and that small touch grounds me to this moment.

But now that I've come back to reality a little, I can't help laughing joyously at the cheers and teasing jeers from our little wedding audience.

"Here," I hear Maggie say beside me as she hands back my bouquet. "Enjoy the wedding night," she adds with a wink.

"Thank you… for just… everything," I tell her, giving her a one-armed hug while still clinging to Cassian with the other arm. I don't know how I'm going to properly thank this incredible woman for everything she did to make this special.

But I will definitely make it up to her somehow.

For now, she pushes me off toward my new husband with a gentle giggle, and I turn back to Cassian, who is gazing at me as if I'm a goddess. "Are you ready?" he asks.

I nod briskly, completely incapable of getting the grin off my face. "More than ready."

He leads me down the makeshift wedding aisle—I have no idea how these decorations made from napkins look so beautiful—through a throng of congratulations from the men on the ship, some of them dressed in their Royal Guard uniforms.

Two guards hold open the galley doors I just entered through as an unmarried woman, and Cassian and I exit together, as husband and wife.

I didn't know my heart could hold this much happiness.

The doors close behind us, and we're finally alone in the hallway. He takes me in his arms again, meeting my lips with his.

That feeling erupts again inside me, and this time, it's more urgent. All I want to do is feel my bare skin against Cassian's and never pull away.

I spend about a quarter of a second wondering why I feel this way when I'm a virgin and don't even know what sex feels like, but that thought melts away as Cassian's tongue explores mine.

Whatever it is, this need is real, and I don't think I can stand it much more before I rip off all his clothes.

He pulls back just long enough to grumble, "Let's get out of here."

In an instant, I feel my legs lift off the ground as if I'm as light as air. I let out a surprised giggle as he puts his powerful arm under my knees. We start moving, fast, down the hallway and up the stairs toward his room, with Cassian skipping every other step on the stairway.

Once there, he takes half a second to turn the knob with the hand under my knees, pushing the door open and kicking it closed with his foot before crossing the room to the bed in two steps and placing me on it gently, never breaking the kiss.

I moan against his mouth, and that seems to make him come undone.

He holds my cheeks with both his palms and kisses me hungrily. My body erupts with pleasure in response, and it feels like he's the only thing tethering me to this world.

Something… different… happens deep in my core. I can feel moisture pooling between my legs, along with a desperate need to feel Cassian inside me.

But at that moment, he pulls back slightly, his famished eyes meeting mine. "I want to rip this dress to shreds," he says, his voice gravelly, deep.

I can't say I disagree, but this dress….

"But I won't," he adds. "You will want to keep this dress, and I won't be the one to destroy it. Let's get it off before I can't help myself."

I let out a light whimper but nod slightly, sitting up a little so he can reach the zipper behind me. I pull the sleeves down off my arms as quickly as I can, and he helps me pull it under my butt and off me. He lays it over a nearby chair and turns back to me.

"The rest of this is fair game," he groans.

I giggle into the kiss, happy to sacrifice my undergarments to any rips and tears he wants to make, so long as he's inside me soon, before I lose myself.

His kisses trail down my neck, and he tears into my slip with his teeth, leaving my nipples exposed to the cold, open air.

I had been self-conscious in our first encounter back at the castle, but I'm not feeling a crumb of embarrassment at the way he looks at me with both hunger and reverence. I'm vulnerable, exposed… yet I trust this man more than anyone I've ever known in my life.

"I will be gentle, but I will not go slow," he tells me, "not this time. We will have years ahead to explore each other with care. Tonight, I need you. Now."

The low growl in his voice has me wiggling my hips trying to stem the ache of need. I don't answer. My breath is caught in my lungs, and I want this as urgently as he does.

I'm almost surprised to find my hands searching his pants, helping him unbutton them and reaching inside. It's like I'm another woman now... no fear, no restraint.

A grin grows on his lips as he assists, and soon his hard, stiff manhood is throbbing in my hands.

I'd never seen one before, let alone held one. But this... this is huge. How is it going to fit?

Again, that's only a passing concern, and my thighs are growing slicker with moisture.

I don't even register how he has taken off my panties, but the stiff tip of him is already rubbing against me. My hips grind against the bed, aching for more.

He goes in slowly, carefully, and I don't know how he has this much restraint.

I feel the stretch against my insides, sharp at first, but then impossibly pleasant as he slides in deeper, and whatever is aching inside me seems to pull him in like a magnet.

He slides in and out, and the tight squeeze against my insides is the most incredible feeling I've ever experienced.

I moan loudly against his lips as he comes in for another kiss.

We're joined. We're one.

Once he seems satisfied that he's not hurting me, he settles into a faster rhythm, and every stroke has my body trembling in pleasure.

And then, the magic–for lack of a better word for it–just erupts. Sparkles of light fill my vision, spreading out in a stunning spiral. My entire body shudders against the pleasant heat spreading across my nerves. I let out an involuntary scream... Cassian's name... in a voice I don't even recognize, heavy with pleasure, with satisfaction.

The effect reaches Cassian, and he pushes deeper inside me with a sudden thrust that takes away my air for a moment, and I feel the hot wetness of his pleasure released inside me.

For a moment, we both stop moving. He stays inside me, and I hold him there with my arms wrapped tightly around him. I feel his heart pounding against mine, his breath rapid and shallow, just like mine.

We lie there, panting together, as our heartbeats slowly return to normal.

"You are mine," he says finally, in a low growl. "And I am yours."

The words make me squeeze against the part of him still inside me, still slightly stiff.

He lifts up a little, propping himself up on his elbows, though he thankfully does not pull out of me. He meets my eyes. "I'm going to mark you," he says, the depth of his voice almost frightening, yet it elicits an involuntary moan from me. "You may be a human, but you are my mate."

I nod, too breathless to speak, and he lowers his warm body back onto me, my skin grateful at its return. I close my eyes as he gently kisses my neck, licks it, sucks on it softly, then slowly, I feel the sharp sting of his fangs piercing the surface.

I'm not prepared for my reaction.

Once his teeth are inside me, they send an iron-hot tingle shooting through my entire body, touching something at my core, stirring it, as though it's… awakening.

With alarm in his eyes, Cassian pulls out of me just as my whole body starts to quake.

AWAKENING

CASSIAN

WHEN LYRA'S BODY BEGINS TO QUAKE, SHE LOOKS AT ME WITH TERROR in her eyes, and I can say I feel the same way. Something is happening to her, and every nerve in my body tenses, ready to protect her from the threat.

But it only takes me a moment to figure out what is happening.

Her scent has suddenly come alive. It was there before, strong enough for me to catch it anytime she was near, but now, it completely envelops me.

I see a new look in her eyes, an easily recognizable glint.

It's all clear now. No wonder the Moon Goddess paired us as mates.

I quickly move from protective mode to reassuring. "It's okay," I tell her, stroking her cheek gently. "She doesn't want much right now. I marked you, and she wants you to mark me."

"She?" Lyra shakes her head. "What the... what in the world are you talking about?"

"Your wolf," I say gently. "Your wolf is awakening with my mark, with our mate bond."

"My—what?!" The delicate skin of her forehead furrows, and her eyes go even wider. "I'm.... Cassian, I'm a human!"

I shake my head, smiling lightly. "You're not," I tell her. "I can see it in you, smell it in you. You're a wolf shifter. You just hadn't awakened until this moment."

"I'm going to shift?!" She sits up in a panic. "I don't want to... I can't.... Cassian!"

"Relax," I tell her, wrapping my arm around her soft shoulders. "I don't think she wants to shift right now. I think she just wants you to mark me back."

She covers her mouth with her hand, probably feeling for the fangs that aren't there yet. "Cassian...."

"Come here," I say quietly, trying to keep her calm. Her brow is still crinkled with worry, but her whole body relaxes when I kiss her again.

Goddess, this woman tastes so good.

I pull back for just a moment, though it's the last thing I want to do. Lyra's body is tense. She needs reassurance right now, and that's what she's going to get.

"Just relax, and let her take over for a moment," I tell her. "You won't shift in order to mark me. That will come later."

I kiss her again, and she nods lightly, her face now relaxing slightly and, like me, more focused on the taste of our passion than anything else.

Slowly, she pulls back and kisses my chin, my neck, making her way to just the right spot, where the kisses turn to light sucking.

My cock grows stiff again as the feeling tingles all the way down my spine. She lingers for a while, and it drives me crazy, until suddenly, I feel the tips of her beautiful fangs cutting in, drawing blood, connecting us forever with the mark of the mate bond.

I just about come on the spot.

I'm ready for a whole lot more, aching to be inside of her, but she suddenly pulls back, and I see fear in her eyes.

"That… how did I do that?!" she asks with a screech.

"It's okay," I tell her, pulling her back into my arms. "Your fangs won't come out like that in human form for any other purpose." Then I add, in our mate-bond mind-link, 'Now, we are one.'

She frowns, sitting up and pulling back a bit. "What did you say?"

"I said, now we are one," I repeat, this time out loud.

She shakes her head. "But before, you didn't say it. But I heard it."

"That's our mind-link," I explain. "Now that we're bonded, we can talk to each other like that."

Her mouth hangs open just a little in surprise, and it's both adorable and sexy. "Oh. All the time?"

I nod. "Yes, so long as we are within range of each other. That's usually about a hundred miles or so. But I've never had a mate-bond link, so this could have a longer range. I'm not sure."

She finally closes her mouth, pursing her lips together.

"Of course, I don't want to test it," I tell her. "I never want to be that far from you."

"Me, neither," she agrees.

She scoots back so she's leaning against the headboard next to me. I link my fingers around hers and stroke her arm. We sit quietly for a while, and I let her soak this in. It's a shock to me. It must be almost unbelievable to her.

"Tell me everything," she says after a while.

"Of course," I assure her. "What do you want to know?"

"Well, first of all, why in the world am I a wolf?" she asks. "Like, how? My parents are humans."

I don't have a real answer, so I shrug. "I'm not sure," I say honestly. "But it must be that one or both of your parents isn't quite who you thought they were."

"Mother," she says, almost instantly.

"Why do you think it was her?" I ask.

She takes a deep breath and lets it out slowly before answering. "My father is… well, he's power hungry. If he were a shifter, he wouldn't settle for ruling a human kingdom. Frankly, I think he'd at least try to come after you or one of the other Alpha Kings."

I nod. It makes sense. "You told me before you had sisters. I suppose they are shifters, too."

She shakes her head briskly. "No, they had another mother," she explains. "I'm the only child of my mother and father."

"She must be a shifter, or at least a half-shifter, for you to have this power," I tell her.

"I guess I have a lot to ask her next time I see her." She giggles a little at the thought. "I'm a shifter!"

I laugh with her, happy that she's beginning to accept it. "Yes, you are."

"Why didn't I know before?"

"I suspect you've always had clues," I explain. "Maybe because you're not a full shifter and were raised with humans, your wolf didn't awaken until brought out by the mate bond, especially after I marked you."

She nods, tracing the lines of the blanket design absently with her free hand. "I guess so. When will I shift?"

"I don't know," I say honestly, shaking my head. "Since I've always known I was a wolf, it happened for me on a full moon during puberty. I'm guessing you could try it on the next full moon."

"Will it hurt?"

"No," I assure her. "Although at first, it feels... different. You'll be in full control, though. Once you do it once, maybe practice once or twice, you'll be able to shift at will, like I can."

"I'm kind of excited for that," she says, biting her bottom lip.

I chuckle lightly. "So am I. I can't wait to see that beautiful red fur."

"Is that what I'll look like?" she asks.

I nod. "It's likely. We usually look similar to our hair and eye color."

"I honestly can't wait," she says again. "I have so many questions still, though."

"I'll answer as many as I can," I assure her. "For those I can't answer, we'll find a priestess of the Moon Goddess Temple. They'll be more knowledgeable about human-shifter hybrids and how things work."

She nods briskly, then we're quiet for a moment until her hand wanders off the blanket toward my thigh. Her touch instantly awakens my wolf.

"Um…." She pauses, biting her lip again. "That 'going slow' bit you talked about earlier," she continues, her eyes narrowed and naughty. "When can we try that?"

A light growl escapes my throat as my cock gets stiffer. "Right now," I answer, my voice gravelly and full of need, before wrapping my arms around her and pulling her on top of me.

LAND HO!

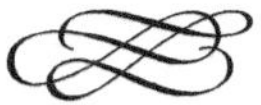

Lyra

My eyes blink open to the sunrise glinting through the small portal in Cassian's room... our room. I'm surprised I fell asleep at all, there's so much pent-up energy running through my veins.

I'm Cassian's wife now! And I'm a wolf!

As much as the first part amazes me all by itself, the second part is nearly impossible to believe, but it's true. I may not have shifted yet, but those fangs that came out to do the marking last night, along with the feeling inside me and our new mind-link, have me convinced.

My mother must be a wolf, or half one at least. I wonder whether my father was her mate. I can't think of any reason she would stay with him and pretend to be human if she wasn't.

What an awful life, having to constantly pretend she was something she wasn't and hiding her true powers. I'm sure Father would be jealous and petty if he knew—or maybe he does know, and he's making her keep it from everyone else.

I also always wondered why they didn't have any other children together after me.

213

I have so many questions, but I won't get answers until I see her again. Boy, is Aisla going to be shocked! I can't wait to tell her.

Scanning the room, I grow more appreciative of everything Maggie did to make our night special. I'd hardly even noticed her decorations last night—we were a bit busy, after all—until Cassian had to get up to blow out the display of candles before they got too low and lit the room on fire.

She must have used every spare candle on the ship to do that for us. She'd also laid out ribbons of lace all around the bed and throughout the room, which makes this cabin look as much like a honeymoon suite as we're going to get on the high seas.

Cassian stirs, wrapping his strong arms around me and pulling me closer, drawing me out of all these thoughts. "Good morning," he says, his voice still gravelly from sleep, deep and sexy.

"Good morning."

He pulls me in for a kiss, and once again, my body alights with tingles of pleasure.

I can definitely get used to this.

But an intrusive voice has me pulling back in surprise. 'Land ho! Ready 'er for port!'

"What was that?" I ask Cassian, who chuckles lightly and pulls me in for another kiss before answering.

"My very rude captain," he explains, our mouths nearly touching still.

It did sound like Captain Kabir, and it must be the mind-link, but it was a lot different from the one I have with Cassian.

"He opened it up to all of us," he explains after another kiss. "I'll talk you through how to sift through those and keep them from being intrusive later today."

I nod as he kisses me again, his lips lingering and his scent filling me as though it tethers me to the world. I've always noticed his incredible scent, something like pine mixed with musk, but when my wolf awakened, it became much more powerful and all-encompassing.

"But now," he adds, coming up for air between our final few kisses, "would you like to see the Winter Realm?"

Enthusiasm rushes through me, along with a hint of hesitation. I know Anastasia was set to marry King Ethan Snowthorne very soon after I left for Oceana. She could be here now, the queen of this land, though royal human power is subservient to Cassian's.

She'd always called me a nobody, always disparaged me as a lower princess. But now, I suppose the tables have turned.

"Lyra?"

"Sorry." I shake myself out of the thoughts. "I was just wondering if my sister was here, the one who… was never very nice to me."

"Ah." He puts a protective hand on my shoulder. "She was marrying the human king here. Her pettiness doesn't matter anymore. You far outrank her now."

I nod. "Yes, but I'm not sure how I'm going to deal with that."

"You'll know if you run into her," he assures me. "And I'll be right there with you."

A wide smile grows on my face. "I like the thought of that."

"As do I," he agrees. "So, are we going to go get a glimpse of the icy port?"

"Let's go."

After some giggles from me and last-minute kisses as we get dressed, we head out the door and toward the upper deck.

I hear the bustle of activity up there before we even ascend the stairs. Crew members dash by, each calling out to each other as they lower the colossal masts. Some of it is in the mind-link, and some of it is out loud.

The rush of words running through my mind is nearly dizzying. I need to have Cassian show me how to keep the mind-link under control very soon.

As we reach the deck, my breath catches in my throat at the scene before us. Giant glaciers cut out ragged cliffs against the clear blue ocean leading to the docks. Above the shore, evergreen trees line a thick forest, their branches dusted with pure white snow, a sight I've never encountered before.

I shiver at the chill in the air, and Cassian pulls me close as we step up to the railing.

"This is beautiful," I tell him. "I've never been here before."

"It is," he agrees. "I'm here rarely, just when we need a show of force or when we're negotiating trade."

I frown as I turn from the icy scenery to look into his eyes. "Why do you need to show force?"

"This place is remote," he explains. "The king here has a habit of forgetting who's in charge. Sometimes we need to remind him."

"Oh." That could be dangerous for Anastasia, and I wonder if she's been threatened.

"We don't harm anyone needlessly," he adds, sensing my concern.

I nod and turn back to the snowbanks that separate the blue ocean from the azure sky, which almost appear to be the same color against the pure white snow.

We're nearing the docks now, heading toward the longest pier. The activity on deck intensifies as they get ready to tie up the mooring and set the anchor.

Cassian turns to his Royal Guard generals standing nearby. "Kellen, go to the temple first and seek out the priestess. Arrange a hero's funeral for the cook right away. Belfor, alert the palace of my presence and arrange an audience with the king."

"Aye," they both say in unison, turning away and preparing to disembark immediately.

"Thank you," I tell Cassian.

He turns to me. "For what?"

"For being so kind to Maggie and the man who befriended her," I explain.

A smile grows on his lips. "I owe that woman everything," he says, clasping my hand in his. "She was there for you when you needed someone, and she helped you escape that ship. And miraculously, she managed to give us the wedding you deserve using only the meager supplies of this vessel."

"She's a wonderful woman," I agree.

I'm about to say more when a bright white gleam catches my eye.

On the next dock over, a ship is loading its passengers in a formal royal procession. I squint to read the ship's name, but I soon find I don't have to because I catch sight of the royal standard.

My breath leaves my throat.

"What is it?" Cassian asks.

"That's… that's my father's ship!" My heart thumps against my ribcage as I scan the boarding passengers. "Oh, my goodness!"

Cassian loosens his grip on me as I run toward the *Ironhawk's* stern, which is closer to the other ship. I wave my arms and holler, praying the woman I spot below will see me before I lose sight of her.

I call to her as loud as I can. "Mother!"

A FAMILY REUNION

CASSIAN

I FOLLOW LYRA AS SHE RUNS TOWARD THE STERN OF THE SHIP. AS SOON as she calls out to her mother, I notice the familiar standard banners of Maelie on the opposite pier, confirming this is indeed her father's vessel.

She waves at her mother violently, jumping up and down and hollering until the queen finally takes notice. Even at this distance, I can see the queen's eyes brighten when she spots her daughter.

The queen takes her husband's arm from behind and prevents him from boarding their ship, excitedly pointing up to Lyra. He pauses for a moment, his expression turning from confusion to disinterest... to disgust. I can feel the tension in my mate at his reaction.

Goddess, I hate that bastard. He'll need to be dealt with sooner rather than later.

But Lyra's cheerfulness continues when she sees another woman beside her mother, younger, with long blonde hair, both of them waving gleefully at the sight of her. Her mother gestures for Lyra to meet them at the dock's landing, which is quite a jaunt given the length of these piers.

"Let's go see them," I tell her, taking Lyra's hand and guiding her to the gangplank that was just laid out by the crew.

Lyra giggles joyfully as we make our way toward the shore on our own long pier, dodging sailors, tourists, and fishermen doing business along the length of it.

We're halfway there when a small boy trips and falls, landing on the hardwood dock with a thump. Despite her excitement at seeing her mother, Lyra freezes in her tracks and offers her hand.

"Are you okay?" she asks.

He nods, accepting her hand and standing, though the broken skin on his shin says he is not uninjured.

Lyra frowns, kneeling beside him to get at his eye level. "It looks like you *are* hurt. Where are your parents?"

The child shrugs. "Papa was bringing me to the boat. A lot of people were around and—" He doesn't finish, starting to cry.

"It's okay," Lyra says, wrapping her arms around him. "We'll find your papa."

"I've already mind-linked my guards," I tell her. "They're combing the pier looking for someone missing a child."

Lyra nods, and I can see the concern on her face, but she smiles anyway and speaks calmly to the boy. "I'm sure he's here close. I'll wait with you until we find him, okay?"

The boy nods again, and I scan the pier across from us looking for her mother. She's not hard to find with several guards escorting her, but she's almost at the end of the pier.

'Intercept the Maelie queen as she exits the pier,' I tell another of my guards in the mind-link. 'Explain that her daughter is assisting a child and will join her soon. Take her to a comfortable location to wait.'

'Aye, Alpha,' the man answers.

"I've sent a man to explain the delay to your mother," I tell her.

"Thank you, Cassian." Lyra's smile is genuine, though it's clear she's still troubled about the boy. I'm about to call for a first-aid kit when a man with eyes as wide as my helmsman's wheel comes sprinting toward us, pushing aside the crowd.

"Christopher!" he yells.

The boy turns around, and his tears instantly fade. "Papa!"

Lyra stands, her hand still clutching the boy's as the man approaches, but she lets go as soon as they fall into a tight embrace.

"My boy," the man says, repeating it in whispers as though it's a prayer. "Why did you run off?"

"I saw a seal swimming over there!" The boy points enthusiastically at the gentle waves around us.

"Goodness," the man says. He turns his eyes to me and Lyra. "Thank you, both of you. I thought I'd lost him…." He trails off, the morning sun catching the moisture welling up in his eyes.

"I'm just glad you found him," Lyra says. "I'm afraid he tripped, and you might need to tend to that knee."

The father looks at the wound, handling his son's leg tenderly, and a policeman arrives with a first-aid kit.

Satisfied that all is well, we give our farewells and turn toward the landing.

"My guard has greeted your mother and taken her somewhere to wait," I explain.

Her eyes shimmer. "Thank you. I can't wait to see her. It's been so long."

"I'm sorry." Guilt washes over me, knowing this is my fault.

She rests her palm on my cheek. "The past is gone, remember? We're married, and we're mates now."

I nod, taking her hand and kissing her fingers before wrapping my hand around hers and leading her down the pier.

Finally, we make it to the boardwalk, which is lined with busy restaurants and shops and dotted with vendor carts selling souvenirs and colorful salt-water taffy. Despite the icy chill in the air and the entire port being surrounded by glacial terrain, the bustling port has always been just as open as one found in the tropics.

In fact, it's in an open-air cabana where we find my guard and the queen's entourage awaiting our arrival.

I had never met Queen Consort Iridessa, having only met with her husband. The queen's hair is bright in the sun, a dark auburn, about a shade darker than Lyra's but very similar.

She stands high and confident with the true air of a queen, and a golden-haired young woman, Lyra's sister, stands beside her. Their smiles are broad as my wife approaches.

Yet, there's something off....

"Mother!" Lyra closes the last few yards with a sprint, practically leaping into the arms of the women, enclosing them in a communal hug.

I step back, giving them room... and also assessing the situation. Now that I'm close, my nose agrees with my initial impression. I don't know how this can be. Lyra is definitely a wolf. But....

'Kabir, detain the Maelie ship,' I tell my captain. 'Something is wrong. Don't let it or anyone associated with it leave this harbor.'

'Aye, Alpha,' he answers without hesitation.

I don't know what's going on, but one thing is for certain.

This woman standing before me is neither wolf nor hybrid.

❀

LYRA

I DON'T WANT TO TAKE MY ARMS OFF THEM. IT'S BEEN SO LONG SINCE I've seen my mother and Aisla, it feels like I'm in a dream.

But they're real, and holding them close grounds me to this moment.

Now that I know I'm a wolf, Aisla's gardenia perfume is a little strong for my heightened senses, but it's just about the best thing I've smelled in ages... short of Cassian's scent.

But I can't squeeze the life out of them forever, so eventually, I pull back. "I can't believe you're here!" I shout, unable to contain myself even though they're right in front of me. "I missed you both so much!"

"We missed you, too!" Aisla says, shouting almost as loudly. There's a crowd here, and it is a little noisy.

But all I see or hear is them.

"We're here for Anastasia's wedding," Mother explains.

My jaw nearly hits the hardwood boardwalk. "She's married now?"

Mother nods. "Yes," she confirms, "just yesterday."

"Why wasn't I—" I stop mid-sentence. I know the answer. Anastasia didn't want me here for her wedding. It's ironic, because I'm sure her husband would have invited Cassian. I should have expected that, but it still hurts being excluded from family events like that. "Never mind. I'm just glad to see you. Can you stay?"

"We were just leaving," Mother says. "But I'm not leaving this city without spending time with you, now that I know you're here."

"Me neither!" Aisla explains. She looks up, and her mouth falls open just as Cassian steps forward and puts his arm around me. I can't blame her. He's more handsome than any man in this city, and he stands out like… well, like the Alpha King he is in this place.

"Mother, Aisla," I begin. "I'd like to introduce my husband, Alpha King Cassian Oliver."

It's my mother's turn to gasp. "Lyra! You had the wedding?!"

I nod briskly and stick out my hand. "Yes! Just last night, aboard the ship!" I can't help but giggle at the black O-ring on my finger, which probably looks pretty silly to the Queen of Maelie.

"I assure you, Your Majesty, this will be replaced with the crown jewels as soon as we return to Oceana," Cassian quickly explains.

I don't even care if it is replaced. I'll always cherish this little ring of rubber and the magical wedding it represents.

Mother giggles enthusiastically. "That's lovely. My daughter looks happy, and that's all I care about." She turns back to me. "We have a lot to catch up on."

I nod once again, enthusiastically. "We sure do. Mother, I know!"

Her creamy white brow crinkles. "You know what, dear?"

"I… know," I say, lingering on the word.

It takes a moment, but I can see the recognition grow on her face… and eventually, it turns to… panic? Then, that turns into something darker.

Is she mad at me? What is happening?

"Lyra, I—" Mother begins. She looks around, particularly back at the Maelie royal ship resting at the end of the pier. "We'd better go somewhere quiet to talk," she says before tightening her lips and avoiding my eyes.

She takes my hand and leads me deeper into the Port of Winter Realm. Cassian follows close by, along with Aisla.

I have so many questions, and now, I'll finally get some answers.

THE UGLY TRUTH

Lyra

THE FURTHER WE WALK, THE MORE I FEEL LIKE A CHILD WHO JUST GOT in trouble for breaking my mother's favorite dinnerware. I start to lag behind Mother, feeling the stretch in our arms as the gap widens between us.

My mother has always been supportive, or so I thought. But now, it feels like everything is different. She's clearly upset about... something.

Cassian walks beside me, his hand firmly holding mine. Aisla strides alongside Mother, sneaking a look behind her to meet my eyes with sympathy and... well, confusion.

She doesn't know what's going on, either.

Strangely, we stop in front of a small hotel, and Mother turns to her guardsmen. "Return to the ship," she orders them.

I furrow my brow, confused. Her Royal Guard never leaves her.

"Tell the king I am staying here for a week... maybe more," she continues. "I don't wish to see the king."

The guards look at each other, each man's wide eyes greeting the same expression in the other. "Yes, Your Majesty," the lead guard says. What else could he say or do?

As they trudge away reluctantly, Mother pulls me into the hotel lobby. It's a large room, considering the size of the hotel, bustling with people lounging on sofas, laughing and chatting with each other. The scent of wine and fresh pastries fills the air.

Mother heads straight up to the front desk like she owns the place. Maybe she does, as mother of the queen in this place now.

"I'd like a room," she says firmly.

The clerk looks at her with wide eyes, no doubt knowing exactly who she is. "Yes, Your Majesty. We have a vacancy in room five. It's small, but I hope it's up to your satisfaction."

"I'm sure it is," Mother says, ripping the key out of the man's hand and walking down the hallway.

I shoot a glance toward Cassian, whose eyes are sharp and distrusting, and I finally stop feeling like a kid in trouble. Even if Mother is mad at me, I'm the Alpha King's wife and mate. She's just going to have to deal with the fact that I'm a wolf, whether she likes it or not.

But all the same, I'd rather have her support.

When we reach the room at the end of the hall marked with a silver-plated number five, Mother opens it and ushers us in. It's a small room, as the man said, but it's quiet, the hushed silence almost ringing in my ears compared to the bustling activity outside.

"Sit wherever you like," Mother says. She turns to Cassian. "Please," she adds. "I'm sorry, Alpha King. I'm used to being casual with my daughters."

He holds up a hand reassuringly. "It's fine," he insists.

The only place to sit is on the bed, so Cassian and I take our place there with Aisla on the other side of me, while Mother paces in front of us, wringing her hands.

She takes a long breath, covering her mouth with her fingertips and dropping them again before finally speaking. "Aisla, this is going to be a shock to you, but you need to know the truth just as much as Lyra does."

"Okay," Aisla says cautiously and slowly, lingering on the last vowel sound.

"Your sister is a wolf shifter," Mother blurts out.

Aisla looks at me, then back at Mother. "What?!"

"It's true," Cassian chimes in. "We only discovered this last night when her wolf awakened."

"But how—" Aisla stops, looking at me and then at Mother. "But how is that possible? You're not a wolf, are you?"

"No, I'm not," Mother says with a light shake of her head.

"Then how is my sister one?" Aisla demands.

I can't even speak. Now, I have to worry about Aisla being afraid of me. What if she never wants to talk to me again?

This is the worst thing ever.

Mother's eyes meet mine again. "Lyra, King Chez is not your father," she says just as suddenly.

I rise involuntarily. "What?!"

Mother waves her palms at me, but not in a dismissive way. "Please, Lyra, sit down. I have a lot to explain, and you deserve to know the truth."

Cassian wraps his arm around my shoulders as I sit back down. Mother paces in front of us.

"Before I begin, I need to say that I appreciate what you've done for my daughter, Alpha King," she says.

But Cassian stops her. "You're the mother of my Luna," he says firmly. "You will call me Cassian."

"Cassian," she says. There's a light twinkle in her eye, despite the tense situation, when she looks up at him. "She must be your mate."

"She is," he confirms.

She nods once, firmly. "Only a mate can be the Luna." She seems to linger on this thought for a while before speaking again. "Let me start at the beginning."

Aisla leans forward, her brow still furrowed in confusion. I probably look about the same.

"When I met King Chez, I was in love," she begins. "Well, I thought I was in love. He was so handsome, so powerful. He was everything I thought I wanted. I felt like a princess, even though I was just a barmaid at the time. I was only eighteen years old, and I was going to be the queen! I was so excited...."

She trails off for a moment, the distant memory glistening in her eyes. After a long moment, she shakes it off. "Anyway, I knew he'd just lost the one woman he loved, but I thought he loved me, too. When he was around me, he seemed to care about me deeply. So, when he proposed, I said yes."

She folds her hands, switching her feet so her ankles are crossed the opposite way. "It was a wonderful wedding, a wonderful honey-moon. I thought it would be that way forever. But he changed... not long after that."

I feel my wolf inside growl and know she's angry. It's a strange feeling, finally recognizing that inner voice as my wolf, but now that I'm mindful about it, I'm more sensitive to her, and she seems to react to my feelings, even when I'm not really sure about them, like now.

"It was just supposed to be one night," she says finally, her shaky voice in a near whisper. Her hand trembles as she covers her mouth again.

"One night?" I ask.

Her chest heaves as she inhales, and I can tell she's fighting back tears. She sucks in her bottom lip hard before continuing. "It was just supposed to be one night with the Alpha King."

"What?!" I find myself saying again.

Aisla and I both lurch forward, kneeling on the floor next to Mother, our hands on her knees. I know this is going to be bad....

"One day, a powerful Alpha King came to our kingdom," Mother begins. She looks at Cassian. "Not from Oceana, of course." She turns back to me. "This was after I'd been there about a year, after my husband became... different toward me. Chez had made a deal with this Alpha King for a cache of gold and jewels. Chez always loved gold and jewels more than anything... more than me...."

"Maybe you should stop talking about this," I suggest softly. I already know what happened, and it's a nightmare she shouldn't have to relive.

She shakes her head. "I need to say this to you, so you know for sure," she explains. "I had to go spend the night with the Alpha," she adds, bursting into tears.

"Mother…." Aisla and I both gasp and put our arms around her.

Mother grasps both our arms with her hands and continues, trembling. "I don't need to describe what happened," she says quietly.

I meet Cassian's eyes and see the rage building in them.

Mother shakes her head. "Anyway, in the morning, I thought I could go home." She turns to Aisla. "I wanted to be with you again. You were so little then, and even in one year's time, I'd grown to love you so much. You needed me. But the Alpha King… he said I had to stay. And he kept me there for a week, I think."

She trails off, and I'm horrified. "Mother, you don't have to explain more. This Alpha King…. he's my… father. Does he know about me?"

Mother shakes her head briskly. "Oh, no, dear," she insists. "I begged Chez never to tell you and never to tell that Alpha King. You had my hair color, so you just looked like you were mine, and you looked like you could have been Chez's, but you… aren't."

I nod. "So that's why my father—why King Chez—hates me and why I'm a wolf."

Mother nods softly. "Yes. He… Chez…. he said that if you believed you were human, you'd never know otherwise. He was so harsh about it. He made you feel like you were nothing so you wouldn't become more powerful than him. He threatened to send me back to that Alpha King, along with you, if I ever tried to stop him from treating you that way. I hate Chez so much, but he also wouldn't let me see you girls ever again if I left."

A low growl rises inside me, but before I can deal with that emotion, I catch Cassian's eyes again. He looks like he wants to rip someone to shreds. If that someone is Chez, I don't think I'll stop him at this point.

"Only one Alpha King is sick enough to do something so... vile." His voice is low, charged with hatred, almost frightening.

Mother just nods. "Yes," she confirms softly.

I glance between her and Cassian, trying to understand. "What are you talking about?"

Everyone is silent.

"Mother, who is my father?"

WINTERHELM CASTLE

CASSIAN

'ARREST THAT FUCKING PIECE OF SHIT KING CHEZ OF MAELIE.' EVEN IN the mind-link, my orders to my Royal Guard are delivered with a holler.

'Aye, Alpha King,' Kellen answers. 'And your instructions for his men?'

'They are all under arrest,' I confirm. 'Throw Chez in our brig. The rest can stay aboard their ship as we escort them back to Oceana. Not one of them is to leave the ship for any purpose.'

'Aye, Alpha King.' This time it's a chorus of the men responding.

Unrestrained rage has my blood boiling. The man is guilty of the greatest crimes in the kingdom, and he will rot in my dungeon for the rest of his days. Even that is too liberal a punishment, but death is too quick for the suffering he inflicted on Lyra and her mother.

"Why isn't anyone answering me?"

Lyra's voice jolts me out of my thoughts, and I leave the handling of that asshole king to my men. They'll take care of him well enough for the time being. My wife is the most important person right now.

I push the anger deep inside me and take her hand gently, pulling her up from where she kneels by her mother and leading her over to the bed. I hate having to deliver this news to her, but she must know.

"Your father is Assanan," I say softly.

Her eyes go wide. "Your enemy? The one who killed your father? You mean he—"

"Yes," I answer quickly. She doesn't need to think about finishing that horrible sentence.

I turn back to the queen, who is sobbing lightly while her other daughter holds her tightly. "We're not going back, Mother," Aisla insists. "We're never going back there again."

"You'll come home with Lyra and me," I tell them. "When we're back, I'll send warriors to fetch your things, along with anyone you want to join you at our castle."

"What of my people?" the queen asks, her voice quiet. "Who will hold things together in Maelie?" Even in such trauma, she thinks of those in her charge. That is a true queen.

"I'll appoint one of my generals to manage the territory," I explain. "He will report directly to you for all decisions."

"Thank you, Cassian." I turn to the beautiful voice floating on the air from the woman beside me. Lyra's smile is wide, despite the horror of this news, but she soon turns serious. "What do we do now?"

"King Chez is being arrested right now by my men, along with all his crew and Royal Guard," I explain, sensing she did not hear the mind-link, perhaps because I initiated it directed at my warriors. "Once we're back in Oceana, we'll straighten out which of these men were complicit in his crimes. Those who were not will return to Maelie. For now, all men except for Chez are confined to their ship."

She nods softly. "Please be sure they have enough food and supplies aboard. I doubt very many of them had any other choice but to obey my... to obey their king."

"Of course," I tell her.

"If Assanan finds out I'm his daughter, what will happen to me?" she adds softly.

"Nothing," I say quickly, my wolf growling in panic at the thought. "He will never come near you, nor will his men. I'll die before I let that happen." I mean every word. No one will come close to my mate.

"But he *will* want me for something, right?" she adds.

"He can try to lay claim to your lands based on your mother's position there," I say honestly. "But that will also never happen."

"I figured as much," she says. "If he sees me, will he know?"

"Yes," I confirm. "He would be able to sense it. But he will not see you, Lyra. He will not."

She nods, slipping into my arms. Her heart pounds in our embrace. She has been through too much in the past several hours, first learning she is a wolf and now… this.

She turns to her mother. "Are you okay, Mother?"

The queen nods softly. "I've had many years to prepare for this moment, but it's still a shock. I wish I never had to tell you this."

I can sense that Lyra wants to go to her, so I loosen my arms, and she returns to her mother, who stands and pulls her into a tight embrace.

'Alpha King.' Belfor's voice calls me in the mind-link.

'Yes?'

'All prisoners are secured,' he explains. 'And King Snowthorne has invited you to his castle for lunch this afternoon.'

Kellen adds, 'And the priestess is prepared for the funeral at sea this evening.'

'Very good. Belfor, you and a force of twenty accompany us to the castle. Kellen, mind the ship.'

'Aye, Alpha King,' they both reply.

Lyra separates from her mother and looks at me. "I heard. I want to go. I need to see Anastasia one more time."

"Are you sure?"

She nods firmly. "I'm not a lower princess anymore. She needs to know that."

I shoot her a grin and turn to the queen and Aisla. "Would you both like to join us or wait on our ship?"

"I'm going," the queen insists.

"Me, too," Aisla adds.

We wait for my Royal Guard to arrive, then make our way inland via coach wagons the king has provided, toward the Winter Realm castle in its capital city, Winterhelm.

The frozen territory is blanketed with snow and ice, but the city streets are shoveled, its sidewalks bustling with citizens engaging in lively chatter as they go about their business. They seem to be satisfied people, without the tension I experienced back in Maelie.

Apparently, the king is doing his job well here.

Soon, we reach the high gates, glistening like crystals in the midday sun despite the chill in the air. The castle inside is modern and somewhat modest compared with some of the others I've seen in human cities.

Snowthorne is wise enough to greet me just inside his palace gate, unlike Chez, who had always made a show of having an audience with me in his throne room, as though I didn't rule over his kingdom.

I exit the coach first. The dark-haired regent in front of us greets me with a warm smile, extending his hand. His queen, standing beside him, is outwardly lovely. But knowing her true personality and the way she has always treated Lyra, I pity the king who just made Anastasia his wife.

"Welcome, Alpha King," he says. "I was thrilled to hear you'd traveled to our modest kingdom. You'll be our guests for the duration of your stay. Oh, Queen Consort Iridessa," he adds when he sees her exit the coach. "It's lovely to see you again. I thought you and your husband had set sail this morning."

Anastasia's eyes widen when she also notices Iridessa. "Mother? Is something wrong?"

Iridessa takes a long breath and shakes her head. "I'm afraid it has been for quite too long."

"That's right," Lyra says, gliding down the coach steps and striding forward.

Anastasia frowns, her brow furrowing into an ugly expression that I know matches her true demeanor. "Lyra? What's a lower princess like you doing here?" She lets loose a high-pitched fit of laughter, and a low growl forms in my gut.

I begin to speak until I hear a musical voice ringing through our mate-bond mind-link.

'I'll handle my sister,' Lyra tells me firmly.

I smile and step aside.

LEAVING THE PAIN BEHIND

Lyra

THE NEXT SENTENCE FEELS GOOD TO SAY OUT LOUD. "I'M NOT A LOWER princess or a slave girl," I tell her firmly. "I am Sea-King Alpha Cassian's mate and Luna."

Anastasia's eyes go wide for just a second before narrowing. "You can't be either of those. You're a human."

I take one purposeful step toward her. I'm not sure when I figured this out or how I know how to do this, but I flash my wolf eyes at her. "I am not," I say simply.

Fear flushes her face. She stumbles backward a few steps, nearly tripping over her gown. It's only now that I notice the king. His friendly smile has faded into a troubled frown as he looks right at her, incredulous.

He isn't acting like a newlywed man anymore. He hasn't made a move to help steady her. In fact, he has put some distance between them.

"Why are you acting like this, Ana?" he asks. "You told me you adored both your sisters."

I doubt it's the only lie she told, and I don't like being the one to have to tell him this since he seems like a nice guy, but someone has to make my half-sister come clean to him. Just in the few moments I've spent in this kingdom, I can tell he's a fair and honest ruler. He doesn't deserve Anastasia's lies.

"She has been harsh and cruel to me since I was born," I explain. "If she's been acting like a sweet, caring woman to you, I'm afraid it's an act to get what she wants. That's what Anastasia is all about. She's selfish and callous."

I feel Aisla brush against my shoulder as she steps forward. "It's true. She has always just... been this way."

Anastasia glares at me and Aisla with horror in her eyes. She opens her mouth, but for the first time in her life, she says nothing. She can't exactly argue with the truth, and I think she knows it, though I can see the wheels spinning as she tries to come up with yet another lie.

I don't know what I thought would happen when I saw her again, knowing what I am, knowing the lies Chez spewed to me, about me. I bought into the lie of the subservient 'lower princess' my whole life, never questioning why the king kept telling me I was less important than anyone else in the family.

I thought I'd yell at her about it, that's for sure. I even played with the idea of giving her the good slap in the face she deserves, though I honestly don't think I could actually go through with that... well, maybe if she really, really made me mad.

But looking at her now, sending a pathetic look of pleading in her eyes toward the husband who just married her yesterday—a man who looks like he already wants to change his mind—I realize something.

Father... well, her father, King Chez, lied to her, too. He told her she was better than me and encouraged all the cruelty she dished out. Now I know it was just part of his plan to keep me from discovering my wolf.

He used her and lied to her, just like he did to me. He made her what she is. And now, there's only one thing I feel when I look at her.

Pity.

"Everything about you—about us—is a lie!" Snowthorne hollers, taking me out of my thoughts. "Dammit! I should have listened to my own gut feeling when I saw you, out of the corner of my eye, looking down on our people, no... *my people*! You think you're better than everyone! You even behave poorly toward innocent children! I thought I had misinterpreted your actions. But I was wrong."

"No, I—" Anastasia begins to speak finally, but the king puts up a firm hand and cuts her off.

"No," he says firmly. "I'm not going to listen to any more of your bullshit. I can't believe I've been such a fool! I told myself I was imagining things. I told myself there was no way my sweet, gentle Ana could ever be cruel to our citizens. But now I know. You're a liar and a monster. And I hate it. Thank the gods I found out before you were crowned queen next week!"

"But—"

"Don't you dare speak to me," he says coldly, cutting her off again. "I'm done, and I won't spend another moment in your presence."

He turns to us, straining to add a polite lilt to his speech. "I apologize, my honored guests," he says. "My servants will see to it that you have everything you need for your stay with me. But I must... I must go find out how to get a goddamn annulment!"

With that, he whirls around, and though Anastasia tries to grab his hand, he slaps her away, and his guards step between them protectively as the king strides off toward the castle entrance.

Cassian's warm hand envelops mine protectively, but though his touch sends a shudder of pleasure through my nerves, I find that I really don't need comforting. Anastasia is what she is, and her bitterness can't affect me anymore.

My mother steps forward, and I see tears welling in her eyes. I suppose she really wanted to be a mother to her. "Anastasia, I tried so hard," she says, her voice shaking. "I tried to give you the love you were missing after your mother passed away, but you just... pushed me away. You were so cruel to everyone around you. Despite that, I don't want to see you destitute. Return to Maelie."

"That's right," Anastasia says, standing and brushing off her dress.

"My father is the king of Maelie, and even if Snow doesn't want me anymore, who cares? Daddy will find a proper marriage for me."

This time, it's Cassian who chimes in with the news. "Your father is under arrest and will never return to Maelie," he says coldly.

"He... he what?" she asked.

"He's under arrest for crimes against Oceana's Queen Mother Iridessa and her daughter, my mate, as well as the citizens of Maelie," he explains, a bit more patiently than I expect. I guess he's picked up on the fact that I'm over her pettiness. "You will never see him again, and you will not reside in the Maelie castle."

"What!?" She dares to take a step forward, but Cassian's towering presence has her cowering a second later.

"Anastasia," Mother says gently. "You have to decide. Go back to Maelie, and I'll permit you to live in the vacant apartment above the Foxglove Tavern."

"You'd have me live above a bar?" Anastasia's eyes narrow at my mother.

"Yes, and it's my only offer," Mother continues calmly. "That, or do not return at all. Go anywhere, though I doubt you're wanted here. Find some honest work and maybe learn how to be an actual decent person. It'll do you some good."

Anastasia tries to speak again, but I shoot her another glare with my wolf eyes, and she shuts up instantly.

The tension is lifted by a voice off to the side. "If you'll follow me, please, Your Majesties, Your Highness." We turn to the gentleman addressing us, a dark-haired man with a warm smile, dressed in high court attire. "His Majesty has had your rooms prepared for you."

I look back at Anastasia, wondering if there's anything I should say to her. Maybe I should explain things a bit more so that she understands why her father is sitting in the brig of the *Ironhawk*, waiting for a grim fate when we return to Oceana.

But then I decide against it. Someone will fill her in. It doesn't have to come from me. It's not like I could comfort her in her confusion. She never made a single effort to even try to love me, and that made it impossible to love her back.

Frankly, I'm done with her.

My mother looks a little hesitant, too, but Aisla slips her arm through Mother's elbow and encourages her to walk forward. If Aisla can pull away, so can Mother, and she moves on.

We walk together as a group behind the cheerful man, with Cassian's strong hand against the small of my back. I hear Anastasia complain loudly, and I can feel her harsh glare as we walk away. But it doesn't bother me, not when I have the love of a wonderful man and the rest of my family, not when I know what I am and what lies ahead of me for my future.

And just like that, I leave the pain of my past behind.

FAREWELL TO THE HERO

CASSIAN

I REMAIN IMPRESSED WITH THIS KING'S APPROACH TO RULING HIS kingdom as I stroll through his castle with Lyra on my arm. Compared with my visits to the kingdoms of Chez and some of the other human rulers, this man seems to value high morals and to truly care for his subjects.

It's evident in the genuine smiles on his staff's faces, something rarely seen in Chez's castle, and the few I saw there were obviously not sincere.

That half-sister of Lyra's must have been quite the actress to fool this king.

Hopefully, he's rid of her.

We pass through the main hall to the white marble staircase, where the scent of fresh bread and garlic fills the air from what must be the kitchen nearby.

"Something smells wonderful," Lyra remarks.

"His Majesty has ordered a lovely feast for your luncheon," the servant escorting us explains as we head upstairs. "It should be ready in about an hour. I'll come to alert you when it's ready." He opens a set of double doors in front of us that open into a large suite of guest rooms. "In the meantime, please make yourselves at home. If you need any assistance, please summon any staff members nearby."

"Thank you," I tell him, escorting the ladies into the room.

"It's nice here," Lyra says when he leaves. "I wish Snowthorne hadn't been fooled by Anastasia. He seems like a really nice man."

"I agree," Aisla adds. "He doesn't deserve to be going through this right now."

"Better now than after her coronation," I suggest.

"I guess so," Aisla says. "It's too bad humans don't have mates like shifters. Then we wouldn't get stuck with huge mistakes like these."

I touch Lyra's shoulder, relishing in the electric tingles it elicits, contentment washing over me. I nearly made a mistake myself, ignoring our bond. I thank the Goddess I came to my senses.

The ladies continue chatting, and the conversation turns to our wedding. Lyra describes it all while I excuse myself to the back of the suite to shower, giving her time to spend with her family.

I'm glad the queen and princess have agreed to come back to Oceana with us. It will do Lyra good to have more familiar faces around our castle to keep her company.

Once we are rested and refreshed, another servant arrives to escort us to lunch, which is served in a small dining room set for intimate meals. I can't take my eyes off Lyra, whose eyes sparkle like diamonds in the flickering candlelight.

"My apologies for the embarrassing scene upon your arrival," the king says when he arrives, "especially since she is your family member."

"You don't need to be embarrassed about her," Lyra insists. "She's very good at pretending to be something she's not. I just wish we could have told you earlier."

"I'm sorry I wasn't involved in the arrangements," Lyra's mother adds. "My husband did not permit me to have an audience with you."

"None of this is your fault, either of you," the king insists. "I've arranged with the council for an annulment based on dishonesty. It should be completed by nightfall. Next time, I'll be more selective."

He leads everyone in a light chuckle, and it removes any tension in the room, though it wasn't thick in the air anyway. The whole castle feels relaxed, a true reflection of this monarch's ruling style. We enjoy the rest of the meal with good conversation.

"Can we spend a few more days here?" Lyra asks me when we're back in our suite. "Mother, Aisla and I would love to do some shopping before heading home. The Winter Realm craftsmen and seamstresses are extremely talented."

"Of course," I tell her. "I've been wanting to meet with Snowthorne more anyway. I have some more ideas for transportation lines that could be mutually advantageous."

The smile on her face is worth the extra time away from home.

While Lyra visits with her mother and sister more, I spend much of the rest of the afternoon meeting with the king. It's a relief to work with someone like him after all the trouble with Assanan and now Chez.

Just the thought of that man makes my wolf growl for what he did to Lyra.

Dinner was another fine meal, and now we're boarding the coaches ordered by Snowthorne to return to the *Ironhawk* for the funeral.

Lyra's eyes are somber. "I just wish we could have helped Cookie," she says sadly. "He was the only one who seemed to care about Maggie after she was kidnapped."

"From what you've told us, he was a good man," her mother says.

"He saved Lyra's life," I add. "For that, giving him this meager hero's farewell seems like so little."

The queen nods thoughtfully. "Well, I'm a mother, and I say that if we always care for the girl he seemed to love as a daughter, Maggie, then his life will have meant quite a bit."

"We'll always take care of her," Lyra says as a pledge. "You're both going to love her. Maybe we can talk her into going shopping with us tomorrow. She wanted to stay on the ship rather than come into the city, and I'm not sure why."

"I'm sure she has her reasons," her mother says.

LYRA

IT'S QUIET ON THE DECK OF THE *IRONHAWK*. THE ONLY SOUND IS A LIGHT flapping of a small piece of the lowered sail's sheet from the cool breeze whisping across us.

Cassian intertwines his fingers with mine, steading me during this unfamiliar experience. I don't know anything about the wolf shifter religion—the mysticism of the Moon Goddess—though I intend to learn all I can when we return to Oceana.

The priestess wears bright white robes embroidered with silver threads, giving her an ethereal glow in the dim moonlight and the soft flicker of the many lanterns, which are lined along the path leading to the edge of the ship. She begins a gentle chant in a language I've never heard before that echoes hauntingly through the breeze.

Maggie sits beside me on the opposite side from Cassian, and I wrap my arm around her when she gasps as the Royal Guardsmen bring out Cookie's body. They carry the ceremonial bier, their white-gloved hands grasping the silver handles inlaid with glowing moonstones.

They march forward slowly, methodically, and Maggie trembles as they approach. A pure white cloth with silver writing embroidered across it, again in a language I don't know, is draped over Cookie's body.

One of the Royal Guardsmen turns his head to Maggie as he passes, a solemn look of aching in his eyes. I can't be sure, but I think Maggie nods back at him.

When they reach the end of the ship, the priestess begins her eulogy. It's a mix of common speech and that mysterious ancient language, and it flows like a song sailing on the wind to join him in his afterlife.

Because the wolf shifters rule all the human kingdoms, there are Moon Goddess Temples in all of them, including Maelie and Winter Realm. Humans rarely visit them, though I've always been fascinated by the beautiful buildings, as well as the Moon Goddess Herself.

I suppose I understand why now.

"Alpha King Cassian Oliver." The priestess says his name in that same musical tone.

He squeezes my hand once then drops my fingers to stand and join the priestess at the temporary altar prepared for the ceremony.

The priestess nods toward the pallbearers, and the two in the front lift the sheet to expose Cookie's head. I pull Maggie closer as her sobs deepen.

"Do you affirm this man to have acted heroically in the name of the Kingdom of Oceana and the Moon Goddess?" the priestess asks.

"I do," Cassian confirms quickly.

The men replace the sheet, and, with another nod from the priestess, place him on the funeral pyre in a small boat. Surrounding him are some of his belongings, as well as bread and ale, and what Cassian has explained to me is a hero's sword in a silver scabbard.

This time, it's Cassian who nods at the ship's crew, and they hoist the small boat up and over the edge.

"Witnesses, come forth," the priestess says.

We stand, and I keep hold of Maggie as we step toward the railings to watch the small boat drift peacefully away. Mother and Aisla, who have stood back out of respect for the foreign ceremony, join us.

The priestess begins chanting again, then raises her hand toward the moon. At that moment, the little boat catches fire.

My heart feels heavy as I watch the boat disappear into bright white flames, their tips raining sparks of silver up into the air.

My heart fills with sadness, and I'm so worried about Maggie.

But soon, that same Royal Guardsman appears, brushing Maggie's arm softly with his hand. She turns around and instantly falls into his arms, burying her head in his chest.

Cassian steps up, and we walk away. "It looks like the Moon Goddess joined two more mates on this journey," he says quietly.

I look back at the couple embracing as they watch the final flames extinguish as the boat sinks into the waves.

"Yes, I guess She did."

SUMMONED TO THE TEMPLE

Lyra

I'VE ALREADY GOTTEN USED TO THE CHILLY AIR HERE IN WINTER HAVEN. Even with all the snow on the ground, it's not really cold. I think it's more accurate to describe it as cool and refreshing.

The streets in the shopping district of Icehaven, the port city, are bustling with activity. Men with shovels hurry to clear the sidewalks that are already trampled from early morning shoppers. On the streets, drivers holler at their golden-maned horses pulling large metal blades attached to wooden frames, driving the snow away for those struggling to make deliveries in the thick snowpack.

No one has waited for the snow to clear, though. Many small groups of women, several with children in tow, scurry in and out of shops, their doorbells chiming pleasantly through the air with every passing. We've been told by one of the lady's maidens in Snowthorne's castle that it's important to get here early to find the best deals.

But I'd rather take the leisurely approach, especially after the heavy emotion of the funeral last night. I am thankful that the funeral pyre had completely sunk out of view in the morning light and that Maggie had found a mate in the handsome Royal Guardsman.

Mother, Aisla, and Maggie stroll along with me, dodging excited children running past with snowballs in their hands. The Royal Guardsmen follow us dutifully, though they keep a respectable distance.

One of those men is Oscar, Maggie's mate. She stops occasionally, pretending to admire merchandise in a store window, but she's not very discreet about turning her head to get a glimpse of him, which always makes her smile.

Her face flushes with a rosy blush when I catch her watching him.

"He seems like a very nice man," I tell her, just loud enough for us ladies to hear but not the guardsmen.

"He is," she says excitedly, maybe a tad too loudly. It makes me giggle. "I suppose you've figured out that he's the reason I preferred to stay on the ship yesterday."

"We have," I confirm.

"I don't blame you," Aisla chimes in. "He's very cute, too."

We all giggle at that, even Mother.

I nearly gasp at a beautiful dress I spot on display in the next window, an emerald-green stunner with a soft, billowing skirt that looks like a cloud.

Mother catches my gaze. "That would look splendid on you, Lyra."

"I do really like it," I tell her. "Maybe I should try it on."

"Let's go in," Aisla agrees.

The small bells above the door jingle as we step into the tiny boutique, where a dark-haired woman with eyes the color of cocoa looks up from her desk in the back. She smiles, and I step toward her, but I stop when I catch sight of another dress in the corner of my eye.

It's deep royal blue in silk cloth so tightly woven it shimmers in the dim lamplight of the store. The bodice is embroidered with bright flowers woven together in a cheerful green vine.

"Maggie, this would look wonderful on you, with your bright blonde hair and those blue eyes to match the fabric," I tell her.

"Me?!" Maggie shakes her head. "That's beautiful, yes, but it must cost a fortune. I don't have any way to pay for that."

I turn to her. "Maggie, you saved my life. Please, try on this dress, and if you like it, I'll buy it for you."

She gasps. "Oh… no. I can't accept something like this."

Mother steps forward, her tone brokering no argument. "Dear, your mate would love to see you in this. You saved my daughter. I'll buy it myself if you like it."

Moisture begins to pool in Maggie's eyes. "You are all so kind to me. I never thought my life would be like this when I was taken from my parents' house. And now I have all you, who are such good friends, and even a mate. I—" The tears start falling, and all of us fumble to step around her and envelop her in a group hug.

"You deserve this," I insist. "You deserve all the happiness in the world. And I'm so happy you found Oscar." I pull back a little. "Now, let's get you this dress so you can knock Oscar's socks off tonight."

I raise a brow, and she nods her head.

"What a great choice," the storekeeper tells us. "The fitting rooms are right this way."

"I'd like to try on the green dress in the front window," I tell the woman.

"Another fabulous choice!" she says excitedly. "Let's get you ladies into fitting rooms, and I'll bring them both in.

The moment I try the green dress on, I know it's perfect, and Maggie looks like a princess in the blue one. After looking around some more, Aisla finds two dresses she loves, and Mother adds a sapphire broach to our haul when we get it all up to the counter.

"Please have these wrapped and sent to the castle," Mother tells the shopkeeper after paying for the items. "Address them to Alpha King Cassian Oliver's suite."

"Right away," the woman says, looking about twenty times happier than she did when we walked in, which is saying a lot because she was already cheerful.

We step out of the shop to see the Royal Guardsmen talking to a woman in a silvery cape, much like the robes the priestess wore last night. I feel my wolf becoming suddenly on guard when she sees us and approaches. The Royal Guardsmen follow close behind her.

"Luna Queen Lyra?" she asks.

I'm shocked into silence at the title, even though I knew that's what I would be when I married Cassian.

"This is she," Mother says for me, gesturing my way. "Although, she has yet to have the Luna ceremony or the coronation."

"Of course," the woman answers. "The Temple recognizes these as mere formalities, for now." She meets my eyes. "I apologize for the intrusion in your city visit. I am Fayth, and the High Priestess Silanya has sent me to request your immediate presence at the Temple."

I raise a brow. "Oh? Is something wrong?"

"No, Luna Queen," she says, and the formal address still sounds foreign to me. "But she does request that you come with me as quickly as possible."

I turn to Mother, who shrugs. "I don't know anything about shifter temple business," she says. "Perhaps we should just go see what this is about."

Nodding toward Fayth, I tell her, "Show us the way."

It turns out the temple is halfway across the city, so the Royal Guardsmen acquire some coaches to carry us there. Fayth sits between me and Mother, with Aisla and Maggie in the back seat and the Royal Guardsmen in the coach behind us.

The horses, regal looking beasts with long white manes and similar long white fur on their legs, trot in front of us gracefully, the silvery bells on their bridles ringing pleasantly throughout the trip.

"Is High Priestess Silanya the one who performed the ceremony last night?" I ask Fayth.

"She is," she confirms.

"Why didn't she speak with us then?" Mother asks.

Fayth shakes her head. "She didn't have the vision until today."

My eyes go wide. "Vision? What did she see?"

"I'm afraid I do not know, but the High Priestess will share it with you as soon as you arrive," Fayth answers.

We're silent for the rest of the journey. I'm lost in my own thoughts, simultaneously worried and curious about what the High Priestess has to say. We reach the temple shortly after, its crystal towers framed perfectly into the snowy mountainside as though it was born there rather than built.

It's strange and beautiful all at once.

We exit the coaches and follow Fayth up the crystal staircase, which somehow seems to chime at each footfall. The cathedral doors are wide open at the top, exposing a huge open room with nothing but a large silver platform in the center holding a glowing purple ball.

Nothing else is in the room, that is, except for a tall, handsome Alpha King.

"Cassian?" I ask. "What's going on?"

CROWN MY LUNA QUEEN

CASSIAN

HER SCENT ENVELOPS ME BEFORE SHE STEPS THROUGH THE DOOR, AND hearing my name escape her lips voice soothes me even more. Now that we're married, even a few hours of separation trouble my wolf.

"I don't know," I answer her honestly. "A messenger from the temple came for me, but she didn't tell me what the High Priestess wanted."

She closes the distance between us, and I take her into my arms. We linger for a moment, but we're both too troubled with what may be wrong here to embrace for long.

She pulls back. "The same happened to me. Fayth said that—" Her words fade when she turns around to see no one else but her mother and sister, who have stayed outside the temple doors. "That's odd. She's gone."

"My messenger disappeared, too," I tell her. "She was behind me, then she was gone."

"This is all so strange," she says before turning back to her mother and sister. "Where's Maggie?" she asks them.

"She's stopped at the bottom of the steps by a statue, kneeling," Aisla answers.

"It's what we do before entering the temple," I explain. "She's asking the Moon Goddess for Her permission and guidance before stepping inside."

"Oh." Worry crosses Lyra's features. "I didn't do that."

"You didn't know about it, so don't worry," I assure her. "Besides, you've been summoned here, which implies permission."

She nods, then turns her gaze to the center platform. "What is this?"

A soft voice answers from behind us before I have the chance to explain. "It's the Crystal Orb." High Priestess Silanya glides into the room, her white and silver robes shimmering. "This is where the Goddess blesses us with visions of the future."

I bow my head at the priestess, and Lyra does the same. "And what is the Orb telling you about our future?" I ask.

Silanya smiles. "I'd expect nothing more from the Alpha King than this direct question," she says. "But I'm afraid the explanation is not so simple. Please, follow me." She looks toward the door. "Your family and companion may join us."

The queen ushers the other ladies through the door, and we all follow Silanya. Lyra shoots me a look of confusion, but I have no explanations to offer. "I know as much as you do," I whisper.

She leads us into the main sanctuary, where Lyra's eyes go wide at the giant statue of the Moon Goddess, crafted entirely from moonstone. A silver light illuminates it from the high ceiling, causing the Goddess's likeness to shimmer like a diamond.

Even after seeing these all my life, it still stuns me for a moment at the heavy presence of the Moon Goddess it projects.

The few worshippers in the sanctuary rise and leave the room quietly at our entrance.

"Please sit," Silanya directs us, and we all gather in the front row of the stone benches.

I'm ready to hear what this is all about, but instead of talking, Silanya steps away through the back curtain.

"Where did she go?" Lyra asks.

All I can do is shrug, but thankfully, Silanya returns soon with a large book cradled in her arms, its edges sparkling silver in the light.

"My apologies," she says. "In order to explain, I needed the *Tome of Glory*."

I instantly recognize the ancient book, which tells of war and sacrifice, the stories we've heard as children about the days when shifters rose up to take their rightful place as leaders in this world. But I'm confused.

"What is it doing in Winter Realm, a human kingdom?" I ask.

Lyra turns to me, her brow furrowed, then glances back at Silanya.

"It was kept here for safekeeping, and it is good that it was," the priestess says. "Danger has reached the shores of Oceana, and this tome holds the key."

Agitation rushes over me, and I stand. "Assanan has made his move? Then we need to set sail right away and take care of the bastard."

Silanya puts up her palm, her long fingernails glistening in the silver light. "Alpha King, please, haste would be a mistake."

"But we have people we love back in Oceana," Lyra pleads, now standing at my side. "Our friends in Maelie... good people at the Oceana castle...."

Silanya nods. "I believe they will hold their defenses—for now," she says. "I'm afraid that returning without the amulet would mean much death."

"Amulet? Ridiculous," I argue. "My warriors can hold their own against Assanan."

"They can," she agrees.

"Well, then, we need to leave," I insist.

"Assanan is no longer your biggest threat," she says. "I'm afraid he has tapped into a much darker power."

"What?" I can't believe it. I know the asshole uses mages, but so do we. "My mages can counteract any of their useless spells."

"It is darker than that," Silanya insists. She sets the book on the pulpit and opens it, the sound of its crackling spine echoing in the vast sanctuary. "It's all in here," she adds before reading from its pages.

"The Dark King Hadrian, a human, employed a witch to cast a spell to keep the wolf shifters at bay. He knew he was weaker than them and could not defeat them on his own," she begins. "She told him that the only spell she knew that could give him enough strength was one that would concentrate darkness upon him, drawn from plains of existence no human or shifter had ever tapped into."

I wrap my hand around Lyra's, squeezing tightly.

"But there was a problem," Silanya continues. "She didn't know how to draw only dark power. She also had to do something with the light that came in with it. So, she took two amulets from the king's treasure and focused all the darkness into one and all the light into the other."

"How come I've never heard of this?" I ask.

"The truth of the human and shifter wars is a distant memory," she explains. "The Moon Goddess has directed all Her High Priestesses to keep these prophecies contained until they are needed again."

"The humans lost those wars," I argue.

She nods. "Because the shifters used the Amulet of Light, which is always stronger than the darkness."

"And I suppose Assanan has that amulet." My wolf growls furiously inside me.

"He does," she confirms. "And there is no conquering it without the Amulet of Light."

"Wait," Lyra says. "So, he has some ancient artifact that even shifters don't know about. How did he get it?"

"Our theory is that he has turned to worship Hadrian instead of the Moon Goddess," Silanya explains.

"But he's just a long-dead human," I argue. "Can't the Moon Goddess stop him?"

She shakes her head solemnly. "When he took the amulet and died with it, he became a god. Besides, these affairs are only for those of our plane of existence to resolve. The good news is that when Assanan awakened the path to the Amulet of Darkness, so did he open that to the Amulet of Light. This is the only way to save all the kingdoms from the darkness."

"What's the bad news?" Lyra asks dryly.

"The amulet is sealed in the Mountain of Crystal," Silanya explains. "It is inland from here in the western mountain range. It's a two-month journey from here, one way."

"Two months?!" I holler without meaning to, and it echoes through the sanctuary. "That's four months inland and a week sailing back to Oceana!"

"I believe your castle will hold until then," she says.

I wish I had her confidence. I can't even mind-link with Turgan. How will I warn him?

"The High Priestess of the Oceana temple will alert your Beta," Silanya continues, reading my concerns. "She will see the visions as well. Also, you should know that once reached, the seal can only be broken by you, Alpha King Cassian, and you, Luna Queen Lyra."

"Why?" I ask.

"Its key requires royal mates of human and shifter blood to open," she says.

Lyra shakes her head. "But I'm only half human."

"It should still work," Silanya insists. "Your bond is powerful. But we will not know until we reach the seal."

"We won't know...." My mind races with thoughts of what my warriors are facing back home. How can they hold off against ancient, magical darkness?

"We need to leave right away," Lyra says, breaking me out of my thoughts. "But how do we open the seal, or try to, once we get there?"

"I will accompany you on this journey," Silanya explains. "There are chants and traditional rituals to perform since it was sealed in stone by the Moon Goddess, to be retrieved only by the chosen Luna Queen. I've already arranged our means of travel. We'll go by coach until we reach the mountain range, where we will need to continue the journey on foot."

"Great." Lyra shakes her head.

"I must perform the coronation and Luna ceremony before we

leave," Silanya adds. "In our eyes, you are royalty, Luna Queen Lyra, but I can't know whether the key will accept it without the Moon Goddess's formal blessing."

"Well," I tell the priestess, "we have no time to waste. Let's get my wife crowned Luna Queen."

THE JOURNEY BEGINS

Lyra

"I suppose we can forget about shopping," I tell my mother and sister, who both shrug. Apparently, now Cassian and I have to trek up a mountain with a priestess to try to open some locked box with a necklace in it that will save the entire plain of existence.

How in the world have I gone from a lower princess of humans to someone who can save all the kingdoms from darkness? I don't know if I'm ready for that kind of responsibility.

But I don't have much time to worry about that because a bunch of priestesses are already piling into the room with lit candles and bundles of herbs.

I guess we're doing this. I'll be the Luna Queen.

Cassian faces me and takes both of my hands in his. "I wanted this to be a special ceremony back in the Oceana Temple, but this will have to do for now," he says. "I promise we will have formal celebrations once Assanan is defeated."

"I don't need any formal celebrations," I insist.

"But my mother will," he says, a light chuckle escaping his lips.

"Believe me. When we return and this war is over, Mother will insist on a large wedding, coronation, and Luna ceremony, all separate events with everyone in the kingdom present."

"As will I," my mother chimes in. "I'm not happy that I missed watching my little girl walk down the aisle."

"And I want to stand next to you," Aisla adds.

"Okay, fine," I say, defeated by these wonderful people. "We'll have the biggest wedding and all those other ceremonies we can get." But a sobering thought hits me. "After my father is dead and gone."

Cassian pulls me in and wraps his arms around me, grounding me. "I promise he will never harm you again."

I pull back. "But I want to see him, just once," I insist. "I need to see the eyes of the man who caused so much pain for my mother."

"And you as well," Mother adds. "Your whole life was influenced by that awful Alpha King, and I'm so sorry about that."

"You owe me no apologies, Mother," I tell her. "None of this is your fault." I look at my mother, sister and my newest friend, Maggie, who stand beside me. "I guess I won't see any of you for a while until we get back from the mountain."

"And why not?" Mother asks, moving her hands to her hips. " When did I say I wasn't going? I have no intention of letting my daughter run off into the mountains without me."

"Me too!" Aisla says.

"And me," Maggie adds.

I turn to her. "Maggie, you don't want to run off to the wilderness when you just found your mate."

"Royal Guardsman Oscar can accompany us," Cassian says.

"Then, it's settled," Maggie says. "We're coming."

"Okay," I say, not that I have any choice in the matter, though I feel tears welling up in my eyes at how much support I have now. I don't know if we'll face any danger, and I hope not. But just having all of them with me makes me feel completely loved.

"Are you ready?"

I'm surprised to hear the High Priestess's voice behind me, but I spin and nod. "Yes, I am."

"We'll begin with the coronation," she says.

I hold Cassian's hand tight through the brief ceremony. The High Priestess chants softly in that language I've never heard, and in a few minutes, I'm wearing a crystal crown studded with moonstones and precious gems that they somehow produced from the back of the sanctuary.

The Luna ceremony follows, and it is just as surprisingly quick. Cassian certifies me as his Luna, and then the line of priestesses approach and circle around me, the smoke from their burning bundles of sage and what smells like other herbs floats around me in gentle waves, then drifts up toward the towering ceiling and passes over the Moon Goddess statue.

For a moment, I swear her eyes glow.

And suddenly, the High Priestess says I'm officially his Luna. She drapes a deep purple silk cape over my shoulders, embroidered with shining silver writing that must be the language of the Moon Goddess Temple.

Cassian pulls me in and kisses me deeply, and everything else around us disappears.

I feel my wolf awaken within me and recognize her emotions of pure joy and bliss. And for a moment, I feel Cassian's wolf reaching through our bond to join with my own wolf.

The place on my neck where Cassian marked me tingles pleasantly.

I guess now we're fully joined, and I've never felt so complete.

With my eyes closed, I deepen the kiss, exploring Cassian's mouth with my tongue, loving the feeling of his flicking against mine playfully.

Until I hear giggles and a throat clearing.

Mother.

With a few more soft kisses, we finally part, and Aisla is smiling wide.

"Sorry, everyone," I say. "I guess I got carried away."

"It is understandable," High Priestess Silanya says. "The mate bond is very strong with you. It is why I believe it will be powerful enough to unlock the key. Now, please excuse me for a moment while I prepare to leave."

We all nod at the High Priestess, which somehow I know how to do in the slightly unnatural way that Cassian does it, which I suppose is the shifter sign of deference to the Moon Goddess. I need to learn a lot more about that, but I suppose it'll be a while before I'm sitting in a library at my leisure reading books about the shifter kingdoms.

Speaking of which…. "High Priestess," I say to stop her before she leaves the room. "Can we take the *Tome of Glory* with us?" It's probably going to be a no. It's not exactly the thing to grab for a camping trip.

"It has already been loaded onto the coach," she says before stepping out of the room.

I look over, confused, and sure enough, it's no longer sitting on the podium. But I never saw anyone take it anywhere.

I guess this wolf shifter religion is… mysterious and complicated.

A voice pops into my head, and it takes me a second to realize it's Cassian giving instructions via mind-link to his Royal Guard and crew. He orders several to come with us, orders others to pack provisions, and tells one to message King Snowthorne immediately.

"You want the king to send his army," I say, more a statement than a question.

"Yes," Cassian confirms. "They won't be a match for Assanan's shifters, but they could help protect the castle and perhaps Maelie. They could set sail and be there in a week at the shortest distance between here and there, which, incidentally, is not the way the ship that kidnapped you sailed. They took a long route."

"I wonder why," I ponder. "And I also wonder why they were even bringing me here in the first place."

"I suppose your oldest sister had something to do with it, but she's out of the picture now," he says. "We'll worry about that later. Perhaps you ladies should gather things from the shops for your needs on the trip. I don't exactly have those kinds of… supplies aboard the *Ironhawk*."

I giggle. "I guess not. Mom, Aisla, Maggie, I guess we're going shopping after all."

Before I leave the Temple, the priestesses gather my crown and cape for safekeeping. I can't exactly go traipsing through the woods wearing those. Then, us ladies head into the city.

In miraculously little time, we've secured more suitable clothes for the trip as well as toiletries and some snacks and supplies the men may not have thought to bring, and we're all watching as the five coaches and two wagons we are using are loaded up.

"Are you ready, my Luna?"

Cassian's voice sends a pleasant shiver up my spine. It's the first time he's called me that, and I can't wait until I hear it from him when we're alone together.

Something tells me the lovemaking is only going to get better from here.

But I can't think about that now. We've got a journey to start, a magical secret amulet to procure, and a whole lot of kingdoms to save from darkness.

It's not about me and Cassian right now. It's about our kingdoms, our world.

"I'm ready," I say confidently, and he holds out his strong hand to help me step up onto the carriage.

I sure hope we can open that lock.

FIRST CAMP

CASSIAN

WE'VE PUT TOGETHER QUITE A PROCESSION FOR A TRIP INTO THE mountains, but half the men will wait at the bottom with the wagons and provisions at the end of the road, and we'll have to make the rest of the journey on foot. Runners will bring up any supplies we can't carry as we need them.

I'm going to hate to see my new queen and Luna trudging up a mountain. If it were my choice, she'd wait in the comfort of Snowthorne's castle. But with the key to the seal requiring both of us, this is one thing that isn't my choice.

And I'm not fucking happy about that.

The procession takes us by the castle entrance, and the king and his men stand waiting as we approach. I turn to Lyra before dismounting.

"I'll be back in a moment," I tell her.

"Mmm," is all she answers back.

I would laugh if I weren't so concerned about the events unfolding back in Oceana. But the way she is leaning forward on the edge of her seat while reading from the *Tome of Glory* is, for lack of a better description, adorable.

I leave her to her studies and exit the coach, approaching the king.

"It's already in motion," he tells me, nodding toward Manning, the Royal Guardsman I'd sent to Snowthorne with my message. "Your Guardsman is more than welcome to stay in the castle to relay messages in your absence."

"The mind-link has a one-hundred-mile radius," I explain.

"Your base camp should be within that distance from here," he assures me. "However, the ascent will take you out of range."

I nod thoughtfully. I don't expect any problems, but I would like to be informed of any news from Oceana. "My men will be acting as runners to the base camp. Any message Manning sends me should be relayed to me within a day."

"Very well then," he says. "I have thirty ships prepared to set sail at first light tomorrow. Besides the crew, each has a contingent of seventy-five soldiers. I've given orders that one of the ships is to be used as a relay, so we expect to receive messages from your kingdom every two weeks."

It's not ideal, especially if I'm up on the mountain, and there's an urgent need for my reply, but it's already been longer than that since I've heard from Turgan.

My greatest concern is my mother being left at the castle that Assanan is more likely than ever to attack. The fact that he has dark magic on his side pisses me off to no end. If he lays one hand on her....

I shake the thought away. Even if the castle were breached, Phelan would protect my mother with his life. He'd guide her away and take her somewhere safe. He is aging as well, but his faculties are sharp, and he's a strong warrior. He has many loyal supporters in our kingdom as well.

My mother will be fine. It is the others in my kingdom I need to concern myself with, and I know Turgan will do everything to protect them until I get back.

With my Luna.

I bid Snowthorne and Manning farewell and return to my seat in the coach next to Lyra, who continues to be enthralled with the *Tome of Glory*. Her mother and sister chat among themselves in the back seat, and Maggie has asked to ride with the High Priestess in the coach behind us.

I settle back, preparing for the long journey.

THE SUN IS JUST BEGINNING TO CAST BRIGHT ORANGE HUES ACROSS THE horizon, and I've instructed the men to make our first camp before nightfall among fragrant pine trees in a clearing just off the main road.

I'd envisioned traveling through a snow-blanketed landscape for the entire journey, but it was mere hours before the scenery around us transformed into greenery, and the chill in the air softened into a warm breeze.

Still, Lyra did not take her eyes off the *Tome of Glory* until now, as the waning sunlight has made reading impossible.

She sighs, setting the book on the floor in front of her carefully before leaning back, turning her head toward the campsite with a distant look in her eyes, biting her lip.

'What's troubling you?' I ask in our private mind-link, sensing she does not want to speak of this around her family.

'Oh, I forgot we could talk this way.' She forces her lips to bend into a smile. 'Nothing.'

'I hardly think that sort of sigh means nothing,' I tell her.

She nods so lightly, I barely perceive it. 'You're right, of course. It's just that the story in there troubles me, the one about Hadrian.'

I frown. 'The evil human?'

'Yes,' she confirms. 'Well, evil, I guess, eventually, but he didn't start out that way. He started out as a good person.'

'I don't think a 'good person' could become like that,' I assure her.

'No, but you see—' She pauses for a moment. 'He grew up being persecuted. Bullies were everywhere, and he really suffered. When he became an adult, he found out his parents weren't who he thought they were and that all the bullies were wrong about him.'

'A bad childhood doesn't justify such cruelty,' I tell her.

'You don't understand,' she insists, turning to me as if we were speaking aloud. 'Cassian, he was just like me.'

'No, he wasn't.'

'Yes, he was,' she argues. 'He grew up just like I did, with people being horrible to him. Other than Mother and Aisla, the whole kingdom treated me like I was garbage.'

'Lyra—'

'And now it turns out I'm a shifter, and I'm your mate and Luna,' she adds. 'So, our stories are almost the same. All I'm saying is that I can see how he would end up that way. Maybe it wouldn't take much to tip me over the edge. Maybe I'm dangerous, too.'

'That's not true.'

By now, we've all exited the coaches and are watching the men hurrying about getting the tents and seating ready. Several men gather firewood, while others form a fire pit from nearby stones.

'What if it is?' she asks.

'I'm not worried about that,' I say. 'You are most definitely not like Dark King Hadrian. You've had nothing but goodness in your soul your entire life. You sacrificed your future, or believed you did at the time, to make a marriage alliance with a terrifying monster.'

She looks at me, her mouth crooked. 'You are not a monster.'

I shrug. 'You didn't know that. But you truly believed the marriage was an arrangement that would let your people continue using the ocean for trade and resources. And you did it anyway because you care about… everybody. That's goodness through and through. And don't think I don't know the rumors going around the human kingdoms about me. I started them, after all.'

There it is—her genuine smile as she gives me a playful tap on the arm. "You did not!" she says out loud, causing all the ladies to jerk their heads our way.

"I did," I confirm. "I didn't want any humans coming near our lands, so I had our people begin rumors about me. I have some very convincing older ladies in my castle who were happy to oblige."

She shakes her head, laughing now.

'That's better,' I tell her, back in the mind-link. 'You are my precious Luna and mate, the kindest woman I have ever met. Do not ever think that you have anything in common with any evil being, past or present.'

She nods. 'I'll try,' she answers softly.

'And if you ever are thinking that again, tell me,' I add. 'I'll help you forget about that.' I wiggle my brows to get the point across.

She raises one eyebrow, and I can see the need growing in her eyes. I can't wait to have her in my arms again, this time in our tent in the middle of the forest.

But it's going to have to wait until later.

PRIMAL

Lyra

It's going to be a long few months, staying in a tent with my mother only meters away, trying to be quiet while Cassian's touch makes me want to holler his name so loud, it echoes through these hills.

But for now, I try to contain myself. We still have dinner to cook and a long night ahead of us before it's time to be alone in the tent. So, I give Cassian a quick kiss, trying not to get any more excited by his touch, before he goes to help his men with the setup.

The ladies and I have our own work to do.

I don't know where the High Priestess is. She'd murmured something about communing with the Moon Goddess and went into the forest before I had a chance to thank her for letting me read that book. I wouldn't ask her to help cook, anyway.

Stepping toward Mother, I can see we're all thinking the same thing—we're going to commandeer the "kitchen" out here. Without a word between us, we walk up to the men clanging pots and pans together and shoo them out of the way. I don't doubt they'll make some delicious grilled meats over that fire, but we brought a few things to make a full meal out of this.

The slender, brown-haired man looks horrified that we're volunteering to do the work. "L-Luna, please," he says, glancing over at Cassian. "This isn't something you need to do."

"Believe me, it is," I argue. "I like to cook. All of us do." I gesture toward Mother, Aisla, and Maggie, who are all nodding furiously. "Look, if you'd like to help, that's fine. We probably need to fill this pot with water."

"Yes, Luna Queen," he says, looking relieved to be doing something I told him to.

This is such a weird feeling.

It's fun cooking with Mother and Aisla again, and it's even more enjoyable with Maggie here, who spent so much time learning from Cookie aboard that ship, which she's told me was called the *Slayer*. Even the name is awful. I'm so glad she's with us now.

She keeps looking over at Oscar, and I can see the cute little flirty glances they give to each other. It's cute. I don't know if they've marked each other yet and can mind-link. I haven't asked. That probably isn't very polite.

The whole time, I think about what Cassian told me. I can't pretend it doesn't still bother me that the bad guy's past seems a lot like mine. But for now, I'm going to try to just trust Cassian's instincts. I can't even imagine doing anything to hurt innocent people. So, I guess I'm different from Dark King Hadrian, after all.

I'm stirring the boiling pasta when I notice something, a strange feeling in my gut that takes me a few seconds to realize it is my wolf. I've only recently been very in tune with her feelings. I guess I need some more practice.

But there's one thing I can tell for sure.

Something is wrong.

Mother and Aisla are oblivious to it, and they continue cooking and laughing, saying something about one of the men back in Maelie Castle. I'm not sure because I've stopped listening and have joined everyone else in this camp by stiffening and listening to the forest.

It's Cassian who makes the call as to what it is, and the tone of his voice is grave.

"Rogues."

I don't know much about my new shifter world yet, but I know enough to understand what that means. Rogues are wolves who have no pack, no kingdom, and no one to answer to.

That makes them dangerous.

"A lot of fucking nerve you have coming anywhere close to this camp," Cassian adds, louder, his voice powerful and commanding.

Mother and Aisla have gone silent now, and I see them looking around nervously and moving closer to each other. Maggie steps over toward Oscar, who wraps his arm around her protectively.

Cassian is on the opposite side of the clearing, so I make a step toward him and see him moving in my direction.

Then I hear it.

A twig snaps behind me, and I should have had enough time to react, but for some reason, I'm frozen to this spot. I'm not used to having to think on my feet like this.

I feel a man's arms wrap around me, then another, their sick laughter ringing in my ear, in the same instant that several other men jump into the clearing and grab Mother and Aisla.

"No!"

The word is a roar that echoes through the forest. It's Cassian, but before he can close the distance between us, no less than twenty grey and black wolves jump on him.

The Royal Guardsmen all shift in an instant, coming to his aid and dealing with the rogues who have attacked them.

They're everywhere. It's like the entire forest has come alive with them, and they keep coming from every direction.

"This one's not a wolf," the man holding Aisla snarls. "I'm going to have a good time with her."

"Let her go!" I holler.

But the two holding me back ignore my pleas and laugh even harder, their putrid breath choking me, their filthy hands grabbing for my chest, but I struggle against them.

"I said, let her go!" I repeat as firmly as I can.

But they just keep laughing. I try to find Cassian, but he's lost in a sea of wolves.

'I'm coming!' he shouts in the mind-link. 'I will not let anything happen to you!'

'Please hurry,' I answer. 'They have Mother and Aisla.'

'We'll make quick work of them,' he promises me.

But I don't see how. There are so many wolves in the campground now, I can't even see the ground anymore, and it's so chaotic, I can't tell which of them are our men and which are rogues.

The food I was cooking is knocked over now, and the logs in the fire pit have been disbursed all over the place, their glowing red embers just one more obstacle for our wolves to avoid while trying to fight off all these rogues.

I finally see Cassian's wolf, a sight I've never beheld. His wolf is huge, bigger than any of the others and twice as large as most of them. His bright white fur glistens in the moonlight, twinged with silver luminescence on the tips that glows like his silver eyes.

He's beautiful.

And he's charging toward me, only to be jumped by about a dozen black, scraggly wolves who bite at his neck. He shoves half of them out of his way like they're nothing but air and sinks his teeth into the others' necks, one by one.

Blood pools on the ground everywhere, letting off a metallic stench that I can smell even above the stink of the men holding me.

I look at my mother and Aisla, who are helplessly trying to kick the men grabbing them. It's not working. I can't find Maggie, and I hope Oscar is protecting her.

Spotting Cassian again, I panic for a moment at the red stains all over his white fur, but I don't think the blood is his. Another set of rogues comes at him, keeping him from crossing the distance between us.

Aisla's blood-curdling scream has me jerking my head in her direction.

The disgusting man is dragging her into the forest.

I have to do something!

I jerk my head toward where I last saw Cassian. He's tearing through the rogues, but he won't get here fast enough.

Aisla is scrambling, but all I can see are her legs as she's being dragged away.

I can't let that happen.

My body trembles, chills reaching the ends of every nerve, and a deep, wailing howl escapes from deep in my throat. I feel my bones ache as something happens.

Something primal lets loose inside of me.

NO CONTROL

Cassian

Shit.

I can see it in the seconds I'm able to glance through the barrage of rogues bearing down on me.

Lyra is shifting.

I haven't had time to talk her through it, to help her understand the process. This was something I needed to coach her through, to tell her it's okay, to introduce her slowly to the different stages and how to control the overwhelming change in sensory perception, in raw emotion.

But she's alone now, on the other side of the vast clearing we've used as a campsite, and she's not even answering me in the mind-link.

'Lyra....'

Her wolf is beautiful, just as I expected. Her red hair is even more prominent in her wolf's fur, and even this far away in the dim moonlight, her green eyes shine like glistening emeralds.

My wolf howls at the first sight of my mate in wolf form.

But she's too far away.

She makes quick work of the assholes who dared put their hands on her, and for that, I'm grateful. I would have taken them out myself if there hadn't been so many Goddess-damn rogues coming, one after the other.

I've sliced through more carotid arteries in the last few minutes than I have in most battles. These rogues are rough, scraggly, and emaciated. They're not fighters. But for some reason, there are at least a hundred of them, maybe more.

Rogues don't usually have an Alpha. That's the definition of the word, after all. But at least one of them must have planned this attack because it's generally organized, though the ones trying to fight aren't smart enough to make a single strategic move against me.

My people are holding their own, but the sheer number of rogues is enough to keep them busy and keep me away from Lyra when she needs me the most.

The next time I catch a glimpse of her through the fur flying at me, she's slipping into the forest and disappearing.

'Lyra!'

This time, she answers. 'My sister!'

But her voice isn't her own. It's raw, primal, and I can tell every sense of self-control has left her.

That's a good thing right now since she's alone out there in the forest. But she needs me. I rip the last wolf in front of me to shreds and throw him aside.

'Handle this!' I holler to my Royal Guardsmen.

'Aye, Alpha King.'

Lyra is in trouble. I have to get to her.

❦

LYRA

. . .

'Sister, save sister.' It's the only thought in my head as I rush into the forest, following the trampled bushes where the man had dragged her.

Her screams drive me forward. Her scent erupts in my nostrils as I get closer.

'Kill. Neutralize the threat. End this. Save her.' The words that come into my mind are simple, commanding.

I catch sight of them. He's on top of her, and she lies on the ground, kicking him and screaming.

I pound my paws on the cool forest floor and leap the last few steps, launching into the air and landing squarely on his back. My fangs—already dripping with the taste of copper from the others— tear into his neck, ripping him off my sister.

But I don't stop there.

With the taste of blood, the joyful feeling of victory consumes me. My jaws keep ripping, tearing off his flesh.

I am unhinged, and I cannot stop.

'Lyra.'

Long after the beat of his heart stops, I keep going, ripping through muscle, crushing his bone. I scent my mate approaching, but I don't stop.

'Lyra!'

My mate's voice is strong, and it stops me cold, blood dripping from my fangs onto the evil man in front of me. But my mate's voice stops me cold. He's speaking out loud now, from beside me, in human form.

"Lyra, shift back," he says, his voice firm. "Focus on shifting back. You can do it."

'No.' It's all I can think of. I want to savor this moment of victory longer. I saved my sister, and this threat must be fully destroyed. He must be obliterated.

"Come out of it," he says. "You are the Luna Queen, Lyra. You've done what you needed to do. This man is dead."

I look back at my kill. He's no longer recognizable in the form he was in when I attacked. He is little more than blood and torn flesh now.

My mate meets my eyes. "Focus, Lyra. Remember who you are. You can do this. Shift back."

'Cassian?' Like lightning, I'm shot into consciousness, remembering who I am, what he is, where we are. I gaze at Cassian, but something's not right. He has to be down on the ground to look at me.

"Yes, that's it," he says out loud. "You're okay. Your sister is okay."

'Aisla….' I turn to look at her, but her eyes are wide, her pupils huge, her face stark white. I've never seen such a gaze of horror before, not from her or anybody. I look down. My feet are paws, and my fur is stained dark red.

Shocked, I look back up at Cassian. 'I'm a wolf.'

"You are," he agrees. "Now, let's get you back to your human form. Focus deep inside you. Just tell yourself to shift back."

'Shift? I—' I follow Aisla's gaze to the man on the ground beside me. 'Cassian, what have I done?!'

"You're okay," he says calmly. "But I need you to shift back."

I shake my head furiously. My head doesn't feel like me. It's elongated, my teeth much too long. 'I don't know if I can.'

"You shifted into your wolf form," he says, again in a soothing voice. "You can shift back. Just tell yourself to do it."

He gives me an encouraging nod. It can't be as easy as just telling myself to shift, and then it happens. It has to be harder than that. 'I can't….'

"You can," he argues firmly. "Don't look at that man again. Close your eyes and focus."

'But….' But I do look at that man, or what's left of him. And when I turn back, Mother is here, holding Aisla, who is still trembling with shock.

She's horrified at what I've done.

So am I.

"Lyra, you need to focus," Cassian says, drawing my gaze back to him. "Focus on me, and tell yourself to shift back."

'Shift back.' I say it in my head, but nothing happens. 'This isn't going to work.'

"It is," he argues. "Look at me. You're the Luna Queen Lyra Oliver. Tell yourself to shift back. Make it an order, and your wolf will obey."

'Shift back!' I say in my mind as firmly as I can.

At first, there's nothing again, but then I feel a strange ache in my bones. It's not pain, just… different, like an overworked muscle.

It starts small at first but then gets so intense I have to close my eyes as my whole body reacts, changes, rearranges.

Then I feel Cassian's touch, soft and gentle, tingling down my arm and back. I have a hand again, an arm, human parts, and I squeeze my hand with Cassian's touch, trying to ground myself as a human again.

I'm a woman, a human; I can feel it now. But that woman has changed forever.

"There," he says soothingly. "You did it."

He wraps a blanket around me and pulls me in close, and it's then that I realize I'm naked.

My arms are trapped in the blanket, so I can't hold him back, but his soothing voice and soft touch up and down my back helps my heartbeat calm.

But then the horror hits me, and I realize what I've done. I've murdered a man, torn him to shreds.

My breath catches in my throat.

Have I become a monster?

THE REAL LYRA

Lyra

I'M SHIVERING. IT'S BEEN SEVERAL MINUTES SINCE I SHIFTED BACK, AND Cassian has been holding me tightly the entire time. Mother has already led Aisla away, though they both turned their heads back toward me a couple of times before exiting the forest.

I pull back from Cassian a little, not because I don't want his comfort, but because I need reassurance that I'm completely back to being human again.

He seems to sense this, loosening his hold on me but not letting go. There's no one else around, so I open the blanket a little to see my feet, my hands, my arms, all the familiar parts of me that have always made me what I am.

They're all there, but now, I'm something different.

"You're completely shifted back," he assures me. "But it's normal, not being sure about that the first time it happens."

I nod lightly, pulling the warm blanket around me again, but this time I leave my arms out so I can hold him. I lean my head on his shoulder, tracing the edges of his chest muscles with my fingers while he strokes my back gently again.

We're silent. I need these moments to breathe, to feel normal again.

"I couldn't control myself," I say finally. "I didn't want to just kill that man. I wanted to rip him up and tear him out of existence."

"Emotions are the hardest thing to control in our wolf forms," he tells me. "They are powerful and primal, free of any of the constraints we hold in our human forms."

"Is it always like that? I don't want to be a monster."

"You're not a monster," he assures me. "You're still Lyra, the woman I love, the one who would do anything to help even strangers, the one who would go to any length to protect the ones she loves. That's what you did tonight."

"It doesn't feel very noble," I say, shooting a glance toward what's left of the man I destroyed.

"It never does," he explains. "Lyra, you have to understand that, as shifters, the rest of us spend our lives preparing for our first shift. We have our families, the entire pack behind us, explaining how it happened for them and how to do it without feeling you're losing control. It takes years of guided training. You didn't even know you were a wolf until a few days ago. Your first shift shouldn't have happened without having more time to prepare."

"I'm not sure if that makes me feel better," I tell him.

"It should," he insists. "Most of us shift because it's our eighteenth birthday, and we're ready. This happened for you suddenly, out of fear, out of your base emotions of protection for the sister you love. Lyra, you saved her."

"I-I guess so."

"You did well," he continues. "Our guardsmen said that as soon as this man went down, the others stopped fighting and surrendered."

"Why?"

"He must have been in charge," he explains.

"He was their Alpha?" I look back at the pile of flesh and blood and have to fight back the bile rising in my throat.

"No, rogues don't have an Alpha," he explains. "But he was their leader of some sort. We'll talk to those who remain to find out for sure, but maybe he used to be an Alpha who was removed from his pack."

A soft voice rings out from the trees in front of us, and we both jerk our heads in that direction.

"I'm sorry to interrupt," Maggie says softly. "I brought you some clothes."

"Thank you, Maggie," I tell her, feeling tears welling in my eyes. "Are you and Oscar okay?"

She steps out from behind the bushes, a handful of folded clothes in her arms. "We're fine," she assures me. "I'll leave you to your Alpha King. We can talk later. But I do want you to know that you were very brave. I'm proud of you, Lyra."

I don't think I feel the same way, but I say, "Thank you."

She hands me the clothes and walks away, and Cassian helps me up and assists me while I put on my undergarments and a pants suit that I'd picked out for hiking in the woods. It feels so foreign all of a sudden, wearing human clothes.

"You see?" he says while putting a sock on me. "Maggie is right. What you did was brave. You saved lives by getting rid of that man. You even saved some of some of the rogues. They fought blindly and didn't even know what they were fighting for. Now, they've stopped, and we have given them some food and care."

"I want to see them," I tell him.

He wraps his fingers gently around mine. "Let's go."

It's hard to get used to the movement of my own legs after gliding around effortlessly on four paws. The ground is littered with broken bushes and tree branches that make up the path I originally followed going after Aisla—the path made by that awful man dragging her into the woods.

I nearly trip over a sharper stick, but Cassian steadies me. I gaze up into that caring look in his eyes, and I know that this man will always be my rock.

But then, we reach the clearing. I can't hold in a gasp, catching sight of what used to be our camp. It's torn to shreds, and there are bodies everywhere, with the thick scent of stale blood lingering in the air. Tents are shredded, and even some of our coaches are tipped over and broken.

But through it all, I sense peace right now. Everyone, even the rogues, are back in human form, dressed in ill-fitting clothes the Royal Guardsmen must have brought for themselves.

Several rogues solemnly drag their companions' bodies aside into a pile near the edge of the forest. Others sit on benches, their wounds tended by some of the guardsmen. Maggie walks along the row, handing a roll to each one.

They gorge on them the second they get them, like they haven't eaten in weeks.

"We lost no one," Cassian explains beside me, and I turn to face him. "These are just hungry wolves who were misled by that leader, whoever he was. We'll learn more about him soon, but for now, we just need to get everyone healed and fed.

I nod. "It's not their fault."

"No, it isn't," he agrees. "I've already messaged the castle. Snowthorne is sending wagons to pick them up, as well as resupplies for those tents and other things that were destroyed, and more food."

"You're a good man for feeding and caring for them," I tell him.

He smiles. "I learned it from you."

I want to kiss him, but with these people dealing with their dead, it's not the time or the place for that. I turn to gaze around the scene again. "I don't see Aisla or Mother."

"I've been told they're in that coach." He nods toward one that hasn't been tipped over. "Go see them. I have to lead the cleanup efforts."

I squeeze his hand and let go, feeling that familiar ache of parting from him, but I need to be sure Aisla is okay. I knock quietly on the coach door. "Can I come in?" I really don't know if they ever want to see me again.

"Yes, dear," Mother answers.

I slip inside without opening the door very wide since Aisla is holding a towel to her front, her backside exposed. Mother rubs a washcloth down her back, squeezing extra water into a basin beside her.

It's filled with blood.

I wince with guilt. I hope that in all my uncontrolled attacks, I didn't accidentally rip her with my claws.

"She's fine," Mother insists as though reading my mind. "She just got a lot of scratches from the sticks on the ground."

Relief washes over me, though my nerves rattle. "I'm sorry, Aisla." I can't believe I did that right in front of her. I can only imagine what she thought, watching me tear that man apart with my teeth. I wouldn't want to talk to me ever again, either.

But she breaks the silence with a soft smile, reaching for me while holding up the towel with her other arm. "Lyra, you saved me. I don't know what that man would have—" She shakes her head. "I don't even want to think about it. And I don't have to, because you stopped him before he had the chance to do anything."

"You don't think I'm a monster?" I ask shyly.

She giggles a little, and it's calming. "Of course not, silly. You saw what he was doing and pulled him away. You did what you had to do, and I'm very grateful."

She squeezes my hand, and now, I feel even more relieved. "I'm glad you don't hate me."

Another giggle escapes her. "Are you kidding? My sister is a badass Luna Queen with a wolf that can rip bad guys to shreds. I love you just as much as I always did, if not more. And I'm so proud of you."

I can't stop the tears from falling down my cheeks.

"Everything is okay," Mother insists. "You're finally getting to be what Chez tried to suppress, and I'm also proud of you."

I guess I still have a lot to learn about controlling my wolf, but I know Cassian will teach me. And now I know that my mother and sister will always support me.

The real me.

THE JOURNEY RESUMES

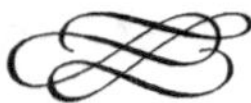

CASSIAN

I CAN FEEL LYRA'S RELIEF AS SHE SPEAKS WITH HER FAMILY. THERE'S NO doubt it was a brutal kill, but it's understandable with her lack of experience and the danger to her sister. I'm glad her mother and sister are supportive.

It makes it easier to get on with cleaning up this campsite. Supplies should reach us soon. Every minute we spend here is one more moment of delay in getting back to Oceana. I fear that what's going on there is dire.

We need to stop Assanan as soon as we can.

Everyone's exhausted. We've been up all night. 'The caravan of supplies will arrive by morning,' I tell my men in the mind-link. 'Everyone, get some rest. We'll want to leave as soon as we have restocked and are loaded up.'

With no tents left standing, the men spread out along the ground. Even a lumpy pile of earth is a comfortable mattress when exhaustion takes over. They position themselves in a circle around the rogues, though I doubt any of them will want to escape.

Their bellies are full, and they're safe. I don't think they've had this level of comfort in years.

Belfor has brought me up to speed with what he's learned after questioning the rogues. These people have families, for the most part, and there is a settlement of women and children to the west of this location.

Through the mind-link and Manning, who is still back in Snowthorne's castle, the king has agreed to handle the rogue community's migration to the castle, and these families will be reunited under better conditions soon... for those who survived the battle, anyway.

I turn my head to see Lyra finally exiting her family's coach.

"How is your sister?" I ask her.

She closes the distance between us in an instant, and I take her in my arms.

"She's okay," she answers. "She has a lot of deep scratches on her back from being... from being dragged through the forest. Mother cleaned them, and we applied bandages."

"She can return with the others to the castle if she wishes," I suggest.

She shakes her head while burrowing into my chest. "She refuses. She wants to come with us the whole way."

"As she wishes," I tell her. "Snowthorne is sending resupplies for the first aid kit as well, so we should be able to re-bandage her as needed." I stroke her soft hair, brushing it through my fingers. Everything about this woman feels so good, I can't even remember what life was like without her.

"That's good," she says softly.

"We should get some sleep," I tell her. "The ladies are safe in that coach. We'll be in another."

She lifts her head off my chest. "Where's Maggie?"

"Safe with her mate," I explain. "They went to a quiet place in the woods with privacy."

She nods. "She's safe then, too."

"I guarantee it." I take her hand and lead her toward our coach, one of those that was not damaged in the scuffle. "These vehicles aren't designed for sleeping, but they're private and quiet. We should be able to lie down on the floor."

When we get inside, it's a bit too cramped to stretch out, but I don't care as long as my mate is in my arms.

My lips find hers as soon as we lie down, and she responds enthusiastically, deepening the kiss. A sense of ease fills me, and the rest of the world disappears.

She speaks when we separate briefly to take a breath. "Are you sure sleeping is what you have in mind?" Her quiet giggles ring like music throughout the coach.

"Yes," I answer, though I kiss her again and let it linger. She needs the rest, but this feels so incredible, it's hard to stop.

"It doesn't seem like it." She giggles again as her hands begin to roam along my chest and down my abs.

But I stop them when she moves lower, wrapping my fingers in hers. "I would love nothing more than to rock this coach until it falls over in the night, but you've just had your first shift."

She pulls up, resting on her elbow, and her eyes meet mine. "I do feel tired, but I want you, Cassian."

"And I want you," I assure her. "But we'll be moving on at first light, which is in only a couple of hours. The ride will be bumpy. You won't get a chance to rest until we set up camp tomorrow night."

Her mouth falls into a crooked, pouty frown.

"If you don't rest after your first shift, you will be weaker the next time," I continue. "Goddess forbid we have any more surprises like that last one, but I want you strong and ready to shift in case you need to defend yourself."

She nods, though her eyes are filled with regret. "Will I be in control more next time?"

"I can't be sure," I answer honestly. "But I think you will be. You weren't expecting it tonight. But next time, if there's danger, you'll be more aware. Also, we'll work on shifting privately in a couple of days after you've had more rest. I'll help you gain more control of it."

"Okay." She moves in for one more kiss, and her scent and the feel of my tongue against hers soothes me. "Goodnight, Cassian."

"Goodnight, my Luna Queen Lyra."

She chuckles lightly then settles into me, her head relaxing against my chest, and I stroke her back lightly until her breathing is soft and steady. Her heartbeat thrums alongside mine, and I close my eyes, drifting off into a blissful sleep.

Lyra

IT HARDLY FEELS LIKE I'VE SLEPT AT ALL, BUT THE CAMPSITE IS ALREADY bustling with activity outside the coach, and the noise of it all wakes me up. It's clear that the reinforcements have arrived with our new supplies.

Cassian is already awake, but it seems like he's just lying still, trying not to wake me. "Good morning," he says, kissing me softly.

"Good morning," I say when we pull apart. "Though it wasn't much of a night." He's still cramped against the coach door with his legs bent, which must have been so uncomfortable.

"And that's why I wanted you to get some sleep," he says. "I'd better get out there."

"Me, too," I agree. "I want to check on Aisla."

Exiting the coach, I can instantly understand why it was so noisy. People are everywhere, loading and unloading cargo and moving the rogues into the wagons for their trip back to the castle, where they'll be cared for until Snowthorne sets up a settlement for them somewhere.

Cassian kisses me one more time before he goes off to direct the activity.

But I'm not alone for long. Mother and Aisla approach, and I give them both hugs, keeping my arms on Aisla's shoulders.

"These people need to be fed again," Mother insists.

"I agree," I tell her. "But we have an awful lot of people here."

Thankfully, one of the wagons at the end of the line is filled with fresh bread. Maggie joins the three of us while we hand out rations to all the people in the wagons as well as the Royal Guardsmen and Snowthorne's people who have come with us.

Even though I'm exhausted, the grateful look on the rogues' faces energizes me. It's probably only the second time they've had enough to eat in a long time, the first being last night after the battle.

Not long after, we're back in our coaches, some of which have been either repaired or replaced, with three wagons of supplies following our caravan.

I can tell Cassian is on edge about what could be happening back at the Oceana Castle. I'm concerned as well since Cally is still there.

I just hope she's safe.

Despite his worries, Cassian gives me a soft smile when I wrap my hand around his. But even in the comfort of his presence, I can't help but feel extra tense, not only about what's happening in Oceana, but also what might happen on the journey ahead.

Cassian seems fairly confident that I'll be able to control my wolf better the next time I shift. But I'm not so sure. For a while there, I wasn't myself at all. I felt nothing but instinct and rage. It's frightening.

He's assured me that's normal. I guess I'll have to wait until the next time I shift to find out. Hopefully, Cassian will have time to give me some training before any danger comes our way again.

As we set off on the road toward the mountains, all I can do is hope that the monster in me never takes over again.

I AM THE RED WOLF

Lyra

"Do you want to try tonight?"

I look away from Cassian's hopeful gaze. It's been two weeks since we were attacked and I'd shifted all of a sudden, so long that Aisla's wounds have actually healed, for the most part.

And every day as we get close to stopping to camp for the night, Cassian has asked me this same question. But each time, I've given him the same answer.

"I'm not ready."

"The further we go, the more likely it becomes that we'll run into more rogues or maybe another problem," he says, just like he does every day. "It would be better if you were used to shifting before that happens."

I'm about to answer when my mother speaks up from the back seat, which she doesn't usually do in this conversation. I guess she figures she doesn't have any say in the wolf part of me.

At least, not until now. "Lyra, you need to practice," she insists. "I can't pretend I know what that feels like, and I completely understand that you're frightened. But Cassian will be with you. And he's right. You need practice before you have to shift in an emergency situation again."

"We'll go somewhere away from all the others," Cassian adds. "No one will see it happen but us."

I bite my bottom lip, feeling a rock growing in my gut. They're right. I have to face this, eventually. "Okay," I tell them. "I'll try it tonight."

Cassian squeezes my hand gently. "There's nothing to be afraid of. I'll be right there."

I nod, knowing that is true, at least from an intellectual perspective. But my emotions are all over the place.

All I can think of is what could go wrong.

IT'S LATE EVENING, AND CASSIAN COMES UP TO ME AND GENTLY PLACES his firm hand on the small of my back. My body reacts, both with that familiar, pleasant tingle from his touch, but also with exaggerated tension.

Because I know it's time. I've got to try to shift again, whether I want to or not.

I nod and catch my mother's gaze, and she also tilts her head lightly in support. Aisla is too busy laughing with Maggie and the men while they roast leftover meat and vegetables over the open fire.

I slip away quietly. I don't want to trouble her with this.

Cassian is already carrying a bag of spare clothes. I don't want to strip naked before shifting. What if I can't do it? Then, I'm standing there in the forest naked for no reason. I'd feel like a fool.

But he said I might tear whatever I'm wearing, so tonight, I threw on some baggy cotton pants and a shirt I don't care about just in case.

He leads me away from the warm light of the campfire into the forest, where only the soft moonlight illuminates our path. It's a bit tricky to walk on, being in the middle of untamed wilderness, but

Cassian is patient and holds me steady while I negotiate all the bushes and fallen logs.

Finally, we reach a clearing, far enough away from the camp so no one can see us, yet we're close enough that I can still hear the jingle of Aisla's laughter. Good. I didn't distract her, and she can just continue to have fun.

While I face this.

"Are you okay?" Cassian asks.

"No," I answer honestly. "I can't believe I'm going to voluntarily turn into a horrible beast that kills people."

"That's not what your wolf is," he insists. "Okay. Let's start with that before you try to shift. Have a seat." He brushes some dirt off a log, though I don't care if these pants get dirty, and we both sit, his hand still protectively enveloped around mine. "I think we need to spend a little time rethinking your mindset," he says.

I jerk my head to face him, feeling insulted.

Apparently, that's clear in my expression, even in the moonlight. "I don't mean anything bad by that. What I mean is that all you're focused on is that one time you shifted. That time, you were scared for your sister and came to her rescue. Your wolf focused on the threat and eliminated it."

I let out a sarcastic laugh. "That's putting it mildly."

"I suppose it is." He softens his tone. "What I mean is that you have a perception of your wolf based on that one experience. But what you need to remember is that your wolf has been with you your entire life. She's been guiding you toward me. If you think about it, you'll realize that she's not evil or bad."

I let out a breath slowly. "That makes sense. I've always had this inner voice, something that was more like an instinct. I thought it was just me trying to make the right decisions."

"It was," he says. "She is you, and you are her. And together as one, you've always made decisions that were in the best interest of those around you, even if they didn't put you in the best position, like when you agreed to come to the castle of an awful Alpha King to become his bride."

I giggle at that.

"You'd better laugh," he warns, trying to stay serious but letting out a light chuckle. "Okay. So now you see that your wolf is an expression of your own emotions, just deeper. She's unselfish, just like you. She's caring, just like you. She protects those she loves, just like you."

I nod slowly. It's all making sense. "So, I tore up that man to protect Aisla."

"Exactly."

"But I went too far, and I couldn't stop," I add. "I'd like to think I'm not that ruthless."

"You're not," he insists. "In that case, you wolf couldn't stop because you weren't directing her. All we're going to do tonight is practice doing that. Tonight, you're not worried about the safety of anyone you love. It's just you and me, no threats. You're just going to shift and experience it... and learn how to redirect your wolf's emotions in the same way you do your own every day. Are you ready?"

"Yes," I say honestly. I guess I haven't given my wolf a break since my first shift. She was just trying to protect Aisla, the same thing I wanted to do.

And besides that, I haven't really given Mother or Aisla a break. I've been so worried they'd hate me because I'm a monster that I haven't paid attention to how grateful they were that I'd stopped what could have happened with that man.

Now, I'm going to learn how to do that.

"Okay," he begins. "Let's go over here."

We step to the center of the clearing, where the moonlight hits at an angle, almost silver as it glows against the forest. It feels sacred here out in nature, silent, yet teaming with life.

And I'm a part of that.

I'm a wolf, though it feels so foreign.

"Close your eyes to focus, and imagine your wolf," he says. "Bring her out from deep within."

I do as he instructs, but nothing happens at first.

"Go deeper," he says. "Find her and pull her out."

With my eyes still closed, I try to find the place where I always feel my wolf... when she's reacting to something happening to me, when Cassian touches me and she lights on fire.

There... I think I catch her, and though it feels strange, I somehow take hold of her spirit and pull on it, helping her grow.

Seconds later, I feel that ache in my bones as they transform my body.

"That's good," Cassian says, encouraging me. "Now, open your eyes."

When I do, he's up higher than usual, and I know I've shifted. I'm closer to the ground, and the world is sharper, crisper. I look down at my paws. This time, they aren't covered in blood. They're clean and fluffy, full of dark red fur.

'Is my coat all the same shade of red?' I ask him in the mind-link.

"Yes," he says out loud. "Your eyes are deeper green. All of it is you, but more you, your natural state of being. And it's the most beautiful thing I've ever seen."

He pulls what's left of my clothes away from me, and I feel free. In an instant, he has shifted too, his white wolf standing by me protectively, the tips of his fur shimmering almost as silver as his bright eyes.

'You see?' he says in the mind-link now. 'You're not evil. You're just... you. Come. Follow me.'

Before I have a chance to ask where we're going, he runs away from me, and I follow on instinct. I see the fallen trees and poky sticks and bushes long before I need to make my leap. And I clear each one easily, effortlessly.

Everything is so clear, bright... even the smells all around us. I sense movement... small animals, insects everywhere.

The forest is alive for me.

A sense of bliss overwhelms me as we power through the forest, slower at first, but then Cassian picks up speed, and I follow him easily, as if the entirety of nature belongs to us, and we belong to it.

I'm aware of everything... the camp's location, where we are relative to where we started, and I sense that he has circled around toward the clearing where we began.

I don't want the feeling of freedom, running blissfully through nature, to ever end. But I also want to learn more, to feel more, to shift back and forth a hundred times until it feels just as natural as being with Cassian.

Back in the clearing, we stop, and he rubs his nuzzle against mine. 'Okay, shift back,' he says.

I reach in and pull back my 'human me' easier now, feeling the change come over me.

"That was incredible!" I exclaim when I return to human form, not even caring that I'm standing here naked in the forest. Cassian is in front of me, his muscular frame glowing softly in the moonlight.

"Yes, it was," he says.

"I was in complete control," I add.

He nods. "Because you weren't in any emotional distress. We'll keep practicing, shifting back and forth so you get used to it. Then, we'll work on different means of control."

We shift and run again, and there's nothing more exhilarating than feeling the light thump of my paws against the moist earth as we sprint through the forest.

Cassian lets out an enthusiastic howl, and I join him, blissfully enjoying this new part of me that's been with me from the moment I was born.

Yes, I am a wolf!

POWER OF THE GODDESS

CASSIAN

EVERY DAY, I'VE BEEN GRATEFUL THAT NO OTHER ROGUES OR OTHER surprises have yet decided to slow us down, but I know my luck is probably going to run out.

I'm especially concerned now that there are so few of us making the trek up the mountain. I've tried to convince Lyra's mother and sister to wait behind at the base camp, but they aren't having it.

I left Belfor in charge of the camp, confident that he can manage the supply rations as well as coordinate runners to communicate with us up on the mountain. It has been days since they set up camp, a large cluster of tents covering a clearing just at the base of the mountain.

The rest of us trudge on; just me, Lyra, her mother and sister, the High Priestess, and two Royal Guardsmen for added protection.

Thankfully, the terrain isn't horrible, but it's a bit of a challenge for a human princess and queen, though they both try to downplay it.

"We can rest, if you like," I suggest. "But we shouldn't linger long."

"I'm fine," Iridessa insists.

"You should at least stop and take a drink, Mother," Lyra says. "We've been walking for quite a while now."

"I'm only stopping if the rest of you are," the queen says.

I nod firmly. "Then we shall do so."

We settle onto fallen logs in a clearing, and Lyra distributes small rations of water to everyone in thin metal cups. I take note of the sun's location in the sky to be sure we don't dally long, but I have to admit, the cool water is refreshing.

Moments after, I sense a presence. The Royal Guardsmen flick their gazes toward me, and I nod to indicate that I've noticed it. I'm proud to see Lyra looking at me with wide eyes, having also detected the intruder.

'Gather together,' I say to all who can hear me in the mind-link, and they do so.

Silanya puts her hand up and remains standing in the center of the clearing while the others gather together near the makeshift benches.

The crackling of sticks and brush underfoot announces the arrival of a beast so large, it has no need for stealth. Soon, we catch sight of him, a giant grizzly bear thumping out of the forest.

The human ladies let out involuntary gasps, having not expected him and certainly not being comfortable around a beast of such immense size. His paws are larger than our heads, and he stands several feet high even with all paws down.

Yet the High Priestess holds her ground.

"He's not a shifter," she confirms, her voice soothing.

I hadn't even considered the fact. I've heard of those who shift into other creatures besides wolves, but none have ever been in Oceana or nearby kingdoms. I'd thought them to be just fairytales, but perhaps not.

"He's a creature of the forest, and we are near his home," Silanya continues. Her hands move gracefully, and sparkles of silver fly off them in a mist toward the bear. "This will reassure him that we are only passing through."

The bear does seem to calm, even setting his giant body down on the edge of the forest. Silanya approaches him, her hand outstretched, chanting in the ancient language of the Moon Goddess.

Hardly any of us breathe as she approaches the beast, reaching forward and petting its neck as the bear leans into her touch. After a moment, she releases him, and he stands and disappears into the forest, the bushes seeming to part for his giant form.

"That was amazing," Aisla whispers when he's completely out of sight.

"The Moon Goddess connects with all creatures of the forest," Silanya explains. "She chose the wolf as the spirit animal of our people because of their connection to the moon, but others have similar souls."

"That's incredible," the queen says.

"We should get moving," I suggest.

Everyone rises, and we continue our journey up the mountain toward the seal. Lyra holds back, walking next to the High Priestess. I don't doubt she has questions, and Silanya is a good choice for those answers.

I continue forward, a new worry festering in my mind. Though it is a relief to see that Silanya has dominion over so many wild creatures of the forest, some of her words trouble me.

There are other shifters around, perhaps in these very woods, who transform into creatures other than wolves.

Wolf rogues, I can handle. But fighting against something new could be a problem for me and the guardsmen. We wouldn't know their moves or their capabilities.

All I can do is hope we have no more surprises.

LYRA

WE CONTINUE OUR JOURNEY UP THE MOUNTAIN FOR A FEW MORE HOURS before I finally have the nerve to ask Silanya. "How did you do that?"

She stops in her tracks, observing me with a calming smile. "It is a gift from the Moon Goddess," she explains. "It is one for which all the priestesses study many hours a day for many years."

"I can imagine," I tell her, and we continue walking so we don't get too far behind the others. "It's really amazing. I'd love to do that."

"As a Luna, you cannot become a High Priestess," she says. "But Lunas have powers of their own that we in the temples cannot emulate."

"Powers?" I doubt I can do anything past turning into a wolf, which, I admit, is pretty amazing. I certainly can't charm creatures in the forest. "What kind of powers?"

"Each Luna comes into different powers of her own," she explains. "You will not know yours until the time has come."

"Oh." I frown. "Well, maybe I won't have any since I'm only half wolf. Most Lunas are pure wolf shifters, aren't they?"

She nods, ignoring my insecurities. "Usually, yes," she says. "But you are clearly chosen by the Moon Goddess. I'm sure She will bless you with a power that will help your people."

My people—I'm not sure if that's Maelie or Oceana anymore. Maybe it's both. But I can't imagine any power that will help them.

"Is opening this key a power?" I ask. "Maybe that's all I'm meant to do, if it works, that is."

"I am confident it will," she tells me. "But I do not believe it is the only power you possess. Visions have told me otherwise."

I put a hand on her shoulder without really meaning to, and she stops. "You've had visions about me?"

"I have visions about all those who influence the people of the Moon Goddess," she says. "And these are sacred things I cannot share. But I do not know what your power will be, if that is your next question."

It was, of course.

"The visions are vague, and I must interpret them," she adds.

I nod. "Thank you for telling me this," I say. "And for letting me read the tome. I have a lot more to study from it on the way back."

"It is yours to peruse at your leisure," she says. "The translated version that you have now is always available to all."

"Translated?"

"Yes, the original is in the Moon Goddess's ancient language, Goslevaere."

"Oh, so that's all the chants and the writing I see," I say, looking down so I don't trip over a rock that's suddenly in front of me.

"Yes, that's correct."

"I'd like to learn it someday, if that's possible," I tell her.

"I'd be happy to teach you."

We fall into silence as we continue climbing the huge mountain toward the seal, wherever that might be, far above us at its peak.

I can't help but feel nervous about whether or not I can open the key, and I'm also excited about the idea that as a Luna, I may have a power that could do some good in the world.

I can't wait to find out what that is.

CAVE OF THE MOON GODDESS

CASSIAN

NATURALLY, THERE'S NO SIGNPOST THAT READS "SECRET SEAL THIS WAY" once we reach the mountain peak. We have to rely on the High Priestess to determine its exact location, something she must do through private chants and prayers to the Moon Goddess, asking Her to send her a vision.

For this, she steps away from us into the forest. Everyone is resting, and Lyra has handed out cups of water again. With the air thinner up here, it's harder to take a full breath, even for me.

Lyra approaches, her eyes weary. "We're running low," she tells me.

"The runner should reach us later today," I respond. "He'll have some limited supplies, water among them."

"Good." She blinks slowly a few times, her eyes red from exhaustion.

"Come here," I tell her, placing my hand on her soft lower back and leading her toward a boulder that will make a decent place to sit. "You need some rest before we go on."

She nods softly and sits next to me, stretching her arms high before leaning on my shoulder. We're silent for several moments, watching the glimmers of the High Priestess's robes through the bright green bushes.

"Do you think she'll get an answer?" she asks.

"I'm sure she will," I reply. "She's had visions of us coming up here, so I doubt the Moon Goddess would have us come all the way up here for nothing."

She sits up straight suddenly, and I instantly miss her warmth on my shoulder. "She told you about the visions? I thought she couldn't do that."

"Not exactly," I explain. "It's true that the visions are sacred and best kept only to the High Priestesses. But they can give some general guidance. From what she did tell me, I just assumed she'd seen us here."

"So maybe she won't get an answer." Her tired face lowers into a frown.

"It's not a zero possibility, no," I confirm. "But I have to believe that since Assanan has the Amulet of Darkness, the Moon Goddess wants us to have the Amulet of Light."

"I think so, too, but I'm not certain," she says. "It's just really hard to believe that I'm meant to help unseal something so important."

I use both arms to pull her back into me again. "You most certainly are," I assure her. "You're special, Lyra, and together, we're going to save our people."

"I hope so."

We're quiet again, and she nuzzles closer into my chest, to the delight of my wolf. Lovemaking hasn't been easy on this trip. Lyra keeps pulling away, always worried about somebody hearing us in the tents nearby.

Though I've assured her that no one would blame two mates for expressing their bond, she keeps insisting she can't do it around her mother.

It makes me laugh, but all I want to do is rip off Lyra's dress and show her how I feel about her.

But now is not the time, especially since the High Priestess has returned from her prayers. Lyra jumps to her feet before I have a chance to get up myself.

"The Goddess has blessed me with an answer," Silanya says quickly before any of us have a chance to ask. "The seal is a mile away, that direction." She extends a slender arm toward the east. "There is a cave entrance hidden in a copse of trees. In it, we will find the seal."

"Let's go." I hardly need to give the order because Lyra is already walking that way, and all the others are following.

Even in this rough terrain, one mile is close. I feel the tension running through my nerves, filled with anxious hope that we find the damn thing quickly so we can get back to Winterhelm and then set sail for Oceana.

Every extra second this trip takes means more danger to our people.

I reach out to the runner in the mind-link to give him our new location.

Thankfully, we make good time, and a thick area of trees and brush sits directly in front of us. "Check there," I order the guardsmen.

"Aye."

They make quick work of pressing the bushes aside. The High Priestess has warned us against damaging the greenery that protects the seal's cave.

"An opening, Alpha King!" one of the men calls out shortly.

I take Lyra's hand and follow the men into the thick brush. It turns out to be not much of an opening, just enough for us to crawl through.

Lyra's mother and sister approach, but Silanya puts up her arm. "I am afraid that only those blessed by the Moon Goddess can enter."

Lyra looks at her with a furrowed brow. "Not even my own mother?"

Silanya shakes her head. "I'm afraid not. This cave is sacred and could be dangerous to those of pure human blood."

"It's okay, Lyra," the queen says. She reaches out her arms and draws her daughter in for an embrace. "We'll wait out here with the guards. This is something you and Cassian need to do together. Just know that we are out here supporting you both."

"Thank you, Mother." Lyra pulls out of the hug and embraces her sister before they turn and follow the guards out to the clearing, leaving only us and the High Priestess for this leg of the journey.

"I'll go first," I insist.

I consider shifting, since this entrance is the perfect size, about the width of a wild wolf den, but decide against it with the clothing issue problematic since Lyra's family is here.

The cave is old, dark, and covered in spiderwebs, which I clear away as I crawl forward. Its dirt floor is dry, but in some places, water seeps through the sides, making my shirt wet as I crawl through and giving the cave a musty smell.

Lyra follows right behind me, and I feel her warm presence as we crawl deeper.

"Are you sure this is the place?" I ask after a long while.

"It is," Silanya confirms from behind Lyra.

"It's dark," I tell her. "I can't see in front of me."

"This will continue for a while, but you will soon see illumination ahead," Silanya explains. "That is the chamber of the seal."

Sure enough, I see a glow ahead of me eventually, first blue, then turning silvery and brighter as we get closer. The circular exit is clear just up ahead.

"About ten more yards," I tell them.

"Good," Lyra says. "Because this place is making me claustrophobic."

I chuckle at the irritation in her voice, but I do regret that she has to crawl through this dirty cave this way. But finally, we reach the end.

The narrow cave opens to a wide room, glistening with some sort of crystals that glow all around us. I step out and turn to assist Lyra and Silanya as they exit the crawlspace.

"Wow," Lyra says, brushing the dirt off her palms.

I have to say, I agree.

"We have reached the chamber of the seal," Silanya announces, though it's clear by its ethereal glow that we have reached a place that is sacred to the Moon Goddess.

I just hope we can open that seal.

RITUAL OF THE KEY

Lyra

It's hard to move from this spot. Crawling through the cramped, dirty cave entrance, I'd thought the end of it would just be a box or something that we'd have to carry back out to open. For a while there, I was wondering how we were going to even turn around.

But this place... it's huge. We must be a hundred feet underground to have the ceilings this high. The chamber is as big as the ballroom in the Maelie castle and far more impressive.

The walls are covered top to bottom in some sort of blue crystals that shine almost silver, the kind of twinkling light that Silanya used when she charmed the grizzly bear. The floor is solid stone—marble, I think, judging by the silver and blue veining meandering through it.

To the right of us is a gently trickling waterfall coming right out of the wall. It flows into a small creek that splits the chamber in half, its water so clear I can see every detail of the stone beneath it.

Other than that, the chamber looks empty. Cassian verbalizes my first question before I have a chance. "Where's the seal?"

We both turn to Silanya, who is dusting dirt off her shoulder. She looks up at us and smiles, with that calm, serene look she almost always carries.

I wish I could be so relaxed about everything.

"Revealing the seal requires a ritual," she explains, pulling out a small book from somewhere in her robes. "We'll begin now. Please stand by the sacred waters."

I look at Cassian, who shrugs and takes my hand, leading me over to the waterfall.

"One of you on either side, please," Silanya asks.

Cassian drops my hand and leaps over the small creek, backing up to stand against the wall by the waterfall while I do the same on the other side.

Silanya begins chanting in that beautiful language of the Moon Goddess, Goslevaere. I'm looking forward to learning some of those words someday so I can speak and write it as well.

"*Onveare, glacoun, omleveare,*" she repeats several times, her voice nearly ethereal, echoing throughout the chamber hauntingly.

I catch a hint of movement in the corner of my eye and turn to the waterfall, which has stopped pouring out and is now fading into a blue mist that floats for a moment before swirling into a vortex between Cassian and me.

With more chants from Silanya, the vortex spins faster. Honestly, I start to get a little worried as it grows bigger.

But then, quicker than it turned into a mist, it dissipates, leaving a giant, shimmering silver plaque where the waterfall once flowed out of the wall.

The seal.

The creek has also disappeared, so Cassian steps over to me, putting a protective arm around my shoulder. "How do we open it?" he asks.

"That is the ritual of the key," Silanya replies, turning to another page in her book. "This has never been tried in known history, so we may not be successful at first. Try standing just in front of the seal to start, holding hands."

Cassian drops his hands from my shoulders and slips his hand into mine, his being warm and strong, steadying my shaking nerves... for the most part.

What if we came all this way, and this doesn't work?

Silanya starts chanting again. I try to catch some of the words, but the vowels and consonants blend together on her tongue so easily, it's hard to catch them.

Sparkles of light come out of her right hand, aimed at the seal. I hold my breath, and the delicate twinkles make their way to the heart of the seal.

But nothing happens.

"This attempt was a failure," she says.

It's hard to swallow with the thick lump growing in my throat. This has to work. It has to.

If we don't come back with the Amulet of Light, Assanan will win. He'll overrun the Oceana castle, and I can't even think about what might become of Cally, Cassian's mother, and everyone else who is there.

He's an evil man, and he will take over all of Oceana. It's easy to imagine what that kind of power will do to make him even more evil than he is now.

After what he did to my mother... he could become something even worse.

A shiver erupts over me.

"Both of you, try touching the seal," Silanya suggests, breaking me out of those horrifying thoughts.

We step closer to the seal, our hands still firmly grasping each other, and touch the outside of it with our free hands. This should work. I think. At least, it seems like it should.

Silanya repeats the chants again. This time, I don't pay attention. I focus all my energy on the seal in front of us, begging it to open. Maybe we have to will it to happen, and it'll work.

But it doesn't.

Silanya finishes the chant and sends forth the sparkles, but nothing opens the seal. She sighs, her face contorting into a frown, something I've never seen on her.

"I do not understand why this isn't working," she says. "I've studied this ritual extensively. The words in the chant are correct."

"Maybe they should be in a different order?" Cassian suggests.

Silanya shakes her head. "The sentences are clear," she says. "Perhaps it's your positioning."

"It makes sense to do it this way," Cassian says. "We've joined hands, and we're touching the seal."

They continue to discuss different possible ways we should stand, or sit, or squat, or lie down, or close our eyes—

"Maybe we need to shift."

They both stop talking and look at me.

"Maybe we need to be in our wolf forms," I repeat.

"That's it!" Cassian says, taking off his shirt and ready to try anything.

"I believe so," Silanya agrees with a firm nod.

Cassian removes his pants in front of the High Priestess like it's nothing, leaving him in his boxers. I look at him with a raised brow.

"It's okay," he says. "As shifters, nudity is not as troubling as it seems to be between humans. Plus, we don't have extra clothes, so we'll need these intact for when we exit the cave."

I hadn't thought of that.

I suppose, if he can strip in front of Silanya, I certainly can, so I do it too. I close my eyes, willing myself to shift. Before I know it, I open my eyes to see my paws beneath me, and all my senses come alive. The cavern has a strong scent of pine and sage, something I hadn't noticed before.

And while I thought the walls were full of crystals before, now, there are thousands of tiny ones I hadn't seen before, echoing the look of the billions of stars in the night sky.

It's beautiful.

Cassian and I both take our places in front of the seal, standing on our hind legs to each place a paw on it as Silanya begins the ritual.

Her chants sound even more powerful to my wolf ears, like a call from the Goddess Herself.

When Silanya sends forward the sparkles of light, the mist returns, this time blue and purple, swirling around in front of the seal. This hadn't happened before.

This is working!

When the mist clears, there's an opening in the center of the seal. Silanya approaches and reaches in, pulling out what looks like a large, silver jewelry box.

Cassian and I shift back. He throws on his pants, and I quickly slip my clothes on before stepping over to Silanya as she opens the box.

A glittering necklace lights up all the crystals in the room even brighter, its large blue stone at the center pulsating along with the rest.

The Amulet of Light is ours.

AMBUSHED

Cassian

Silanya holds the box open with the bejeweled amulet. I've never seen anything like it, even among my family's crown jewel collection.

The chain of the necklace is made of moonstones, each one intricately carved into the shape of a diamond or star. These lead down to an oversized broach in the center, one large blue stone that I don't recognize surrounded by precious gems of all colors.

We're all mesmerized for a moment at the sight of it until a sound starts gurgling up from the wall behind the seal.

"Step away," Silanya warns.

I take Lyra's hand and do so, and within seconds, the seal is completely gone, with the waterfall pouring out in its place again. Crisp, clear water flows down into the stone creek bed.

"The seal will remain, should we ever need to conceal the amulet again," Silanya explains before we ask.

I nod. "Hopefully, we won't need it for long."

She closes the box and hands it to me. "I think it will be safest in the Alpha King's hands for now. But when it comes time for its use, I believe it is the Luna who must wear it."

"Me?" Lyra asks. "Why?"

"It is just my feeling," Silanya says. "I will do more research. But I do believe that soon it will become clear how to use the sacred amulet."

"Well, for now, we need to get it out of here and back to Oceana," I say. "Let's go." I tuck it into my waistband to keep it from prying eyes and lead the ladies toward the exit. "The guardsmen are outside. I'd feel better bringing up the rear in case there's something we don't know about in here."

This chamber could be home to some wild animals that might come up the narrow cave behind us.

Lyra nods and takes the lead, though I would have preferred she stay closer to me. I just keep telling myself it will only be a few minutes before we reach the outside and that my guardsmen are already there standing watch for when she exits.

Silanya follows, and I give her a few moments to get a bit ahead of me before crawling in myself.

I'd forgotten how cramped the tunnel was, having enjoyed plenty of space in the chamber of the amulet. It's slow-going, and the cave turns almost pitch-black, but before long, I can see the ladies' shadows against the bright sunlight ahead.

"No!"

Lyra's sudden scream sends a cold shiver down my spine, and I see her snatched roughly out of the tunnel. My blood goes cold. I want Silanya to move so I can kill whatever bastard was stupid enough to dare touch my Luna, but she freezes instead.

'What happened?' I ask Silanya in the link.

'There are men outside,' she answers. 'At least twenty of them. They are holding her mother and sister.'

'Exit,' I order her. 'We'll deal with all of them quickly enough once I can shift.'

She obeys, quickly moving toward the exit, where another man grabs her and pulls her out. I look down at the amulet box tucked into my pants. If I shift now, I'll drop it, and these men will get it.

I have to play it cool, no matter how much rage is boiling inside me.

I slap their hands away when the bastards try to pull me out. I make quick work of landing on my feet outside the cave entrance, my palm on the amulet box just to be sure I haven't dropped it.

"Alpha King Cassian," one of the assholes says, "it's good to meet you in person."

The tall, lanky man is wearing the colors of Assanan's kingdom.

I snarl as I catch sight of Lyra, her hands held behind her back by a smirking man who is as good as dead for touching her. "Let her the fuck go," I order in my Alpha voice.

All the bastard does is laugh. I flick my eyes around to take in the scene. The Royal Guardsmen are shackled, and I don't understand why they're still in human form and not shifted and ripping everyone's heads off. Lyra's mother and sister are near her, shackled as well, and the High Priestess is struggling against the man who just pulled her out of the cave.

"All we need is the amulet, Alpha King," the asshole closest to me says dryly. "And none of them will be harmed, at least, not today."

I'm more than glad that Silanya suggested I hold it. Better me than them searching Lyra....

I reach out to my runner in the mind-link. 'Return to base camp. Get everyone up here and ready to fight.'

'Aye,' the man replies.

"You get nothing," I say out loud. "And you release them all before I tear your heads off and feed them to the wild creatures."

He laughs, a loud cackle that grates on my nerves.

"You've been busy," he says. "You haven't been out here for us to grace you with our newfound powers. Allow me to demonstrate."

He makes a gesture that looks like a pointed finger, but I can see a flicker of something metal hidden in his hand. He aims it at one of his own guards.

The man's eyes go wide. "No! Please!" he screams. But any other words are lost to the wind as the man starts... disintegrating, for lack of a better word, until all that remains of him is dust on the forest floor.

What kind of a monster does that to his own warrior?

This asshole is just as evil as Assanan himself.

He chuckles as if happy with the result. "He was a slacker anyway," he says, as though anything could justify the horror. "Now, we wouldn't want the Luna Queen to meet the same fate, would we?"

I growl, feeling the tips of my fangs protruding slowly. "Don't you dare fucking touch her."

The asshole moves closer. "I don't need to touch her to make her disappear from this plane. Now, hand it over."

'Don't, Cassian!' Lyra begs in the mind-link. 'There's no defeating them if we don't have the amulet.'

'I will not lose you!' I argue, pulling out the jewelry box and handing it to the dickhead. 'We'll get it back later. Backup is on the way.'

She says nothing more but gives me a slight nod.

The asshole in front of me opens the box, letting out a long whistle. "My, but it is a pretty piece, isn't it?" he says with a smirk. "My Alpha King will have a joy of a time destroying it." He turns to his men. "Release them."

The moment the man lets go of Lyra, she runs into my arms. "We can't let this happen," she whispers into my ear.

"I know," I reply simply.

The piece of shit man slips the jewelry box into a backpack that's already strapped onto the back of a shifted warrior. "It's been lovely doing business with you, but I'm afraid we're in a bit of a hurry."

He shifts, and the rest follow, and they run off down the mountain into the woods.

Lyra looks toward her mother, so I let go of her so she can check on them. "Mother, Aisla! Are you okay?" she cries.

They assure her they are fine, but my attention turns to Silanya, who is chanting and swinging her arms in a graceful swirl, building a sparkling mist in front of her. I stand back as she pushes it forward into the forest where the men have disappeared.

Whatever it is, I hope it helps.

She shifts into a pure silver wolf, but before I shift, I approach Lyra. "Stay here with them," I tell her.

"No!" she replies defiantly. "I'm shifting and coming with you!"

"It's too dangerous," I warn her.

"And I don't care!" she snaps. "We are in this together, Cassian. It's my... it's my evil father behind all of this. I *will* be a part of putting a stop to him. We can't let him have the amulet."

Reluctantly, I turn to one of my guardsmen and order him to stay with the woman. Lyra and I shift, and we follow Silanya's wolf into the forest.

I don't like it, but Lyra is right. Whatever happens from now on, we are in it together.

No matter how much it terrifies me to lead her into danger.

NO CHOICE

Lyra

There are times when I wish I'd never opened my mouth. Now is one of those times when we're chasing a pack of wolves with some sort of power to dissolve people in an instant.

I'd insisted on coming, demanded it, in fact, telling Cassian that we were in this together. I know we are, but I can't help the fear that's crawling up my nerves as my paws pound the forest floor beneath me.

I don't know if I'm built for this kind of thing. At least, I have no formal training in fighting. I don't know what in the world I thought I was going to do when we confronted them. I guess I should have Cassian teach me how to fight sooner rather than later.

If we live through this.

But we have to. The only way we can beat that awful Assanan is if we have the Amulet of Light. I don't know how he got the darkness power, but I can't think of a worse person to wield it.

Fear or no fear, I have to help Cassian get the amulet back.

Cassian runs ahead of me, along with the one Royal Guardsman who came along while the other stayed back with my mother and sister. I'm thankful that someone is there for them. They must be terrified.

I know I am.

Cassian runs like a hurricane-force wind. When we were frolicking in the forest in our wolf forms before, he stayed right beside me. But now, he's showing his true skill because he can't hold back just for me.

He has to catch these people.

Silanya's silver wolf streaks through the forest beside me. I was in awe when I saw her transform. She's pure silver, gleaming against the landscape with a sparkling mist surrounding her. Her irises are like crystals, pure white.

I know she sent some magic in the forest in front of her, and I sure hope it's something that can help us. She hasn't had time to explain.

'They're ahead by fifty yards or so,' Cassian tells me in the mind-link.

I'm surprised when Silanya answers. I didn't think she could communicate with us, being from another kingdom, which I suppose is called a pack from a wolf's point of view.

'I was able to call the forest creatures for help,' she tells us. 'I've asked them to set up a blockade ahead of them. We should catch up soon.'

'Excellent,' is all Cassian says before closing the mind-link.

And now that I'm not connected with Silanya, I can't ask her any questions, like what a bunch of little forest creatures are going to do to block a pack of wolves who are barreling through the forest with the Amulet of Light.

But I suppose I'll find out when we get there.

That happens sooner than I expect. I hear snarling up ahead, followed by yelps and wolf screams, which are actually pretty terrifying. We catch up with Cassian and the guardsman. Cassian already has blood dripping from his fangs from taking out the wolves near the back of the pack.

But we have at least eighteen left to go.

Cassian opens the mind-link again, and this time, I can somehow tell that Silanya and the guardsman are included. 'Be safe,' he says to me first. 'Don't engage unless one comes at you. If they do, go for their neck. You'll be able to sense where the carotid artery is as you move in.'

'Okay,' I say.

'Hang back,' he adds. 'Our reinforcements will be here soon.'

Silanya chimes in. 'I do not believe they can activate their disintegration powers in wolf form. It seems to require a device.'

'I caught that,' Cassian says. 'He was trying to hide it, but there was something shiny in his hand when he pointed. If anyone shifts, take them out.'

'Okay,' I say again, deciding that will be my job. I feel a lot more confident attacking someone in human form.

There's no way I'm going to let them use that device on Cassian, Silanya, or anyone. I can't believe that man would use it on his own men. It's horrifying. And it's a glimpse of what the whole world will be like if Assanan takes over with his dark power.

We have to stop that now.

I slow down as we reach the wolves, watching Cassian rip the necks out of the slow ones running in the back of the pack. It should terrify me. It does, but I know what's at stake. It's them or the entire kingdom of Oceana.

Silanya joins him with elegant grace. Yet, her wolf is just as brutal as Cassian when it comes to making the kill.

I'm still not sure I can do that.

Everything stops cold up ahead—no fighting, no running, just a stand off with Cassian at the front. I pad up quietly behind him.

Even in my wolf form, I feel my eyes go wide when I see the scene before me. A row of giant grizzly bears, about the size of the one that was in the clearing before—along with angry mountain lions—has stopped the awful pack of wolves in their tracks.

I suppose these are the forest creatures Silanya was talking about. I guess they're not so small.

Silence echoes around us. Even with my wolf's sharp senses, I can barely hear anything but the smallest of insects hopping around on nearby leaves. Even the birds are silent and have either flown off or sit still as statues in the trees above.

In the next moment, there's chaos. Bears and mountain lions attack wolves. Cassian, Silanya, and the guardsman rip through some of the wolves, but others look like they're more formidable enemies that know how to fight.

I'm just standing here frozen. I don't know what to do. I should jump into the fray, but I'll probably get myself killed before I even figure out where that carotid artery is that I'm supposed to be aiming for.

I can't do this.

I can't.

Every nerve in my body is screaming for Cassian. I want him to stop fighting. I don't want him to die this way. I want him to come hold me and tell me that everything is okay.

I'm definitely not built for fighting.

But then I see it. One of the wolves sneaks over to the side, away from the others. He starts to shift, and I recognize his face even before it's fully formed. It's the man who disintegrated his fellow warrior.

Oh, no.

I glance back at Cassian, and he's too busy to notice. They all are. I'm the only one who sees the man as he grabs something out of the backpack that used to be strapped to him before he shifted.

An icy chill runs down my spine. He's reaching for whatever it is he used to disintegrate that man, and he's going to use it on Cassian.

I can't let him get it.

I don't care what I'm built for anymore. I don't care that I don't know how to fight. I'm the only one who can stop this man, so I have no choice.

I tear through the forest toward him and push off in a flying leap, aiming for his throat.

LITTLE BRAVE

Cassian

I don't have time to think about what all the wild animals are doing or why they've agreed to fight on our behalf. I'm just glad they're here. My warriors are approaching, but there's no time to wait for them. We need to end this now and get the amulet back.

The weak wolves toward the back of the pack were easy to dispose of. It seemed as if they had no training at all, being too slow to react.

But these wolves, the ones protecting the pack with the amulet, are proving harder to dispatch. Without the extra help, it would have been a challenge for us to keep up. But now, Silanya, my guardsman, and I are holding our own.

I've lost track of Lyra, and I hope she listened to me. I haven't had a single moment to train her to fight. I didn't think it was necessary since I can handle rogues by myself. I believed it was enough to help her get accustomed to shifting and feeling the sensations of just being a wolf.

But I'll start training her as soon as we get through this.

I have just dispatched another formidable opponent when I hear a twig break. I turn to see the asshole who took the amulet, the one who killed his own man, is standing in full human form, completely naked, his hand outstretched in my direction, though it's currently pointed slightly above my position.

The next moments happen in slow motion as though time itself has stopped. Lyra, in her sleek and stunning red wolf form, is wrapping her sharp fangs firmly around the man's neck. Simultaneously, he lets loose with whatever it is he's holding in his hand, and a beam shoots in our direction, though it misses by several feet.

I follow the beam as it flies past into the forest behind the fray. A loud boom echoes around us as no less than four trees completely disintegrate, the pure dust that remains floating to the ground.

In shock for a split second, I hesitate for a moment before dropping the corpse of the wolf I just attacked and rushing to Lyra's side. She stands there, still in her wolf form, breathing heavily, her fangs dripping with blood.

'It's okay,' I tell her in our private mind-link. 'You did well, Lyra. You were so brave. You saved us.'

My gaze flicks over to the man, who lies dead and bleeding on the ground next to her. A shiny object glints silver in the sun—the deadly device. It's slender, surprisingly small, narrower than the man's finger but filled with the power to instantly kill.

I turn toward the rest of his wolves, who have all lowered themselves onto their front paws, their heads down in the sign of surrender.

A fearsome pack of wolves bursts out of the forest beside us—my warriors.

'Arrest them,' I tell them. 'Let none escape. And bring clothes for your Luna.'

One of the men drops a backpack next to me as I shift, grab the backpack and the device in the man's hand, and turn to my wife. "Lyra," I say.

It seems to snap her out of her daze, her eyes locking with mine.

"It's over," I tell her softly. "You did it. Let's get you to some privacy where you can shift back."

But she doesn't move, still in shock.

"Lyra," I repeat. "Come on." I nudge her lightly, and she turns robotically and steps behind some bushes with me. "You can shift back now," I tell her gently.

It takes a moment, but she closes her eyes and shifts back, her slender, perfect naked body shivering as she crouches down, wrapping her arms around herself. I pull her in, trying my best to ground her with my embrace, feeling her shattered nerves calming slightly at my touch.

We stay here for several moments, not speaking, with me just holding her, until her arms loosen and she reaches for the clothes I've pulled from the bag for her. I help her dress, her hands shaking, then pull her next to me again, kissing the top of her head.

"You did it, Lyra," I tell her repeatedly. "You saved us all."

"I—" She finally speaks. "You were busy. I saw him reach for it. I had to stop him. I had to."

"Yes," I agree. "Yes, you did. It's okay. We're safe now."

Lyra

I still don't feel completely like myself, but Cassian's touch is calming. I don't know how long I stood there staring at the man I killed. And I have no idea how long I leaned naked into Cassian's arms in the middle of the forest.

But what I did was real. We're alive. We are safe.

And now, I just want to go home.

After throwing on some clothes, I start to walk, and he keeps one arm around me. The forest is a mess of blood and bodies, some wolves, some bears and mountain lions. I feel horrible for the wild animals that had to become entangled in our problems. But I'm very thankful that they agreed to help. I don't think Cassian and the others could have held everyone back long enough for our warriors to get here.

Everyone is in human form now, with our people tugging at the prisoners to lead them out of the forest.

A woman approaches, and I barely recognize her as Silanya. She looks so different in ordinary sweatpants and a T-shirt and out of her silver ceremonial robes.

A weary smile covers her face, and she's holding the jewelry box. "The Amulet of Light is intact, Alpha King," she says, handing it to him.

He takes it and immediately hands it to me, much to my surprise. I look at him with wide eyes. "Isn't it safer with you?"

He shrugs. "I'm the one they took it from. Maybe they'll think twice before messing with you next time, little brave wolf."

I open my mouth to protest, but he just gives me a wink and a smile. I shake my head at him and laugh.

Little brave wolf? I guess I was that, for a moment anyway.

It's a long trek down to the base camp, where my mother and Aisla are waiting, having been escorted there by guardsmen. They both run to me as we approach, and I wrap my arms around them. "Oh, my goodness, it's so good to see you both," I say.

Mother pulls back. "We were so worried. But we knew Cassian wouldn't let anything happen to you."

Cassian smiles. "She's the one who saved us all," he tells them before launching into a brief recap of what happened.

Aisla gasps about ten times throughout the story. "Lyra, you're such a badass now! I have the best sister in the world. You took down the bad guy and saved the amulet!"

"And all of us," Cassian adds.

I shake my head. "I had no choice. I just did it. I think my wolf is braver than I am."

"Impossible," Cassian says, pulling me into a kiss.

"Ooohh, there go the lovebirds again!" Aisla teases.

I just smile, then I watch my mother as she approaches Silanya. "Here," she says, handing her a bundle of silver cloth with the High

Priestess's prayer book on top. "I'm afraid some of the robes are torn, but I just couldn't leave such lovely garments in the forest."

"Thank you," Silanya says gratefully.

I feel Cassian's strong arm tighten around my shoulders. "Are you ready to head home, Luna Queen Lyra?"

I giggle lightly. "More than ready," I say.

We all get to work packing up the base camp so we can head back to the Winterhelm castle.

I just hope we don't run into any more trouble along the way.

NEXT STOP: HOME

Lyra

FOR SEVERAL DAYS OF THE RETURN TRIP, I'M GLUED TO THE *TOME OF Glory* once again. It's as if an entire new world has opened up to me between my new experience shifting and learning everything I want to know about wolf shifters.

Well, not quite everything—I still have a whole treasure trove of books from the Oceana castle library waiting for me to explore back home.

For now, I'm enthralled by this one, which explains much of the history of the wars between humans and shifters long ago. The struggle lasted hundreds of years. In the beginning, shifters were thought to be inferior. They were so drawn into the propaganda of that nonsense that they began to think it was real. They didn't even try to fight. They thought being shifters made them outcasts, mistakes.

That sure hits home for me.

But I'm past all that now. I think the people who thought we were

337

inferior were inferior beings themselves—like King Chez, who pretended to be my father while holding back my powers.

It's such a waste. People like that should have been celebrating differences and learning from each other rather than trying to dig out some weird dark power so they could control everything.

I can't understand what drives people like that.

But I know what inspires me. Dark King Hadrian, that horrible man–the dark power he pulled out of the universe is now threatening the future of all the people I love. And I'm going to play a big part in putting a stop to that.

I hold the Amulet of Light in my crossover bag close to my heart. And I'll put everything I have into stopping anyone who tries to take it away from me.

Of course, they'd need to get through Cassian first. I don't think that's even possible.

Just like with every journey, the return trip seems so much faster than the trek toward the mountains. Yes, we have to stop and camp for a few nights, and yes, it's a lot of work cooking for all these people and packing up every morning only to do the same the next day.

But knowing we got what we came for, and that it's going to help us defeat my horrible biological father, Assanan, makes time fly.

So, we arrive at the Winterhelm castle in no time. King Snowthorne greets us at the gates with several soldiers, who take control of the prisoners we've captured.

Silver shackles flicker with a shimmering mist as his guards lead the prisoners out of the wagons. "The Temple has provided us with chains that will prevent them from shifting," the king explains. "We can handle them in our dungeon, unless you plan on questioning them, Alpha King."

Cassian shakes his head. "No, and I thank you for your efforts. I'll pay for their care while in your custody. But that one—" He points toward a man being coaxed out of the wagon. "I'll be taking him back with me. Something about him tells me he has information I can use."

I glance at Cassian.

"Of course," the king says. "I'm happy to host you all in the castle for as long as you'd like. I would love to have my chefs prepare a celebratory meal."

"I appreciate the offer," Cassian says. "But I'm afraid all celebrations will need to wait until the threat of Assanan and his followers is eliminated. The sooner we return to Oceana, the better."

"I understand," the king says. "Anything you need, my men will provide. I'll continue to send messengers back and forth for our mutual benefit. Speaking of which, this man here has your first report." He points to a man in the crowd behind him and waves him forward. "This is Drewbaker. He was aboard the first ship back after we sent soldiers for combat."

Cassian nods toward him. "Good to meet you. What do you have to report?"

"The Oceana castle was secure at my last meeting with their representatives," Drewbaker begins. "They did speak of fighting near the Pearl Coast."

Mother, Aisla, and I all gasp simultaneously. "Are they attacking Maelie?" I ask.

Drewbaker shakes his head. "I hadn't heard the name. I know that the Alpha King's warriors were fighting hard in that area, though. I'm afraid that's all the news I have. You should pass the messenger ship midway. They will have a more updated report."

"Thank you," Cassian says.

After all our other necessary business is concluded, Cassian turns to Snowthorne. "We'd better head toward the ship. I'm afraid we have no time to waste." He offers his hand, which the king grasps firmly in a handshake.

"I understand," he says. "I'll await your return with news of victory. I pray it will be sooner rather than later."

"As do we," I say.

He inclines his head toward me. "It's been a pleasure to meet you, Luna Queen Lyra."

"Likewise," I tell him.

When all the supplies are restocked, we continue with the caravan to the port of Icehaven, where the *Ironhawk* awaits. I catch sight of her sails from the mountain that we descend just before we reach the port city.

It's a beautiful sight.

Soon, we'll be headed home. I don't know what's waiting for us there, but I know they need us, and I hope the wind is in our favor.

While all the deckhands busily load the new provisions and prepare to sail, Mother, Aisla, Maggie, Silanya, and I linger on the boardwalk.

I turn to Silanya. "It's hard to say goodbye," I tell her. "I feel like I've known you forever, and I don't want to leave you."

"I feel the same kinship, yet, my place is in the Temple of the Moon Goddess here," she says. "Trust the Goddess that She will provide me with visions of your progress overseas. I must admit that I will miss all of you as well. I look forward to your return to our shores."

I don't know if it's proper decorum to embrace a High Priestess, but I don't really care right now. I reach forward and wrap my arms around her. "I can't wait to return," I say when we step back from each other. "Oh." I turn toward my carriage and step inside, bringing out the *Tome of Glory*. "This belongs to you."

"Take it with you," she says.

My eyes go wide. "Are you sure?"

"Yes," she says. "You are the only Luna Queen we expect on the shores of Winter Realm for many years to come. You should have the opportunity to study everything within its pages." She turns to a group of priestesses in white gowns approaching us. "In fact, I have asked the Temple to provide you with this." She turns to the women, one of whom hands her a package, which she hands to me. "Inside are other tomes that will be of interest to you," she explains. "The more our Luna Queen learns of our ways, the better she will serve her people... and wield the Amulet of Light."

"Thank you," I say, accepting the package. It feels like at least four or five books are inside.

Silanya smiles. "May the Moon Goddess bless you on your journey. Farewell."

"Farewell," I repeat. I stay glued to my spot on the boardwalk while she walks away with the other priestesses until they vanish into the crowd.

"Well, sweetheart," Mother whispers into my ear. "I think it's time for us to board."

Her words take me out of my thoughts and have me turning toward the *Ironhawk* at the end of the long pier. Cassian has gone ahead of us to direct the men and help ready the ship.

"Well, then, let's go." I smile wide, carrying my load of books and leading the ladies toward the giant battleship.

It's a long journey ahead, and I know I'll read every one of them.

I'll need as much information as I can get to face what is coming back in Oceana.

I'M READY

CASSIAN

LYRA LEADS THE OTHER LADIES UP THE GANGPLANK, CARRYING A HUGE bundle. I scoop it out of her arms. "What's all this?" I ask.

"Silanya gave me some reading assignments," she explains, clutching the jewelry box holding the Amulet of Light to her chest. "I have a lot of work to do, studying to be a good Luna."

"You're already a perfect Luna," I tell her, planting a kiss on her cheek.

"I'm not, but I appreciate your support." She looks over her shoulder at the other ladies. "I need to get my mother situated in her stateroom."

'Assist the Luna with her family's stateroom assignments,' I tell the nearest guardsman in the mind-link. He steps over to us immediately, and I hand him Lyra's package of books. "He'll show you there."

"I'll see you soon," she tells me, stealing a light kiss.

"I look forward to it." I watch her walk away down the staircase, her traveling pants clinging tightly to her perfect ass. There's a lot more to look forward to tonight, finally being in a real room and not in a tent where she's been so self-conscious about her mother and sister hearing us.

No matter how many times I remind her that we're mates and newlyweds and that no one will mind, she hasn't been able to relax and enjoy being together knowing we have an audience within auditory distance.

I cannot wait for tonight.

I'm surveying the action on the deck when Kellen and Belfor approach. "The guardsmen are very eager to get back and kick some Assanan warrior ass," Kellen quips.

"And I am in their company," I agree. "I don't know what that bastard is up to right now back in Oceana, but we need to deal with him swiftly."

"I hope I get a piece of him," Belfor adds. "But with that nasty black magic on his side, I'm not sure I'll get close to him. How will that amulet work?"

I shrug, meeting his gaze. "Your guess is as good as mine. I suppose, when the time comes, our Luna will put it on and wield its power somehow."

"I'm looking forward to that moment," Kellen says.

"As am I." I turn to the sound of solid footsteps against the polished deck behind me.

"We are ready to set sail, if that's agreeable to you, Alpha King." Captain Kabir gives me a smile and a wink.

"More than ready," I tell him.

"Cast off!" he orders the crewmen. The deck comes alive again with activity, crew members running purposefully in all directions, knowing exactly their task to bring the *Ironhawk* out to sea.

Several minutes later, we are moving away from the long dock, heading into the inlet surrounded by a snow-covered coastline. A chilled breeze alights across the deck, and my nerves awaken with the rush of being out at sea.

And being one step closer to home.

With everything settled for the *Ironhawk*, I have another rush of excitement I want to satisfy.

So, I head below deck.

I find Lyra in the open doorway of her sister's cabin. "We've set sail," I announce, though that's probably obvious given the ship's movement. "Is everyone settled here?" It's hard to be patient, smelling my mate's scent rushing through my nostrils and lighting a charge over every ounce of my being.

I've waited for this too long.

"Yes," she says calmly, as though my blood hasn't been boiling with passion. "Mother, Aisla, do you need anything?"

"We're fine, dear," her mother insists, and my wolf is grateful. "I think I would just like to rest for a while."

"I'll see you at dinner," Lyra says before turning back to me, her gaze finally meeting mine.

And I can tell right away she registers the heat in me. I see the startle in her eyes as they go wide, but then they narrow and soften, matching my sense of need.

I wrap my fingers around hers, feeling joy at even this simple touch as I lead her toward my—our—stateroom. I want to touch her body from head to toe. I want to stop right in this hallway and bury her lips in mine, running my hands up her shirt and feeling the warmth of her skin against mine.

But there are so many guardsmen and crewmen filing down the halls, I don't do any of it.

Not yet.

We reach the stairs that take us one floor down to our room. "I can't help but notice—" she begins.

I glance over at her, my eyes landing on the soft, pink lips I want against mine. "Notice what?"

"That we're far away from my mother's room," she says with a giggle.

"Oh? I hadn't noticed."

My blank expression doesn't fool her for a moment. "Alpha King Cassian," she says, "I believe you planned this arrangement."

We reach our room, and I throw open the door, pulling her inside and against me, kicking the door closed behind us. "And if I did?"

I don't give her a chance to answer because my mouth has already engulfed hers. She closes her eyes, melting into our kiss, holding herself steady on my hips. She tastes so good. She feels so good. And finally, I don't have to stop.

"Then you've done well," she whispers against my lips when we pull away for a breath, and I come undone.

I want to say something else, how much I love her, how incredible she feels against me, how I never want to let her go, but all my words come out as a low, guttural groan of need.

Standing against the wall isn't allowing me to worship this woman the way she deserves. But the few feet between us and the bed is too much real estate to cross without her body against mine.

So, I bring my arm down, lifting her and pulling her in for another kiss while I carry her to our bed. I set her down gently, and she smiles as I let my gaze wander over her. Her shirt lands off-center, leaving her velvety soft shoulder exposed, just below my mark, the symbol of our matehood.

It's the sexiest sight I've ever seen, and that's where I place my lips.

She lets out a little whoop of surprise as I devour her, kissing softly at first, then harder, then grazing her alabaster skin with my teeth, which leaves a trail of goosebumps everywhere I've touched.

My cock stiffens impossibly harder, but this moment isn't for me.

I pause just long enough to lift her shirt over her head, letting out a bit of a growl at the lacy red bra beneath, to which she giggles, jiggling her flawless breasts in the process and adding yet more stretch to my already struggling pants.

Hoping for a matching set, I tug on the loose elastic waistline of her traveling pants and am rewarded with exactly that, a tiny pair of red ace panties in the shape of a steep V.

"I bought these in Icehaven," she says. "I thought you might like them."

A rumble of approval escapes my lips, and she's laughing when I first crush them against hers, but then she quickly stops, moaning against me.

"Let me feel you inside me," she begs.

"Not yet." I give her a smirk before kissing lower, right between her perky breasts. I don't stop there, kissing a trail all the way down to the top of the red lacy V, so close to her sweet pussy, I can almost taste it already.

Grabbing hold of the panties with my teeth, I pull them down, just far enough that her beautiful mound is on full display for me. She can't spread her legs yet with her panties in the way, but I can get my fingers in, pushing against her lower lips and feeling the sweet moisture pooling on me.

"Goddess," I moan, yanking the panties all the way down. I don't need to pull her legs apart because she's doing it for me.

"Cassian, I can't wait," she groans. "I want you inside me."

"You'll get it, my sweet mate," I tell her in a low whisper. "But not yet."

Her scent is stronger now, flowers and the sweet scent of maple wafting into the air around us, driving my wolf to howl inside me. When I finally bend down onto her, she tastes as good as she smells, and I lap up every drop of her moisture before flicking my tongue against her clit and sliding in my fingers.

She feels so good.

She erupts underneath me almost immediately—I suppose she's been wanting this as much as I have—and my name escapes her throat in a hoarse moan as I feel her juices pour over my fingers.

Now, I'm ready.

THE JOURNEY HOME

Lyra

MY HUSBAND IS NOT EVEN UNDRESSED YET, AND I'VE ALREADY LET loose an explosive orgasm. I guess that's what happens when I hold back for weeks, always getting started but then backing off, afraid I'm going to scream his name so loud it echoes all over the forest, while my mother and sister are lying there horrified in their tent.

Yes, I guess that's what happens when I hold back what I really feel.

But not anymore. I've barely stopped quivering from it when I grab his arm and pull him toward me, tugging at the button on his pants. I guess he's decided I've had enough, or maybe it's that he's so stiff he's about to burst, so he can't play hard to get anymore.

His manhood just about spills out of his pants the moment I unbutton him, and he is just inches away from where I want him. I take it in my hand, and it's almost like a rock, it's so hard. I guide him over to my entrance, and he doesn't stop me, not when I rub it against my wet entrance.

He doesn't need much convincing after that, pushing it in, almost roughly, but my wolf inside screams so loud for it that it doesn't even hurt. The stretch against my insides is a pleasure and a relief all at once, and I start screaming his name the way I feared I would all those nights in the forest.

I don't even care. It's heavenly, feeling him inside me.

He bends down and takes my mouth with his, swirling his tongue in circles so I taste every bit of him, completely lost in the feel of him so deep inside of me, he feels like he's a part of me.

It takes me over the edge again, a primal, blissful release, and I feel him quiver inside before he joins me, getting impossibly harder before exploding with a loud call of my name that echoes through the room.

Even after his release, he keeps pumping a few more seconds, and I feel him soften inside me, though not all the way. He doesn't pull out, and I don't want him to.

We hold each other, panting and trying to catch our breath. Being in this man's arms means everything to me. Any place feels like home with his touch, even the inside of a giant warship.

After a while, I look up to meet his gaze. "I promised my mother I'd be there for dinner," I say with a naughty giggle.

"Well, we're going to be late," he replies, and I feel him stiffen in me again.

CASSIAN'S HAND FEELS SO WARM IN MINE AS WE WALK TOWARD THE galley. I'd be lying if I said I didn't wish I were back in bed with him, just enjoying the feel of him against me, inside me. But we have to eat, eventually.

Got to keep up our strength, after all.

He smirks as if he's reading my mind, so I stop and face him. "Are you sure there's not some secret telepathy beyond the mind-link that lets you know my every thought?"

He chuckles, pulling me in for a kiss and whispering against my lips, "No, there's not. I promise. I'm just thinking the same thing you are, so it's not that hard to tell."

I pull back, laughing with him. "I sure hope no one else can tell what I'm thinking. If my mother knew, she'd be horrified."

"She'd be happy for you for finding your mate and husband," he corrects me. "Don't you think so?"

"I guess." I frown a little and start walking again. "It's just that it's so embarrassing. We never really talked about... sex."

"Never?"

I shrug. "I guess she tried to fill me in on what I might expect when she thought I was marrying the evil Alpha."

This gives him another laugh. "And what did you think of her explanation?"

"I was horrified," I reply honestly. "The idea of a man sticking his... well, you know. Just the idea of that sounded gross."

It's his turn to stop walking as he wraps his arms around me and draws me in for another kiss, stretching his large palms across my bottom. The sensation goes straight to my core and makes me want to turn around and go back to our room.

"Do you still think it's gross?" he asks, his voice gravelly and deep.

Now I laugh. "No." The word comes out with a giggle. "It's wonderful. But you'd better stop because my mother is waiting for us."

"Mm," he moans against my lips, sneaking in one more kiss before he pulls back and takes my hand again as though he didn't just light up every nerve in my body with pleasure.

"Maybe you are the evil Alpha," I suggest teasingly.

"Only if you want me to be," he answers.

I'd tease him more, but we've already turned the corner toward the galley, where a guardsman opens the door for us and we enter the now-packed galley. Most of the crew and guardsmen are already eating.

Mother, Aisla, and Maggie are all seated at the main table, which has two empty chairs. Oscar is handing Maggie a biscuit when she looks up and gives me a smile.

"It's about time!" she says, and all heads turn to us.

I can't stop the blush I feel rising in my cheeks. How many of these men heard me screaming Cassian's name?

I guess I'll need to get used to that.

Dinner is delicious. King Snowthorne ensured that our supplies were well stocked with fresh meats, vegetables, fruit, and ground flour for bread. The cooks must have been baking all day since the table is filled with biscuits, muffins, and buttered rolls that look like they would melt in my mouth.

They do.

As we eat, I look over at the people surrounding me. It's so good to have my family around me.

For a while, I wondered whether I'd ever see my mother and Aisla again. And now, they're moving in with me at the castle in Oceana. I've made a new friend in Maggie, and I'll see her all the time when she moves in with her mate in the walled city surrounding the castle. I can't wait for her to meet Cally.

So, I have a husband I adore, close family right down the hallway, and two best friends to enjoy my life with. Not to mention that I'm the Luna Queen of the Oceana kingdom. I'll always have people to see and places to go, and I'll always be sure to be the best Luna I can, a Luna Queen the people of Oceana can be proud of.

I can't wait to meet everyone in the kingdom.

After dinner, Cassian and I head up to the deck to stand by the railing at the tip of the bow. We're out on the open ocean now. It's pitch black out except for the bright stars in the sky. There are billions of them visible, some impossibly thick in a band that stretches straight across the sky so dense that they almost look purple.

There is no moon out tonight, just the stars twinkling lightly above the moving ocean, its now-gentle waves lapping against the side of the *Ironhawk*.

I turn to Cassian and see the stars sparkling in his silver eyes. "What are you thinking about?" he asks me.

"All that waits for us ahead," I say, facing forward to watch the mesmerizing waves. "It's exciting and terrifying all at once."

"That's true," he tells me, rubbing his arm up and down on the small of my back. "But you don't need to be afraid of the terrifying part. I'll never let danger threaten you. I'll always be at your side. And you have the Amulet of Light. Remember that our kind once defeated the darkness with it many centuries ago."

I nod sharply. "Yes, and we can defeat it again." I'm surprised at how confident I feel. "Still, I wish things didn't have to happen like this."

"There will always be someone somewhere who gets a taste of power that leaves them wanting more," he says. "Once Assanan is gone, another will come along. But there will also be times of rest and peace in between."

"I hope we defeat him soon and that the peace lasts for many more centuries."

"I hope so, too." He turns to me and places a palm against my cheek. "I love you, Lyra, my Luna Queen. Peacetime or war, I will always feel that love."

"I love you too, Cassian, always."

Our lips meet gently, and I enjoy the taste of him for several minutes before a cooler breeze presses by us. We both turn back to the vast ocean ahead.

Tonight, we can relax and be together, but we have only a few days before we need to brace for the battle ahead.

There is so much uncertainty waiting for us in Oceana. But there's one thing I know for sure: Love and light will get us through it, no matter what.

THANK YOU FOR READING! BOOK 2 IS COMING SOON!

ALSO BY OLIVIA BHELLE KILDARE

Pregnant With Four Alphas' Babies (writing with Bella Moondragon)

Chosen As the Breeder

Mated to Four Alphas

Threats Against the Breeder

At War for the Breeder

The Stolen Breeder

Four Alphas, Four Babies

Becoming the Luna Queen

Descendants of the Breeder

My Secret Billionaire Series

Finding My Secret Billionaire

Falling for My Secret Billionaire by Bella Moondragon

Sea King Alpha

Bride of the Cruel Alpha